"Cain?" she said in a voice usually reserved for pleas to the executioner. *"Will you marry me?"*

Following a moment of protracted silence, he laughed out loud. "Man, for a minute there, I thought you asked me to *marry* you."

Maggie's face had gone two shades of red. "I did."

The smile slipped disbelievingly from his expression. Cain stared at her, dumbfounded. Standing up to his ankles in the horse dung and straw he'd swept out of the stables, he nearly sat down where he was.

"Not a real marriage, of course. Don't look at me that way. I know how this sounds."

Cain snorted, thinking he'd been transported to some weird alternative universe while he wasn't looking. "You do?"

"I—I said it all wrong. Actually, there is no right way to ask a complete stranger to marry you."

Dear Reader,

There's so much great reading in store for you this month that it's hard to know where to begin, but I'll start with bestselling author and reader favorite Fiona Brand. She's back with another of her irresistible Alpha heroes in *Marrying McCabe*. There's something about those Aussie men that a reader just can't resist—and heroine Roma Lombard is in the same boat when she meets Ben McCabe. He's got trouble—and passion—written all over him.

Our FIRSTBORN SONS continuity continues with *Born To Protect,* by Virginia Kantra. Follow ex-Navy SEAL Jack Dalton to Montana, where his princess (and I mean that literally) awaits. A new book by Ingrid Weaver is always a treat, so save some reading time for *Fugitive Hearts,* a perfect mix of suspense and romance. Round out the month with new novels by Linda Castillo, who offers *A Hero To Hold* (and trust me, you'll definitely want to hold this guy!); Barbara Ankrum, who proves the truth of her title, *This Perfect Stranger;* and Vickie Taylor, with *The Renegade Steals a Lady* (and also, I promise, your heart).

And if that weren't enough excitement for one month, don't forget to enter our Silhouette Makes You a Star contest. Details are in every book.

Enjoy!

Leslie J. Wainger
Executive Senior Editor

Please address questions and book requests to:
Silhouette Reader Service
U.S.: 3010 Walden Ave., P.O. Box 1325, Buffalo, NY 14269
Canadian: P.O. Box 609, Fort Erie, Ont. L2A 5X3

This Perfect Stranger

BARBARA ANKRUM

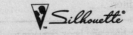

INTIMATE MOMENTS™

Published by Silhouette Books

America's Publisher of Contemporary Romance

To Babs
For throwing me your reserve chute on this one and for
reminding me daily why we do this very difficult thing.
Thanks.

 SILHOUETTE BOOKS

ISBN 0-373-27173-5

THIS PERFECT STRANGER

Copyright © 2001 by Barbara Ankrum

All rights reserved. Except for use in any review, the reproduction
or utilization of this work in whole or in part in any form by any
electronic, mechanical or other means, now known or hereafter
invented, including xerography, photocopying and recording, or in
any information storage or retrieval system, is forbidden without
the written permission of the editorial office, Silhouette Books,
300 East 42nd Street, New York, NY 10017 U.S.A.

All characters in this book have no existence outside the imagination of
the author and have no relation whatsoever to anyone bearing the same
name or names. They are not even distantly inspired by any individual
known or unknown to the author, and all incidents are pure invention.

This edition published by arrangement with Harlequin Books S.A.

® and TM are trademarks of Harlequin Books S.A., used under license.
Trademarks indicated with ® are registered in the United States Patent
and Trademark Office, the Canadian Trade Marks Office and in other
countries.

Visit Silhouette at www.eHarlequin.com

Printed in U.S.A.

Books by Barbara Ankrum

Silhouette Intimate Moments

To Love a Cowboy #834
I'll Remember You #972
This Perfect Stranger #1103

BARBARA ANKRUM

says she's always been an incurable romantic, with a passion for books and stories about the healing power of love. It never occurred to her to write seriously until her husband, David, discovered a box full of her unfinished stories and insisted that she pursue her dream. Need she say more about why she believes in love?

With a successful career as a commercial actress behind her, Barbara decided she had plenty of eccentric characters to people the stories that inhabit her imagination. She wrote her first novel in between auditions, and she's never looked back. Her historicals have won the prestigious Reviewers' Choice and K.I.S.S. Awards from *Romantic Times Magazine*, and she's been nominated for a RITA Award from Romance Writers of America. Barbara lives in Southern California with her actor/writer/hero-husband and their two perfect children.

SILHOUETTE MAKES YOU A STAR!

Feel like a star with Silhouette.
Look for the exciting details of our new contest
inside all of these fabulous Silhouette novels:

Chapter 1

The idling Harley-Davidson rumbled beneath him with an impatient growl. All power and muscle and ragged edges, the machine—like its rider—waited for some sign that the town that lay at the foot of the pass whose crest they straddled was better or worse than any other.

Dawn was just beginning to ease the darkness from the sky. Lights winked from the small constellations of buildings scattered across the valley below. Cain MacCallister had seen a hundred towns just like it in the past few weeks. Even stopped in a few. But destinations, like dreams, were temporary things, and a man like him didn't stay long in either one. Still, his dark gaze prowled the compilation of roads and ranches crisscrossing the picturesque landscape below the way a hawk's did a potential landing spot. And for a moment, Cain dared to imagine himself belonging there. It was foolish, he knew, because he hadn't belonged anywhere in so long, he'd forgotten what it felt like.

Tightening his fist around the throttle, he glanced to the

west. The road forked here toward Missoula. If he wanted to, he could take it. Ride another hundred miles. Not much farther than that. He'd poured the last of his money into the gas tank of his bike just outside of Butte. He might find a job in Missoula, lose himself in a city of that size for a while. A man with choices would do that. But it had been two days since he'd eaten, and hunger gnawed at his insides. He needed food and sleep and most of all, he needed a place to be. At least for a while.

A cool night wind swept down off what some called The High Lonesome, tugging at his thick, dark hair and stirring the restlessness in him. He understood loneliness the way only a man who'd been behind bars could. Most of the time it suited him. But today he felt it in his bones with a deep and abiding ache.

His skin went hot as memories of holding Annie skittered across his mind. They tended to catch him off guard at moments like this, but he tamped those memories down. No use thinking about her. That chapter of his life was over. Whatever needs still eddied inside him, he could assuage with an anonymous roll in the hay. And even as that urge crystalized low in his loins, he realized his decision was made.

He gunned the throttle with a brutal twist of his big hand. The engine answered him with a roar that echoed through the pass and drifted down toward the rushing Musselshell River like the call of some wild thing. Somewhere in the distance, an animal howled in reply.

"So, that's it then." Maggie Cortland stared disbelievingly at the bank manager, Ernie Solefield, who was studiously avoiding eye contact with her. For that, she was almost grateful, because she didn't trust herself not to start blubbering like a baby.

"I'm afraid so, Maggie," he said curtly, shuffling papers

on his perfectly ordered desk. "I wish it could have gone the other way."

She stared blankly at the shiny bald spot at the top of his head. The smell of money permeated this place, but it dangled, as usual, just out of her reach. "Ernie, you've known me for seven years. You know my land—what it's worth. You knew Ben. We had you and Sarah to our house."

He shook his head regretfully. "I'm sorry, Maggie. You know I did everything I could."

"Everything within the prescribed limits, you mean."

His head came up with a snap. "What's that supposed to mean?"

The expression on his face, somewhere between anger and guilt, told her she was right. Somehow, that comforted her. After all, she knew the drill. She'd been through it at every bank in town. Lead Maggie Cortland by the nose. Let her think there's a chance, then pull the rug out from under her. She just hadn't expected it from him.

She glanced around at the people milling in the teller line, at the bank officers handing out forms to perspective clients. People she knew and once trusted. Her throat felt like it was closing up.

Maggie got to her feet, gathering up her purse and paperwork from the desk that stood between them. "I think you know exactly what I mean, Ernie. Thanks for your time, but you know what? I don't need your money. I'll find a way, with you or without you. If you think I'm going to fold just because Laird Donnelly has every man in this town by the short hairs—"

"This has nothing to do with Laird Donnelly," Ernie sputtered, shoving to his feet as Dorothy LaBecque, the pretty, thirty-two-year-old blonde watching them from the express window, ducked her head and pretended to be counting her drawer. "Our decision was based solely on your ability to—"

"Play my part? Is that what you were going to say?"

"No, of course not." Flustered, he glanced around at the stares they were beginning to draw, then, in a lower voice, stammered, "Based on—on your, uh, potential to show a profit." He hesitated and leaned closer, as if what he had to say embarrassed him. "You're all alone out there, Maggie. The bank...they don't put a lot of stock in a single woman's ability to..." He shook his head. "If you were uh, still married..." He let the rest drift off.

The laugh that escaped her made him flinch. "Still married? Since when is that a requirement for loans these days? Isn't there something in American jurisprudence about discrimination in regards to single—"

"This isn't about discrimination and you know it. It's a hard life up here. Hard enough for men, let alone women. Now...you need to calm down, Maggie. I think you're overwrought."

Overwrought? With slow deliberation, she placed one palm flat on his desk, leaned closer to him. "It's *Mrs.* Cortland to you. And you can tell Laird Donnelly for me that I will never roll over for a man like him, no matter how many people he's got on his payroll." She glanced meaningfully at the tall blonde behind the express window, then back at Ernie.

Ernie absorbed the blow, then leaned one smooth hand on the desk himself, coming inches from her face. "Watch yourself, Maggie. You don't know what you're playing with here."

"If I were a man, we wouldn't even be having this conversation. But this isn't the nineteenth century and Donnelly's not the only one making up the rules."

Ernie slid his gaze to the bank's only window, where

clouds were crowding the morning sky. "Ben would've wanted you to sell."

His words hit her like a ringing slap, and the sting of them made the room go blurry for a moment. When she'd gathered her control again, she pinned Ernie with a look that had all the color rushing out of his florid cheeks. "That," she said quietly, "was beneath even you, Ernie."

Ernie lowered his eyes, searching for somewhere safe to land his gaze as Maggie turned and headed out of the bank. In the glass reflection of the door just before she pushed past it, she could see Dorothy hurrying over to Ernie's desk.

Outside, the air was crisp, even for May, and the dark clouds that scudded along the shanks of the Bitterroots carried the promise of weather. She wished she had foregone the dark business suit today and worn her usual work clothes. It was cold and no one gave a damn about her experience running a business anyway. No one gave a damn, period.

There were a million things to do this morning, but at the moment, she couldn't think of a single one that sounded more important than drowning her sorrows in a steaming cup of coffee at Moody's. Not that she wanted to talk. She didn't. She simply couldn't face heading back alone just yet.

Her hands were shaking as she pushed the door to Moody's open. The rich aroma of coffee hit her the moment she entered the shop and settled over her like a balm.

"Hey, Maggie," the attractive, middle-aged woman called out to her from behind the counter where she held court with her coffeepot. A half-dozen men of various ages gathered around her on the vinyl-covered counter stools like a bunch of hungry old roosters, pecking for crumbs. They turned to look as Maggie walked in the door.

"Hey, Moody," she said, ignoring their stares. "Can I get a cup of coffee?"

"Comin' right up."

The café was warm and cozy with gingham-checked curtains and a different Victorian lamp hanging down over each table. Old books covered the shelves that rode above the windows and antiques and greenery dotted the wall space that wasn't taken up by windows. Moody had done more than convert this old diner into something special. She'd created an ambiance that made Maggie feel at home here. She suspected that half of Fishhook felt the same.

Her name, of course, wasn't really Moody. But anyone who still remembered her real one lived under penalty of death if they divulged it. No, Moody Rivers was as much a fixture here in the valley as the river that had earned her her nickname. A free spirit, who, at fifty, answered to no one but was adored by all.

She set a steaming cup of coffee and a pitcher of cream down on the booth table, tilting a sideways look at Maggie. "Wanna talk about it, hon?"

Maggie thought she couldn't stand kindness right now. Her eyes glistened as she shook her head.

The older woman smiled. "Well, then, I know just the thing." A minute later, a plate appeared under Maggie's nose filled with a "Moody's Dutch Double-Fudge Brownie," last year's county fair grand prize winner.

"Chocolate," Moody sighed. "The elixir of life. It's on me. Talk's free, too, if you want it."

She *wanted* to wail, but prudence prevailed. She thanked Moody and stirred cream into her cup, watching the white slowly spiral into the black. A gaff like public crying would instantly be fodder for the wags of Fishhook and a mere two degrees of separation from good ol' Laird Donnelly— a man who regularly ate the young for breakfast and was already licking his chops at the prospect of her next falter. No, she couldn't show weakness. Not for a moment. She took a sip of coffee and sank back against her seat. Exhaustion pulled at her, even though the day had barely begun.

Peripherally, she heard the little bell above the café door jangle, felt the men at the counter turn to take in the newest arrival with a collective, male bristling. To her left, Moody looked up too. The perpetually easygoing woman fumbled a coffee cup against its saucer, then juggled it still again, seeming to attempt the same thing with her expression.

Cool air from outside slithered against Maggie's face as curiosity tugged her gaze in the direction of the lace-covered door that still blocked the newcomer from her view.

"C'mon in," Moody invited, still a bit wide-eyed. "Find yourself a seat. I'll bring ya a menu."

"Just coffee," he said in a deep, baritone voice as he cleared the door, tugging off his black leather gloves one finger at a time.

The coffee cup poised at Maggie's lips froze where it was. For a moment, she actually forgot to breathe. Big, was the first adjective that leapt to mind. No less than six foot-three and used to ducking door frames. Drop-dead handsome was the second. No, that was three adjectives, she amended stupidly, unable to tear her gaze from him. Square-jawed, with shockingly blue eyes hooded by thick brows, the dark-haired stranger took in the small café with a quick turn of his head. His gaze locked with hers for an assessing moment before it swept away again. And like a blow to the solar plexus, it left her heart inexplicably racing in her chest.

He moved with the graceful efficiency of a caged cat, prowling to a table in the corner of the room and sitting with his back to the wall. If this had been the Old West, she would have guessed him a gunslinger, but she supposed he was just another loner on his way to somewhere else.

Here, machismo was as much a part of the landscape as

cattle, but there was no pretense about the pure, unadulterated maleness that lurked beneath the black clothing this man wore from head to foot. His self-contained intensity made every head turn his way as he walked in the room. And her response to it was as obvious and as primal as that of everyone else in the room. Unbidden images tumbled through her—of sweaty sheets and his big hands on her skin.

She managed to get her coffee cup to her lips, trying to comprehend her completely carnal reaction to the man. It had been years since a man—any man—had made her think of…sex. But this stranger had managed it in the space of ten seconds. And he hadn't said more than two words.

Lust at first sight, she thought. It was more than shocking. Ernie was right. She was overwrought. She forced herself to stare at the brownie on the plate in front of her, realizing that she'd lost all interest in it.

Moody crossed the room in the unhurried way she had and set a cup of coffee down in front of him. "Take cream?" she asked.

"Just black," he replied.

"We've got the best hash browns this side of the Rockies and omelettes that'll make you think you died and went to heaven. How 'bout it?"

Maggie could've sworn the man's gaze slid longingly at the plates of food being cradled by the old roosters at the counter, before returning to his coffee.

"This'll do," he said, and pulled a long sip as Moody watched.

"Suit yerself, darlin'. Enjoy." She breezed by Maggie's table with a little grin and a wink as she passed. Maggie, who was concentrating on swallowing a bite of brownie, nearly choked.

"Reckon we ain't seen the last o' winter by the smell o'

that air,'' old Bill Miller announced to no one in particular from his spot at the counter. ''Storm's rollin' in.''

''Ah,'' Bob Tacumsa replied with a shake of his gray head, ''Just the leftovers. T'won't be much.''

''Yeah,'' Wit Stacey replied, glancing pointedly at the stranger. ''Them Northers blow in all sorts o' riff raff this time a year.''

Maggie watched the stranger tap his finger against the rim of his cup, trying to ignore them.

Moody slapped at the counter with her damp towel perilously near to Wit's plate of eggs. ''And it mostly accumulates at my counter,'' she said sharply. ''Mind yer tongue, Wit, or you'll find yourself wearin' my best breakfast plate.''

Wit ducked his head and forked in a mouthful of eggs.

Score one for Moody.

Maggie glanced back at the stranger. To her dismay, he was staring right back at her through a sweep of dark lashes. She flashed him an automatic smile, then looked away, tamping down a racing heartbeat.

What was wrong with her anyway? Tightening her hand around her coffee mug, she wished she'd gone straight home from the bank. Instead, she was sitting here fantasizing about a man she didn't even know, wondering what his smile would feel like against her mouth.

Lord.

The bell above the door jangled again. This time she knew who was coming through the door before she saw him because she heard his voice. The sound of it sent a shiver through her.

Laird Donnelly and two of his men brought the cold air in with them as they swept into the café like they owned the place. Barrel-chested and just as big as the stranger sitting across the room, Laird looked every inch the cattle baron he was. At thirty-five, he owned the biggest operation in northern Montana, not to mention half the men in this town. Maggie slid her eyes shut, wishing she could gracefully slide under the table and disappear.

"Well, well, if it isn't Maggie Cortland," Laird said, strolling her way, slipping off his gray felt Stetson. "How ya been, Maggie?"

"Laird." She sipped her coffee and stared out the window.

"Been keepin' to yourself a lot lately. Why, we were just talkin' about you, weren't we boys?"

The "boys" nodded like good little soldiers.

"That's right. We were wonderin' why you hadn't fixed that fence up on the north pasture yet. A couple of your mares wandered onto my land yesterday."

Damn him! She'd fixed that fence twice in the last two weeks. Someone had been cutting it, and it didn't take an rocket scientist to figure out who. "Where are they now?"

Laird smiled magnanimously. "Your mares? Oh, I imagine right about now, they're happily grazin' with my best heifers. I planned on bringin' 'em on by later today."

Her knee hit the table with a *thwack* and the old roosters jumped as a single entity. "No!" she said too loudly. "Don't bother. I'll come get them later."

"No hurry," Laird told her, draping his muscular arm across the high back of her booth. "'Cause from what I hear this hasn't really been your day."

"I suppose I have you to thank for that," she said without a glimmer of a smile.

He did though—a wry, foxlike grin that set her teeth on edge. "Me? Hell, I can take credit for lots of things, but makin' your day bad isn't one I'd care to claim."

Maggie couldn't actually remember hating anyone the way she did Laird Donnelly. He made her skin crawl. Crowding her the way he was now was something he did for fun. He loved to see the terror leap into her eyes. But she swore she wouldn't let him do it to her. Not here. Not now.

Thankfully, Moody interceded, nudging Laird out of the way so she could refill Maggie's coffee cup. "Why don't you and your boys have a seat, Laird?" she said pointedly. "Maggie's not in the mood for talkin'."

"Another time then," he promised with a wink that sent a shiver through Maggie.

It wasn't until Laird moved out of the way that she noticed the stranger watching her. Rather, watching Laird watching her. The muscle in his jaw worked rhythmically as his gaze collided with hers, then he looked back at his coffee.

She dragged her purse up from the seat and began rifling through it for money. Moody intercepted her again, setting the coffeepot down on the table. "I told you. It's on me today. You go on home, honey. Put your feet up. You're pale as a ghost. You could use a rest."

Maggie slid an anxious look at Laird and his bunch before sending Moody what she hoped was a reassuring smile. "Don't worry about me. Okay? I'm just a little tired is all. I'll be fine."

"You sure? When you gonna get some help out on your place? Lord knows, you shouldn't be handling all that on your own."

"Soon," Maggie lied. "Thanks, Moody. For everything."

The older woman just smiled. She was nosy, Maggie thought, but she wasn't dense. She always knew how far to push, and Maggie had just drawn the line. Gathering up her purse she headed toward the door, deliberately avoiding eye contact with the stranger. He'd disappear in a few hours like the cold wind off the Bitterroots.

And she'd still be spitting into it.

Cain MacCallister made no pretense of ignoring the fragile-looking beauty named Maggie as she unfolded those long legs of hers from the booth and walked by him without a second glance. More to the point, he couldn't take his eyes off her. Perhaps, he reasoned, it was her resemblance to Annie that had caught him like a sucker punch to the gut. Slender and pale, with that blond, pinned-up hair and swanlike neck of hers, she could've been a dancer. Maybe it was the elegant way she held herself as that cow-chaser hassled her.

Maybe it was the way she smiled—the little flicker of that wide mouth of hers that had nearly stalled his heart. All of which had forced him to reassess the "fragile" description he'd pinned on her. Oh, she was delicate all right. Delicate the way centuries-old bone china was delicate, with a tempered core that belied the translucence.

Damn, he thought, sipping his cooling coffee. What the hell was wrong with him? He had no business thinking about a woman like her. She was probably married with three kids, a picket fence and a dog. He was in the market for something considerably less permanent.

But that didn't stop him from watching her pull away in her beat-up old pickup truck, or from wondering who'd put the sadness he'd glimpsed in her eyes.

Swivelling a look at the trio of men seated a few tables away, Cain tightened his fist. He'd known plenty of men like them. In lockup, a man got familiar with the lowest common denominator quickly. In the real world, men like Laird got off on using intimidation. Especially on women.

Cain smiled grimly. He'd give that bastard five minutes behind bars before men much better versed in arm-twisting put him in a place he'd wish he'd never seen. But men like Laird—men with money—rarely found themselves in the black hole. Even if they'd earned a spot there.

Cain reached into his pocket for the last of his change

and tossed it on the table. The waitress who'd filled his cup smiled as she cruised by him again. "Finished? Sure I can't get you something else?"

The smell of cinnamon buns had been making him almost sick with hunger for the past ten minutes and if he didn't get out of here soon, he might just have to ask her for a job as a dishwasher to earn one.

"Thanks," he said, managing a smile of his own as he shrugged into his denim jacket. "This is it. Unless you can tell me who might be hiring around here."

"You're looking for work?" she asked with a surprised lift of her brows.

He nodded curtly. "I've got some experience with ranch work. Horses, mostly."

Her eyes narrowed thoughtfully, looking him up and down for a moment. "Funny, I didn't take you for a ranch hand."

He slid his gloves back on.

"Horses, huh?" She glanced at Laird. "The Bar ZX is always hiring at this time of year."

Laughter erupted from the men's table as they shared a joke. Cain glanced out the window. "Anywhere else?"

The woman smiled slowly, then gestured to Cain with a tip of her chin to follow her. "As a matter of fact," she said softly, walking him to the door, "I just might know of something."

Chapter 2

The sleeting rain started after lunch, but by one-fifteen it had turned into hail—a sharp, biting deluge that rattled against the tin roof of Maggie's barn. It had scattered the horses in the paddock in a blind panic. Marble-sized balls of ice pummeled the mares, reducing them to quivering masses huddling against the barn.

One by one, she managed to catch them and lead them into the barn, out of the weather. But Geronimo, a green-broke three-year old gelding, was too frightened to be caught. She'd already missed him three times with her rope as he skidded around the paddock, eyes white with terror.

The gelding was the most unpredictable of her new horses. With the temperament of a scared bulldog, he'd resisted her every attempt at training. But Maggie knew he'd been mishandled as a young horse and she believed he had real potential as a cutter.

The heels of her boots slipped in the mud as Maggie threw the lariat. She missed, going down painfully on one knee. Geronimo crashed into the split-rail fencing and shrieked. Struggling to her feet, Maggie hauled back the spooled out rope, cursing the weather and imagining the bruises she'd have on her before she was done.

Thunder rumbled, shaking the ground and blurring the roar of the hail against the barn. Frigid rain dripped off the brim of her hat and slid down her neck. The stinging hail beat against her slicker-covered back. Instinct warned that she should leave the damned horse where he was. But she knew she didn't have the heart to do that either. Geronimo had been through enough in his short life to fill a book. She wasn't about to compound his misery by abandoning him when things got tough. In his state, he could break his neck trying to break out of the paddock.

"Shh—Geronimo—" she called, approaching him again as he pranced madly back and forth on the north end of the enclosure. She knew he hated the rope, but she couldn't get close enough to him to grab his halter. "Whoa, boy. Settle down, now. Here we go. That's it. Let's just get you outta this weather."

Geronimo rolled his eyes in terror as she tossed the loop one more time, this time, miraculously, dropping it over the gelding's head. Maggie hauled back on the rope feeling the resistance before she'd even gotten it tight.

The big gelding shuddered for a moment, legs splayed, before he exploded with a high-pitched squeal. Nine-hundred pounds of fury, bone and muscle bore down on her like a shrieking banshee.

There was no time to react. Nowhere to go. She heard a scream and knew it had come from her.

Too late, she lunged sideways, diving toward the fence rails, but Geronimo slammed into her with the force of an oncoming locomotive. The impact sent her careening against the railing and slammed the breath from her lungs. Lights exploded in her skull, and the rain and the sky and even the mud beneath her cheek winked in and out like a flickering lightbulb.

She felt, more than heard, the thunderous pounding of Geronimo's hooves against the ground nearby. She gasped and coughed. Her lungs burned. The world, as she opened her eyes, was spinning. The only thing that was holding still was the post she was curled around.

Get up!

The voice was hers. Wasn't it? She willed herself to try. Her fingernails sank into the mud in her pathetic effort to drag herself toward the nearby rail, but found no purchase around the cold chunks of ice that littered the ground. She could hear the frantic barking of her dog, Jigger, coming from inside the house and she suddenly wished she hadn't left him there, safe from the storm.

Dimly, it occurred to her that this was a sloppy way to die. Slogged in mud, trampled in her own paddock by a dumb animal who depended on her for its very survival.

Embarrassing, really—

Before she could finish the thought, someone was tugging on her wrists. Pulling her effortlessly away from the sound of oncoming hooves. She felt the heavy, pounding closeness of them as they barely missed her legs. Somewhere in the distance, thunder rumbled with a fierce howl.

And then she was sprawled outside the paddock with someone leaning urgently over her, shielding her from the hail. Touching her face.

"Can you hear me?"

It was a man's voice. That realization only dimly registered. The sky above her was still doing a slow rotation. "I—" she croaked, licking the rain off her lips. "Ben—?"

The shadow above her shook his head. "Don't move. You might've broken something."

Not Ben, she thought. Of course, not Ben. Someone else. She tried to sit up. "Who—?"

"Lie still," he commanded, pressing her back down. "I'm not gonna hurt you."

He didn't have to. Everything ached. Maggie squinted up at him past the rain as he ran his hands down the sides of her ribs. Big was the first word that came to mind.

And just like that, her head cleared.

Oh, no.

Pushing his hands off her, she tried to sit up again. "Don't—"

He swore under his breath, but let her sit.

She couldn't think. Not coherently anyway. And not while he was touching her. "I'm all right," she told him. "I just…just had the wind knocked out of me, that's all."

Her shaking hands were muddy, but she fingered her aching cheek, taking in the beat up old motorcyle parked twenty feet away.

"You—you were…at Moody's."

"That's right."

"What—" she shook her head "—what're…you doing here?"

"Saving your pretty little behind apparently." The hail was still pelting them, but he scanned her empty yard with a look close to anger. "Where the hell is everybody?"

Everybody? Maggie tried to get to her feet and failed, bracing a hand against the post. A soft curse spilled from her lips.

In one effortless movement, he scooped her up in his arms as if she weighed nothing at all and headed toward the house.

She gasped. "No, wait! I'm perfectly capable of—"

"The hell you are." Unmoved, he trudged through the mud toward her front door. His arms were strong and thick and she felt unreasonably small in them.

She swung a look back at the paddock and the gelding still racing around in a froth of panic. "But Geronimo—"

A humorless laugh escaped him. "You mean that loco horse that just tried to trample you to death?"

Her head ached. "He's afraid of ropes. He wasn't trying to hurt me."

"And if you had the sense God gave a flea, you'll call the knacker's truck for him tomorrow."

The knacker! She would've argued if she had the wherewithal, but she couldn't seem to muster it.

They reached the door then, and he yanked open the screen and gave the handle a twist, shoving it open the rest of the way with his foot. A low growl froze him in his tracks. It was Jigger, who'd planted himself just inside the doorway, poised to do battle with this stranger. But at the sight of Maggie in the man's arms, the dog whined happily and jumped up to lick her hand.

"It's okay, Jigger," Maggie told him. "He's a friend." She looked up at Cain, whose expression was considerably more guarded. "Don't worry. He only bites when I tell him to."

"That's reassuring," he said, carrying her into the warm room and setting her down gently on the corner of the pine-planked kitchen table.

Maggie braced a hand behind her, surprisingly unsteady. She had every intention of getting immediately to her feet, but her knees had the tensile strength of water.

Wordlessly, he tugged off his gloves, reached for her mud-covered right boot and began pulling it off.

"I can do that," she argued, even though she wasn't precisely sure that was true. Her head felt like a fractured egg and her hands wouldn't stop shaking.

"Moody was right about you," he said, as the boot released her foot with a watery pop.

She frowned. "Moody?"

"She said you were stubborn as mud."

"She actually said that?"

"Which I see now is true."

She stared down at the top of his head as he worked on her other boot, at his dark hair, slicked with rain and hanging in dripping hanks against his forehead. His shoulders were thick and wide with a man's strength. "What else did she say?"

He cupped his palm against her calf and tugged at the heel of her boot. "That you need help." That boot came off with a pop and his hands followed her muddy sock up her calf and pulled it down.

Help. Yes, she needed help right now, she thought, inhaling sharply at the touch of his hands on her skin. Lord, what was she doing letting this stranger undress her?

As if he'd heard her thought, his gaze lifted to hers, his cool palm still cradling her leg. The penetrating blue heat of his eyes seared her and she tried to remember ever feeling more off balance than she did right now.

"I...don't even know your name," she said, reclaiming her leg and scooting backward on the table.

"Cain," he said. "Cain MacCallister."

Biblical references of the dark kind flitted through her mind. Cain. As in the second original sin. She watched him pull a hand towel off a towel rack and run it under the kitchen faucet until the water got hot. Jigger was watching him, too, with a proprietary sweep of his tail across the floor.

"Listen, Mr. MacCallister—" she began.

"It's just Cain."

"Okay. Cain. Thank you for helping me. I mean, I owe you, but if you don't mind, I can certainly—"

He was back at her side then, lifting the hot, damp towel to her cheek. "Hold still."

She blocked him with her hand. "Please—"

"You're bleeding."

"I *am?*" She raised a hand to her cheek and brought it back stained with red. Oh, God...

The heat stung and she winced, but he was gentle. Very gentle as he soothed the towel across her cheek, cleaning away the mess she'd made of it.

"How bad is it?" she asked. He was close enough that she could feel the heat of his nearness.

"It's not too deep. I don't think you need stitches. But you're gonna have a nice shiner."

She sank lower as he moved back to the sink to rinse the towel.

"You're lucky," he said. "It could've been worse. A lot worse."

He was right, of course. She'd come close many times. But never as close as she'd come today. "So...do you mind telling me what you were you doing riding all the way out here on a motorcycle in the middle of a hailstorm?"

"It wasn't hailing when I started out. But we can talk about that later."

She grabbed his wrist as he lifted the towel to her face again. "I think we should talk about it now. I mean, it's not every day I let a strange man carry me into my own house and—" she stared at the towel "—pull my boots off."

A small grin softened the hard line of his mouth. Maggie felt her resolve slipping as he lifted the towel again and smoothed it across her jawline.

"I suppose it's not every day you nearly get yourself trampled either," he said. "Or are you in the habit of putting yourself in harm's way?"

"Not in the habit, no. What about you?"

"Oh, it's definitely one I'm trying to break."

The low baritone of his voice vibrated through her. Outside, the hail still battered the window. "So...Moody sent you out here, you said?"

"That's right. I'm looking for work."

An unreasonable disappointment sluiced through her. "I wish I could've saved you the trouble. I'm not hiring."

He lowered the towel. "Correct me if I'm wrong, but you're out here all by yourself."

Uncomfortable with his closeness, she slid off the table and stood, taking a moment to get her balance. "Mr. MacCallister—"

"Cain."

"Cain. I don't know what Moody told you, but—"

"That your husband left you alone with this place awhile back and that you've bitten off more than you can chew. She said you need help. It just so happens that I know a little something about horses and I'm in the market for a job."

Maggie pressed her hands together. "You don't understand. I can't hire you. I can't afford to hire anyone."

Folding up the towel, he walked back to the sink and stared out the window. "I don't need much. Three squares and a roof."

She blinked at him. "Room and board?"

Slowly, he turned back to her, but she didn't miss the way he'd balled his fist against his stomach as if trying to grind away an ache there.

"I noticed your fences in the south pasture need fixing." He glanced up at her ceiling where water droplets swelled and dripped in a steady staccato into a dented metal bucket on her kitchen floor. "One more good storm like this one and you can probably kiss your roof goodbye. Not to mention your stock. You need help. I need a place to be for a while. It sounds like a fair trade."

The tattoo of hail stopped abruptly on the window and silence invaded the room. Was it her imagination, or had he gone suddenly pale? She dismissed the thought as a trick of lighting. Besides, nobody who looked like he did worked for room and board. His grasp of the English language told her he was educated too, which put him miles beyond most of the itinerant hands that drifted through here. And then another thought occurred to her. "Are you in some kind of...trouble, Mr. MacCallister?"

Sweat beaded on his upper lip and he braced a hand on the counter behind him. A low curse escaped him.

"Mr. MacCallister?"

Without answering, he bolted out the kitchen door. Maggie stared after him for a heartbeat before following him. Jigger shadowed close on her heels.

She found him leaning over the boxwood bushes around the corner of her house, retching. Maggie watched helplessly, uncertain whether to stay or leave him alone. In the end she found she couldn't simply walk away from him.

When he'd finished, he straightened slowly, his color not far off from the winter-pale green leaves beside him.

He wiped the back of one hand across his mouth. "Sorry about that."

"You're ill?"

He shook his head. "Moody's coffee on an empty stomach. Not a good idea."

She remembered the way he'd looked at those plates of food at the café. The way he'd hugged that cup of coffee as if it were gold. "How long since you've eaten? I mean something solid."

His posture stiffened and he blinked as if he were considering lying. "I'm looking for a job," he said, "not a handout."

"That's not exactly an answer, is it? How long?"

"A couple of days ago, I guess."

"A couple of—?" Maggie blinked at him incredulously.

He stared first at his feet then off toward his bike. "I'm

sorry to have troubled you, Mrs. Cortland. I'll be on my way."

"*Troubled* me? You saved my life, Mr. MacCallister. I...I owe you something for that."

"You don't owe me a thing."

"I can't offer you a job, but the least I can do is feed you a decent meal. In fact, I insist."

His gaze traveled slowly down the length of her, then moved to his own mud-coated boots.

"Please," she repeated softly. "Come inside."

Reluctantly, he followed her back in the kitchen. Maggie pulled a glass down from the cupboard, filled it with milk and held it out to him.

"Mrs. Cortland, I—" he began.

"Drink this. It'll settle your stomach." She looked down at her mud-covered clothes. "Look, I'm...a mess. I need a shower and a change of clothes. And then I'll come back down and fix you some lunch." She pulled a chair out from the table for him. "Will you let me do that for you?"

Some of the steel went out of his spine as he took the glass she offered. He was proud. She could see that. But he was hungry, too. Too hungry, she decided, to refuse her.

"I'll be outside." Sliding his gloves back on, he left her standing with Jigger pressed protectively against her, and the screen door screeching shut in his wake.

It took her a ten minutes under a steaming shower to get the mud out of her hair and another ten to gingerly pull on her clothes, past the ache in her shoulder and left hip. And her cheek... Well, her cheek was another matter altogether.

She supposed the bruises she saw when she looked in the mirror were minor compared to the battering her confidence had taken today. She'd always believed she could do anything she put her mind to. Today, however, she'd failed. Failed not only to save her ranch from the fate to which her husband had consigned it, but failed at the simplest of tasks required in running it.

She leaned over the vanity, inspecting her battered cheek with a frown. She'd been lucky today. If it hadn't been for that stranger downstairs, she might well be lying dead in the paddock right now instead of contemplating how a scar would add character to her face.

She closed her eyes against the dull ache throbbing at the back of her skull. Lord, what had she been thinking chasing Geronimo that way? She should have read him better. Anticipated what he'd been about to do. Sure, she was overtired, overworked, but who wasn't? running a day-to-day operation like this one. Maybe Ernie and the bank and all of those men were who were waiting for her to fold were right. Maybe she couldn't do it. Maybe Big Sky Country did belong to the men of the world.

Maybe a husband was a requirement up here in this wild country. And in the best of worlds, she'd have one. But Ben had taken that option right out of her hands six months ago. So what choice did she have? Husbands didn't grow on trees. And except for the one man she'd never, ever consider, no one had offered. And even a ranch hand wouldn't help her now, she realized, thinking of Cain's offer. It was too late for that. She needed the loan. And they'd turned her down.

She'd failed. Utterly. It was only a matter of dotting the i's and crossing the t's. And after that, Laird Donnelly would finally get what he'd always wanted. At least, she amended, half of what he wanted.

Maggie moved to her bedroom window and looked down at the yard. She couldn't explain the relief she felt when she saw Cain's bike still parked there. Nor could she comprehend the almost palpable rush she got at the prospect of seeing him again.

Who was he and what strange twist of fate had brought

him onto her ranch exactly when she'd needed him? More troubling, perhaps, was why that very coincidence didn't alarm her? After all, she reasoned as she made her way downstairs, she didn't know anything about him. What if he worked for Laird? What if Laird had sent him here to make trouble for her from the inside?

Unlikely, she decided, pulling a jacket from the clothes tree by the front door. He'd come into the diner off the highway. And there hadn't been even an exchange of glances with Laird or his men that she could recall. No, he'd said Moody sent him and Moody would never knowingly send a dangerous man to her ranch.

But then, she reasoned, real monsters rarely have fangs.

Shrugging into her jacket, she headed outside to find him. She'd promised him food and she would feed him. And that, she told herself, would be the end of that.

"Whoa, son," Cain soothed, rubbing a dry blanket over Geronimo's soaked haunches as the gelding blew out a nervous breath and backed against the rear wall of the stall. Cain tightened his grip around Geronimo's lead rope and brought the animal's head down closer to him. "Nowhere to go now, is there? It's just you an' me here, pal. Nothin' to be afraid of."

Geronimo nuzzled Cain's clothing for a scent and exhaled sharply.

Cain's mouth twitched with a smile. "Yeah, I know. Life's a bitch, isn't it? But you could do a lot worse than to end up in Maggie Cortland's barn. A helluva lot worse. You keep that in mind the next time she steps into a paddock with you, you hear?"

A sound from the doorway had Cain whirling around with an instinct honed over the last few years. It was an old habit and hard to break, and his shoulders relaxed fractionally when he saw it was only Maggie walking toward him with a curious expression on her face. Her hair was still damp from her shower and as she walked, she pulled her fingers through it unselfconsciously.

The sight of her did things to him. Made him remember how long it had been since he'd been with a woman. Any woman. Locking down the thought, he turned his attention to the wool blanket in his hand.

"I can't tell you," she said breezily, "what a relief it is to know I'm not the only one who talks to horses."

"See?" he said, tossing the blanket over the stall half door. "I told you I could be useful."

As Jigger prowled the hallway of the barn near her, Maggie nodded at the gelding. "How did you do that?"

"Do what?"

"Settle him down like that? He's never let anyone but me touch him."

Cain ran his palm down over Geronimo's velvety nose and the horse quivered with pleasure. "We came to an understanding."

"Ah," she said, "you mean, he understands he's not to trample you if you understand his heartfelt desire not to be sold to the nearest glue factory."

"Something like that." He grinned at her as he ran his hands down the animal's flank and across the thick, well defined muscles of his chest. "He's got decent lines. More than decent, actually. But he's got a shaky history."

She braced her elbows over the half door and studied the horse. "You're right. I've had him for less than a month. God knows what happened to him before I found him in that auction. But I'm not giving up on him just yet."

"Horses like this are unpredictable at best, dangerous at worst, like today. He could kill you in a heartbeat if he took it into his thick head."

Maggie reached up to scratch Geronimo under his chin. "He's scared, not mean. I know the difference."

"Dead's dead. Nobody will care later what his intentions were." Cain turned his back on her and finished rubbing the horse's flanks with the blanket.

"You're right, "she said evenly. "I'll be more careful."

He nodded without reply.

"So…you seem to know your way around horses."

"Yup."

Maggie braced her arms across the half door of the stall, resting her chin there. "Huh. A monosyllabic résumé. That's a unique approach."

He relinquished a small smile. "I thought you weren't looking for a résumé."

"I'm not…exactly. Just curious, I guess. You don't look like the sort of man who'd be drifting, that's all."

He gave Geronimo a final pat, then gave her damp hair and battered cheek a fresh perusal. "And sad-eyed beauties dressed in city clothes who sit alone in cafés don't usually run ranches. So there you go."

Color crawled up her neck as Cain drew near enough to smell the scent of soap on her. And for the briefest of moments, he had the crazy impulse to bury his face in her hair and simply breathe in the scent of her.

"You're not the first person who thinks I don't belong here."

Cain narrowed his eyes. "I never said that."

"Well, that puts you miles ahead of the competition."

"Competition?"

"Never mind."

She turned and he knew he'd said something wrong. Dammit.

"No, wait. Mrs. Cortland. I may be a little outta practice, but I think I just stepped on your toes. I'm…sorry."

Maggie turned around, her expression thawing as she hugged herself with her arms. She exhaled slowly. "No,

I'm sorry. I didn't mean to— It's been a bad day. You have nothing to do with that.''

"Look—" He stared down at a callus on his hand. "Maybe I should just go."

"No, *don't.* I mean…'' She pressed her hands together and he had the oddest feeling that what he'd heard in her voice was desperation. ''What I mean is, I still have to feed you. You did say you'd stay for lunch? Right?''

Her eyes had gone dark. Not desperation. Fear. Not of him, but of something. Like a child scared of being alone in the dark, afraid the boogyman would come out of her closet.

He shouldn't care, he told himself.

No, make that, he didn't care.

He couldn't afford to get involved with this woman's troubles. He had enough of his own. But something about her—maybe it was her stubborn pride—made him want to tell her that everything would be all right. Hold her against him until the worry melted from her eyes.

Hell.

As if he could. As if he had it in him to try. She was a means to an end. That's all. She'd offered him food and he'd take it and go. Simple. Clean.

No fuss, no muss. That was his motto. And he'd damned well better stick with it if he was ever going to—

''Why don't you come in and wash up,'' she said, before he could finish his thought. Turning abruptly, she headed toward the house. ''I hope you don't mind chicken. I thought I'd fry it.''

Chicken? His mouth watered instantly at the very sound of the word and his empty belly growled.

No fuss, no muss, he thought, falling in behind her with all the self-restraint of a back-door dog.

Yeah, right.

Chapter 3

Four hours and a dozen chores later, Maggie stood in her doorway holding the glass of lemonade she'd poured for Cain, watching him wield an axe over the ancient limb of the oak that had fallen across her yard in the last storm. She hadn't asked him to do it. He'd insisted. Something about paying her back for the chicken and biscuits she'd fixed him.

She allowed herself a smile, remembering how he'd devoured the meal she'd made him. She suspected that it had been more than a couple of days since his last full meal. It made her wonder about him. A drifter, but not like any drifter she'd ever known. What had brought him to this? Where had he been and what had happened to him?

It was none of her business, of course, and she settled for the fact that she had, in a small way, repaid the debt she owed him for saving her life. How odd, she thought, that it could give her such pleasure, such a simple, old-fashioned thing as watching a man sate his hunger with her cooking. It made her feel useful. Necessary.

But now, as the rhythmic sound of the axe echoed across the shadow-drawn yard, she realized that "necessary" didn't adequately describe what she was feeling as she watched him. She felt her pulse skitter and told herself she shouldn't stare. But with his back to her, she indulged herself.

Where Ben had been compact, Cain's build was lean and powerful. The muscles in his back and arms bunched and flexed as he hefted the axe over his head and brought it down hard against the ancient wood. There was a controlled violence to the way he dismantled that limb. Piece by piece. Stroke by stroke. The only break in his rhythm had come when he'd paused to add the chopped wood into a neat and growing pile that stood now to his left.

He was thinner than he'd been once. She could see that in the way his jeans fit—loose and low on his hips—and in the definition of his ribs. But whatever muscle mass he'd lost to hunger was more than compensated for by the sleek, animal-like grace with which he moved.

It wasn't so much an economy of motion, she decided, studying him, as it was a deliberateness. She wondered absently where a man like him learned that kind of self-containment. And what in his past that had taught him to always watch his back.

Almost as if he'd heard her thought, he stopped chopping, catching sight of her watching him. Jigger, who'd been lying in the shade watching Cain, too, lifted his big, dark head and thumped his tail happily against the damp soil in greeting.

"You've got quite a rapt audience," she told Cain.

"He's just keepin' an eye on me." Cain wiped the sweat from his face with the back of his wrist and reached for his black T-shirt. "That for me?" he asked, indicating the lemonade.

She pushed away from the door and started toward him. "I thought you might be thirsty."

He tugged his T-shirt on, then took the glass from her and guzzled down the contents in four serious gulps. Maggie stared, unable to take her eyes off him, or off the stray rivulet of moisture trickling down his chin.

He gave a sigh of satisfaction and dragged a forearm slowly across his mouth, all the while watching her. "Thanks."

She swallowed hard. Lord, what was wrong with her?

Taking the empty glass, she fixed her gaze on the stack of wood. "You must have been a Boy Scout once."

"Nope. My old man never believed in team player mentality," he said, stroking the old oak handle of the axe as though he was prepared to tolerate her interruption politely. "Whacked apart my share of tree limbs, though."

"I'll bet. Grow up on a farm?"

He tossed a look in her direction. "Ranch."

Ah. "That must account for the laconic cowboy conversationalist you've become."

He grinned, staring off at the sun as it settled between the peaks of the Bitterroots. "You wanna talk? Or you want me to chop up this limb?"

She hugged herself against the chill beginning to settle in the air. Maggie glanced at the sinking sun, too, remembering how many sunsets she'd watched alone lately. "It'll be dark soon."

His gaze slid to her. If another man had ever made her feel utterly naked with one look before, she couldn't remember it. "You know," she began, "I really...appreciate what you've done here, but you don't have to finish."

"I said I would."

"I mean, it's a big limb and when you volunteered you didn't even know my chain saw was broken and now I really owe you so much more than a chicken dinner for all that you've done for—"

"Do you want me to go?"

She blinked up at him. "No, it's just—"

"If you want me to leave, I'll leave." He leaned the axe handle against the wood pile and stepped back.

She did want him to go. Wanted him to stop making her brood about things she couldn't have anymore. But she found herself shaking her head. "I—I don't—"

"—know me." He ran a hand across his stubbled chin as if realizing his appearance might have something to do with the look on her face right now. "I'm afraid I don't have any references in my back pocket. It's been a while since I held down a job."

"I...told you I couldn't afford to—"

"—hire me. I know." He smiled ironically. "But you already paid me for this. See, it's been a while since I've had more than truck-stop food either. Food, in any case. I figure that's worth this whole damned tree limb. And I mean to finish it."

"But it's...getting dark."

He glanced around, as if noticing for the first time that daylight had nearly disappeared. He slid his fingers along the smooth wood of the axe handle with a self-deprecating laugh. "Sorry. I'm a little slow on the uptake these days, too. I'll just get my things together and be outta your hair." He leaned the axe handle against the woodpile and reached for the jacket he'd left draped there.

It took Maggie a moment to react. "Cain. That's not what I meant."

"It's okay, Mrs. Cortland," he said, as if he were used to being dismissed.

"But where will you go?"

"That's not your worry," he said, shoving his arms into his jacket. "I'll manage."

"Do you have somewhere to stay?"

He started toward his bike parked across the yard. "I'll manage," he repeated.

"Wait. Cain." Maggie crossed the distance between them stopping a few feet from him.

He stopped, but didn't look at her.

"There's a cot in the tack room. It's not much, but it's clean and dry and—"

He pivoted toward her, surprise clearly etched on his face. "You...want me to stay the night?"

Maggie bit the inside of her lip. "I'm...yes. If you want to. For the night. In the barn."

His shoulders relaxed a fraction and he looked at the barn. "Whatever you're afraid of, you should know I'd never hurt you. You don't know me, but you should know that."

A shiver ran through her. A dark inkling that this stranger had the potential to break her heart.

Ridiculous, she thought. Tomorrow, or maybe the next day, he'll be gone. After everything she'd been through in the last year, her heart was every bit as bullet proof as Cain's appeared to be.

She brightened and forced herself to smile. "Then it's settled. I have a stew on the stove. Come in when you're hungry."

She could feel his eyes on her back as she turned and headed back to the house. Jigger trotted along beside her.

"Yes, ma'am," he called to her back.

She turned, walking backward and tossed him another smile. "It's Maggie. Just Maggie."

The last of the sun had sunk behind the mountains limning Maggie's valley by the time Cain finished with the fallen limb. He stacked the last split of wood on the pile beside him, then wiped the sweat off his face with the ban-

dana he kept in his back pocket. The muscles in his arms
and his back burned like hot embers and he could feel the
blisters rising on his palms, but he walked toward the water
spigot near the paddock feeling a sense of satisfaction. The
physical labor made him feel alive—useful—something
that had become almost foreign to him over the past four
years.

He'd missed being able to walk outside when he wanted
and feel the sun against his skin. He'd missed seeing the
sunset and the sunrise. Four months since his release and
he hadn't missed a single one. He didn't want to remember
the man that place had made him. But neither could he
leave him behind. He was the sum of his life and it had
made him hard.

He gave the faucet handle a twist. The water spilled out
in an icy cold rush, but he splashed it against his face and
across the back of his neck, energized by the shock.

He glanced out over the pastures to the west, where the
land rose to meet the mountains and Maggie's herd of
mares and foals grazed in the dusky light. The small herd
of black Angus she used for training were finishing off the
hay she'd laid out for them.

Once he'd dreamed of having a place like this of his
own. With a string of horses and cattle and land as far as
the eye could see. Not the Concho. That had never belonged to him. That had been Judd's domain. And always
would be. But somewhere, Cain's dreams had fallen away
to make room for plain old survival. For now, it was
enough that he'd sleep tonight with a full belly and a roof
over his head.

He glanced at the light spilling from the kitchen window
and saw Maggie's silhouette moving around near the stove.
It was simple gratitude he should feel toward her for offering him the chance to get back on his feet. But some
other, less well-defined feeling complicated the simplicity

of that. It wasn't as easy as sex. Sex was simple. Lust, even simpler. He couldn't honestly deny feeling either one. But what man could? She was a natural beauty with vulnerability and loneliness written all over her. And he'd been too damned long without a woman to overlook what she had to offer.

He wasn't, by choice, a curious man. He had no interest in getting to know anyone better than what he could learn from a handshake. But he was curious about her. Who was she? And what the hell was she doing out here all by herself in a country that devoured the strongest of men? What was that jackass of a husband of hers thinking, leaving a woman like her alone?

And, Cain wondered darkly, if he hadn't ridden out here today in that storm, would she be in her kitchen now, puttering over the hot stove? Or would that damned horse have precluded any speculation on his part at all?

Which, he reminded himself, he shouldn't be doing anyway. Tomorrow, he'd be moving on and Maggie Cortland and whatever problems she was facing would be miles behind him.

She was setting the table with dishes when he knocked quietly on the door. Jigger announced him and Maggie called for him to come on in. The door was open.

The aroma hit him first: savory beef and vegetables simmering on top of the stove. The warmth of the kitchen hit him next, followed immediately by the gut-punching view of Maggie's backside as she leaned over the table with a handful of silverware. She'd changed out of her work clothes and into a slender pair of black slacks and a sweater the color of the sky in April.

"Hi," she said brightly, turning toward him. "All finished?"

He cleared his throat. "Just about." She smiled at him and he felt something stutter inside him. "Smells good."

"It's almost ready. I thought…maybe…you might like a hot shower before dinner."

A hot shower? Cain blinked. He hadn't even dreamed of that small luxury.

"Down the hall, second door on your right. Towels are in the cupboard. And a fresh razor if you want one."

Cain swallowed hard and nodded. "That's…that's kind of you. I'll just," he said, backing out of the kitchen, "get something clean out of my gear."

Maggie smiled and turned back to the cupboard, fishing out a pair of water goblets for the table.

Cain headed for his bike, praying that he had something clean to replace the clothes he had on his back.

When they'd finished eating the stew and biscuits Maggie had made for supper, she poured Cain a cup of coffee and they walked out onto the porch together. Evening had brought out the blanket of stars overhead and the chill in the air required Maggie to throw on a soft jacket over her sweater. She'd gotten used to being alone. It felt strange to have company, Maggie thought. Their meal had been awkward and full of long silences, and now he stood, staring out over the mountains, his look, a thousand miles away.

"Penny for your thoughts," she said.

He looked up, then took a sip from his coffee. "They might be worth almost that."

"The mountains are beautiful, aren't they?" she said, taking a sip of her mug.

His gaze scanned the silvery trace of the mountaintops. "Yes."

"Even in moonlight," she said. "They never cease to steal my breath."

"How long you been here?" he asked.

"Six years. Not long enough," she replied. "Never long enough."

"It's an easy thing to fall in love with the land."

Pulling her gaze from the darkness beyond, she swivelled a look at him. "Have you? I mean, ever fallen in love with a piece of land?"

He took a sip of coffee. "Ancient history."

Maggie nodded. "I can't imagine living anywhere else now. I'll do whatever it takes to keep it."

He filled his lungs with the scent of the snow off the mountaintops and the burgeoning green covering the hills. "It's worth fighting for."

She held her mug up to his for a toast to that sentiment. He smiled and returned the favor.

"To the good fight," she said, and slugged a drink of the bittersweet coffee. He did the same and she had trouble taking her eyes off the way his muscular throat moved as he swallowed. The sight made her skin go suddenly tight.

Jigger nudged between them and Cain dropped his hand on the dog's furry head for a scratch. The dog's whole body quivered with pleasure.

"Can I ask you something?" he said as the silence stretched between them.

"Shoot."

"Who was that guy in the coffee shop this morning?"

She tightened her hand around her cup. She knew instantly who he meant. "Guy?"

"Tall. Blowhard. Bent on ruining your day?"

Maggie smiled in spite of herself. "Oh, *that* guy." She didn't want to talk about Laird. "He was nobody. Just a rancher."

"Not according to him."

"True," she agreed. "He's under the misguided impression that he owns this valley."

"Does he?"

"Not everything." Maggie smoothed her right palm

across the wood railing and a splinter slid neatly under her skin with a vicious prick. "Ow! Darn it!"

"Lemme see," he said, grabbing her palm and inspecting it in the moonlight.

She tried to pull away, but his strong hand held hers firmly. "It's nothing," she complained, ignoring the sting. "Just a splinter." But it felt like a ponderosa pine trunk had found its way under her skin.

"Hold still." He bent over her hand, and turned it toward the kitchen light spilling through the open door. She didn't mean to inhale the clean, soapy scent of him, or stare at the worn seams on his dark leather bomber jacket where his shoulders had strained it. And she couldn't help herself from taking in the deep, dark brown of his hair or the way it curled over the edge of his shirt collar.

Lord, Maggie thought, giving herself a mental shake. You've been alone way too long.

It took less than ten seconds for him to get a grip on the splinter and pull it out. He lifted a smile up at her triumphantly, only then seeming to realize how close he was to her. His smile faded as he dropped her hand and stepped back. "Better put something on that."

She rubbed at the spot gingerly with her thumb. "Thanks. I will."

His large hand seemed to dwarf the railing as he brushed at the loose paint and splintery wood on the rail. "This could use some sandpaper and a fresh coat of paint."

"Along with nearly every other surface on my property," she said, shaking her head. "I'll get right on that. In my spare time."

"Sorry, it's none of my business."

"Don't apologize. I've gotten way behind on things here. But painting railings isn't exactly a priority when I'm barely managing to pay my bills. That's why I was in town today," she said with a sigh of resignation. "Getting turned down for a loan."

He shook his head, "I always did have good timing."

"Need I remind you that I probably wouldn't be standing here now if you hadn't ridden up on your bike when you did?"

He turned to look out over her darkened pastures again. "That was just lucky."

"I used to believe in luck," she said. "But now I don't think there are any coincidences."

"You mean you think I was supposed to ride up and drag you out from under that horse of yours?"

She laughed. "I don't know. Maybe. Maybe you just needed a meal so you could get on to the next thing. Maybe that's all this is."

"Pretty deep for a horse rancher," he said with a smile.

She returned it. "That's what I get for spending too much time with the animal kingdom. I get philosophical."

"And lonely?"

She smoothed her hand over her palm. "Sometimes. Mostly I'm too tired to be lonely."

"That's my cue," he said. "I'd better turn in, too."

For reasons she couldn't explain, she wasn't ready to let Cain go yet, but could think of nothing to stop him. "There's fresh bedding in the trunk beside the cot. Blankets and... It get's a little cold still at night, even for June."

He reached a hand out to her and she took it. His fingers curled around her palm with gentle firmness. "Make sure you take care of that hand. I'll be out of your hair first light. Thanks for everything." He let her go and smiled. "Goodbye, Mrs. Cortland."

She watched him head toward the barn. Before he could disappear into the shadows, she said, "It's Maggie."

He turned back to her.

"My name," she explained. "And you don't have to

rush out first thing. I mean, I could probably find one or two other chores around the place if…you aren't in too much of a hurry to get back on the road.''

He cast a restless look around her dark yard. ''Are you askin' me to stay?''

She pressed her hands together. ''Asking? No. That wouldn't be fair of me. I can't really pay you. Not what you're worth. But I still have to cook tomorrow and well…you'll still be hungry. Right?''

He thought about it for a minute, rubbing a hand absently against his belly. ''I'll move that stack of wood closer to the house in the morning,'' he said at last. ''Maybe…sand down that railing of yours. Then, we'll talk.''

Relief washed over her as he turned and melted into the darkness. She shook her head and wrapped her arms around herself against the chill. ''Crazy,'' she told herself. ''You are definitely, unquestionably, nuts, Maggie.'' But something told her that Cain MacCallister might just be her one last chance.

Cain lay with his hands propped under his head on the cot in the tack room, staring up at the blackness above him. The cot was comfortable, if a bit too short for his six-three frame, and the room smelled comfortingly of leather, horses and hay. It wasn't the sound of the animals moving restlessly in their nearby stalls that kept him from finding sleep. Or the songs of coyotes far off yipping to each other.

It was Maggie. She was interfering with his dream.

He closed his eyes and sighed, trying to shove her out of his mind. He'd spent the last hour trying to call up Annie's image in his memory. He almost had it once: the blond hair that framed that oval-shaped face of hers; her eyes, not quite blue, but not really green either, but always a pool he'd wanted to dive into. He was having trouble with her nose and her mouth. It was the mouth that bothered him most, because he could always remember her mouth. More specifically, her smile.

He kept confusing it with Maggie's, the way her mouth turned up at the corners and that little dimple dented one cheek near her mouth.

Focus, man. Don't get distracted.

But the little bruise above Maggie's eye popped into his mind again...the soft feel of her hand in his...even the smell of her hair.

Damn. He squeezed his eyes shut. What the hell was wrong with him?

Annie's voice. Remember it. Yeah. There it was. He could hear it now: *"Be right back. Save me some popcorn. Be right back, save me some...be right...save me—"*

Shoving off the blankets, he sat up, finding the cold floor with his bare feet. He felt dizzy and his chest, dammit, his chest was doing its usual timpani roll.

Seven little words that had changed his life.

Snapping on the lamp parked near the cot on the little wood table, Cain dragged in a few deep breaths. He re-oriented himself as he reached for his backpack. He shoved things aside, then threw them on the floor, one by one, until his hand closed around the thing it sought. Cool, smooth glass. It took shape in his hand.

The whiskey inside the bottle sloshed against the sides with a magical sound, calling to him. He cradled it in his hands, tempted by all reason to break the thin paper seal that stood between him and true destruction.

He craved it right now, something that he hadn't done in a long time. Even when he'd gotten out, he'd managed to steer clear of bars where he knew he might be tempted. But he'd bought this bottle to remind himself what was back there in that dark place he'd visited in the months after Annie's death. The ones that had nearly killed him.

He'd spent the last three years building his strength, finding the quiet place inside him that could silence the noise outside. The guilt and the pain. He could call it up when he needed it. Except tonight.

Tonight, he found himself tempted again, not just by the siren of oblivion, but by a woman he hardly knew who had already made him forget the curve of Annie's lips.

Cain turned the bottle over in his hands, smoothing the cool glass with his fingers. It would be easy, he thought. One twist, one sip or two and the noise would stop.

But he wouldn't stop at two or three, or even four. Not until he reached the bottom of the bottle and the darkness it promised. And slow suicide, as appealing as it had once been, wasn't his style anymore. If it was going to end, it wouldn't be slow and it wouldn't come in a liquid form.

So with its paper honor code still intact, he slid the bottle back inside the leather knapsack and reached instead for his wallet, resting on the table beneath the lamp.

He pulled out the dog-eared photo, soft from years of handling. Annie smiled up at him from the picture and Cain stared at her hollowly. He rubbed his thumb over the image. How many times had he wished he'd gone that night instead of her? Maggie had said she didn't believe in luck, good or bad. He figured a man was only born with so much of it and he'd used all his up when he'd met Annie and stolen those few short years with her. Their luck had run out simultaneously that night even though they'd been miles apart. And a man like him didn't get second chances.

Minutes later, he didn't know how many, Cain reached for the light switch and flicked it off. For a long time, he just sat there in the dark, counting the seconds 'til morning. If he could just make it to dawn, he'd be all right.

He wouldn't think about luck, or about the woman sleeping a few hundred yards away, or anyone who reminded him what it was to be alive. Because he owed Annie that much.

* * *

Dawn had barely lightened the sky when the phone beside Maggie's bed rang. Groggily, Maggie looked at the clock. 5:45 a.m. She frowned. Who would be calling her at this hour? And why, after a sleepless night, did they have to pick this particular morning to wake her up?

She dragged the receiver to her ear across the sleep-rumpled bedclothes. "Hello?"

There was only silence on the other end of the line.

"Hello?" she repeated, sitting up on one elbow. "Is anyone there?"

Nothing. Angry, she began to shove the receiver back in its cradle when she heard a voice, the words too indistinct to make out.

Pulling it back to her ear, Maggie listened. "Hello? Is someone there?" Nothing. "Okay, I'm hanging up now."

"Don't," said a man's voice.

A shiver went through her and her hand tightened on the receiver. "Who is this?"

"A friend." The voice was cigarette hoarse and unfamiliar.

"I know my friends' voices. And I don't know yours."

"Your husband…" the man continued, undeterred. "Ben?"

Her heart started to pound. "What about him?"

There was a long pause. "He didn't fall on his own. He had help."

"Wh—what are you talking about?"

"If you want to know more, find Remus Trimark."

"Who?" Maggie scrambled into the bedside drawer for a pen and a scrap of paper. "Who's Remus Trimark?"

There was another long pause before the caller said, "It's not over," and clicked off.

"Hello?" The dial tone buzzed in her ear. Maggie stared at it, feeling dizzy and off balance. Not over? What's not over? She hung up the receiver and scribbled the name he'd mentioned down on the back of an old Hallmark anniversary card from Ben.

She remembered to breathe.

Remus Trimark? What kind of a name was that, and what did he have to do with Ben's death? And why had the man on the phone waited six months to tell her about it?

She eased back down on the pillow, clutching the card between her shaking fingers. Her mind raced over those last days with Ben, trying to remember something, anything he'd said about a Remus Trimark—what an odd name—or *anyone* he'd mentioned for that matter. She came up blank. Completely blank.

It wasn't as though she hadn't already racked her brain for months on end, trying to piece together the how's and why's of his death. Trying to deconstruct those last weeks. The only conclusion she'd come to was that she and Ben had been so far apart by then it was as if they were strangers.

She turned the card over in her hands, running her fingers over the picture on the front of a yellow rose in a slender glass vase. He'd given her this card on their first anniversary. Inside, the sentimental Hallmark greeting had nothing to do with why she'd kept this particular card. It was the handwritten inscription there that had made her tuck the card away here years ago.

Happy Anniversary, sweetheart. When we're old and gray, sitting around the fire on some cold winter night, remind me to thank you for taking a chance on me.

All my love,
Ben.

It seemed so far away now, those days when he'd loved her so completely. That fire had been banked long before he'd died. He'd gambled that away along with nearly everything else.

He had help.

The stranger's words echoed in her ears. Help? What did he mean by that? And how was she going to find some man named Remus Trimark? In the phone book?

The sound of thunking came from outside Maggie's window. Silently, she slid out of bed and padded barefoot to the window. The filmy drapes billowed as the cool night air slid through the one inch crack between window and sill. She wrapped her arms around her waist and searched the dusky yard for the source of the sound.

She spotted him half-hidden beneath the ash tree in her yard, shirtsleeves rolled halfway up his elbows, hacking away at what was left of that old tree limb.

Cain.

What was he doing up so early? Maybe he figured to finish the job and leave before she could get him to change his mind.

Maybe he hadn't slept any better than she had.

She'd spent most of the night thinking about him, her situation, and the impossible scenarios she'd constructed around how she could save her home—everything from auctioning off the nonessential contents of her house to taking up striptease dancing at the local hangout. But none was as far-fetched as the one that had hit her sometime before she'd drifted into an uneasy sleep. It was too insane to even consider. Really. And Cain would probably call the men in the little white suits to come and take her away for even suggesting it.

Maggie chewed on her thumbnail, watching him bend over to scoop up an armload of wood. The muscles in his thighs bunched like liquid iron. He was strong. And if she didn't miss her guess, a little reckless and maybe even a little desperate. Exactly the sort of man she needed.

It's not over, the voice on the phone echoed in her mind.

Neither was she, she decided. Not while she still had a shred of hope.

With a grateful smile, Cain took the glass of lemonade from her hand and guzzled the cold liquid down. The afternoon heat had backed up in the barn where he was shoveling out stalls and he'd taken off his shirt again. He didn't miss the way her gaze traveled across his bare chest, or the way that little bead of sweat had gathered above her lip.

"Where's yours?" he asked.

She jerked her gaze upward with a flustered little flush of color. "What?"

"Your lemonade," he said.

"Oh. Um." She took the empty glass from him. "I…I'm not thirsty."

He nodded, not believing her for a second. She'd been working her butt off in the pole corral with that demon seed, Geronimo, for the last two hours, getting nowhere. But she looked like she had more important things on her mind.

She'd been quiet at lunch, but he'd figured those dark circles under her eyes might explain that. She looked like she hadn't slept any better than he had. But work, for him, was like a tonic. It made him feel useful. She looked plain worn down.

Or maybe she'd decided he'd worn out his welcome.

He braced a hand on his pitchfork and stabbed at the dirty straw near his feet. "I got that gate latch working again. It just needed a little grease, a couple of screws."

"Gate latch?" she asked, lost.

"By the paddock." When she still looked blank, he pointed. "By the north pasture?"

"Oh! The *gate* latch! Of course…the gate…latch. Thank you. Thanks…" She squeezed her palms together, as if she were looking to enhance her bustline. Something, as far as he was concerned, she didn't need to do.

"Somethin' wrong?" he asked.

"Wrong? No." She smiled broadly. "Nothing's wrong."

Her teeth tugged nervously at her lower lip for the second time since she'd come in here, and she turned away from him, pacing to the other side of the barn hallway.

He couldn't help but notice the way her jeans hugged those long legs of hers, curving against her backside. Nor did he miss the way that little sleeveless cotton blouse of hers outlined the slenderness of her waist and pulled against the fullness of her small breasts. Thoughts he had no business having pulsed through him with little jabs of awareness in regions he'd been ignoring for far too long. But, hell, no matter what his convictions, he was still a man. And she was a—

"I'm just going to say it," she blurted out, whirling back toward him. "There's no point beating around the bush. I have a proposition."

His eyebrows went up. He liked the sound of this already.

"Cain?" she said in a voice usually reserved for pleas to the executioner. "Will you marry me?"

Chapter 4

Following a moment of protracted silence, he laughed out loud. "Man, for a minute there, I thought you asked me to *marry* you."

Her face had gone two shades of red. "I did."

The smile slipped disbelievingly from his expression. Cain stared at her, dumbfounded. Standing up to his ankles in the horse dung and straw he'd swept out of the stables, he nearly sat down where he was.

"Not a real marriage, of course. Don't look at me that way. I know how this sounds."

Cain snorted, thinking it sounded like he'd been transported into some weird alternative universe while he wasn't looking. "You *do?*"

"I-I said it all wrong. Actually," she said, wrinkling her brow, "there is no right way to ask a complete stranger to marry you."

He let the pitchfork's handle thunk against the silvery old wood of the stall door. "Stranger being the operative word."

"I know." Maggie turned and paced to the other side of the barn's main hallway. "I *know*. Don't you think this sounds crazy to me, too?"

He shook his head, still not comprehending. "Then why—?"

"Because I need a husband, Cain. Technically. I need a husband or I'm going to lose this place."

The gears began to lock in place in his brain. "Look," he began, "I'm sorry to hear that. But I don't see what that has to do with me."

"Believe me," she said, pacing from one side of the hallway to the other, "no one is more surprised by what I'm suggesting than I am."

"Really." Cain tore off one work glove and slapped it against his knee. Fragrant bits of straw dust swirled in the air between them. "I don't think I want to know...but what exactly *are* you suggesting?"

She stopped pacing. "An arrangement."

"Arrangement." Even his voice sounded odd. And was it suddenly hotter in here?

"Yes. It would be strictly a business arrangement. With a contract. Guidelines. That sort of thing."

"Guidelines."

"You're horrified."

Cain rubbed his temple. "Horrified isn't exactly—"

"Because I'd be horrified if I were you. I mean, after all, all you did was ride onto my place and innocently ask for a job and here I am—"

"Speechless is more the word I'd go for."

"Right. I understand. But this could benefit us both."

This he had to hear. "How?"

"Well, first of all, there's the obvious. I need a husband to qualify for the loan I need to save this place. You seem to need a place to be. I just thought, since you weren't heading anywhere in particular—"

"Did I *say* that?"

Her lips parted in surprise and he cursed himself for snapping at her.

"I...I—" she stammered, "maybe not."

"I never said that."

She nodded. "All right. At any rate, I wouldn't ask you to do me this favor without compensation. I'm prepared to offer you—"she swallowed hard "—five hundred acres of my land in exchange for posing as my husband."

Five hundred—! Cain nearly choked.

"To be delivered *after* our arrangement is terminated."

Cain was still stuck on the five hundred acres of prime cattle country she'd offered. Something old and rusty lurched back to life inside him. A dream he'd thought long dead. *Land.*

Land that he could call his own. Maybe the old dream wasn't as dead as he'd thought it was.

"Cain? Did you hear me?"

He dragged himself back. "What?"

"I said, you'd have to promise to stay—play my husband that whole time. If you broke your end of the bargain, or if we fail to make this place work...I'll lose the ranch. And your part with it."

She was right. It was a gamble. If she lost, he'd be out six months and the prospect of a place to start over. If she won, though...what? He'd settle down? Build a house and a picket fence and pretend he could ever have go back to the life he'd walked away from?

He reached for the pitchfork again, and just for the hell of it, asked, "How far do you mean to take this little fantasy of yours?"

"What do you mean?"

He turned back to her. "You and me. How far do you intend to take this marriage charade?"

"I told you. It's a business arrangement. You will, of course, sleep in the tack room."

"The tack room. You want me to play your husband from the tack room."

She cleared her throat. "Yes. No one needs to know."

Images of another wedding and another time clicked through his brain. Pictures that turned like a Rolodex in his mind whenever the hell they wanted to. He turned away from Maggie. Hell, what was he thinking? That he could ever start over? Be that man he'd been once? That anyone would ever let him forget where he'd been?

"No," he said, shoving the pitchfork into the last of the soiled bedding in the stall.

Maggie let her arms drop to her sides. "No…as in you won't sleep in the barn? Or—"

"No…as in I won't marry you." He dumped the load of dirty straw at Maggie's feet and turned back to toss the fresh flake of straw around the clean floor.

Behind him, Maggie was silent for the space of ten heartbeats. But that didn't last.

"You could…think about it." Her voice was small and sounded thin. "We could…discuss—"

"I don't need to think about it. I'm not in the market. I told you. I'm just passin' through."

"I could even pay you a small salary when I get the loan. Enough to get you started—"

"Not interested."

Maggie studied one of her palms. "Right. Okay."

Cain leaned against the pitchfork, staring at the dirt floor. He should've left this morning. Early. He didn't want to hear the need in her voice or ponder what it meant to leave her alone here on this place when she was begging him to stay. The flash of anger her offer had set off in him subsided. He wasn't sure where it had even come from. All he knew was that it was time to get out of here.

He combed a hand through his hair. "It's probably best if I go now. I've stayed too long already."

Straightening her shoulders, she started backing out of the barn. "Right. You have to do what you have to do. I'd, uh, better get back to the horses. Please, say goodbye before you go." She turned on her heel and walked out of the barn like a queen. Untouchable. Surrounded by glass.

But he suspected that underneath all that glass was a real woman whose passions ran deep. A woman who, in some other time or place, he would have wanted to get to know.

Did that make him a heel for turning her down? For not wanting to get involved in her troubles? Hell, he'd had enough troubles of his own for more years than he cared to remember. He didn't need anyone else's.

He ground the tines of the pitchfork into the dirt, and headed into the tack room to gather up the few things he'd unpacked there and shove them back in his knapsack.

He'd get on his bike and ride to the next place. And after that, he'd ride some more. Because he had places to go and things to forget.

Maggie managed to reach the pole corral at the far side of the yard before she allowed herself to crumble inside. Grabbing hold of the bark-covered lodgepole fence rail, she climbed up it and wrapped her arms around the top rail. Inside the corral, Geronimo was doing his imitation of a caged cat in the afternoon sun. She knew just how he felt.

Dammit all!

She'd had her share of humiliating moments in this lifetime, but this one just might be the topper.

What had she been thinking? That he'd say yes? That he'd bite on the bribe she'd dangled in front of him in exchange for yoking him with a marriage he didn't want? God. What idiot would want to burden himself with a woman he didn't even know? One that was sinking up to her neck in troubles? Certainly not Cain MacCallister. Nor could she blame him.

Fine, she thought. Let him go. Let him ride off into the sunset. She'd find a way. With him or without him! She wouldn't fail. She simply couldn't. This was the first real home she'd ever had. The ranch meant everything to her and they'd have to physically drag her off, kicking and screaming, before she'd allow them to take it from her.

Geronimo cruised by her, his tail set high, his ears pitched forward at full attention. A shrill sound came from his throat, like the sound wild stallions make when they're gathering their remuda of mares together. He was beautiful, with the conformation of the champions that ran in his bloodline. He wasn't meant to be put behind fences or separated from his kind. Headstrong and a more than a little wild, he had a good heart. A strong heart. She recognized the same qualities in Cain, too. But he was meant for the road, too. A man like him didn't operate under contracts or guidelines. The man was like the horse. Probably untamable and most definitely dangerous to her.

The sight of a truck and a horse trailer coming down her road made Maggie hop down from the fence rail and brush away the moisture that had dampened her cheeks. She cursed under her breath.

Donnelly.

Her heart began to race and she backed toward the house, trying not to panic. She'd left Jigger sleeping inside, dreaming about chasing rabbits. She hadn't had the heart to wake him. But now he was barking worriedly inside the house.

The truck pulled into the yard, spitting gravel and crunching it beneath its tires. Laird was behind the wheel. The passenger seat was empty.

She actually pictured Ben's rifle, tucked safely away in the closet of her bedroom. Too far to help her now. And it was probably just as well because in the mood she was in, she might be tempted to use it on him for simply getting out of his truck.

Laird pulled to a stop not five feet from her. "Told you I'd come by with your mares."

"Don't bother to get out, Laird," she told him. "I'll unload them."

He opened the door anyway and unfolded himself from the truck. "That wouldn't be very gentlemanly of me, would it? After all, I brought the ladies all the way back here…"

"I mean it. Don't come near me."

"I came to pay a simple, friendly visit, Maggie."

"Nothing you do is either simple or friendly." She moved toward the back of the loaded horse van. She lifted the slide bolt and whacked it open with the heel of her hand. But as she swung the door open, Laird appeared beside her.

"Anybody ever tell you you've got a touch of paranoia, Maggie Mae?"

She shot an ugly look at him before climbing up into the trailer. "Don't call me that."

He followed her, crowding her in the dark, narrow space as she moved to unhook the first mare's halter from the stabilizing tether. She fumbled with the metal latch several times before she got it.

Laird moved to unhook a second mare, all the while watching her. "What?" he drawled. "I get no thank-you for goin' to all this trouble? It's not like I didn't have better things to do with my afternoon."

"You could have sent one of your men. God knows, you have enough to spare."

"True. But to tell you the truth, I was curious to see how you were holdin' up on your own out here. Without Ben."

Maggie ignored him and backed the mare down the

ramp, clucking at her as she went. "Atta girl. There you go," she crooned.

Laird followed with the other mare, but he wasn't paying much attention to the horse. "He was a fool, your husband. Abandoning you the way he did."

"Go home, Laird. I mean it," she said, leading the mare to the paddock where she tied it up to the fence rail. Laird did the same with his horse but cornered her there against the fence before she could move.

Maggie swallowed hard. "Get out of my way."

"There's nobody else here, Maggie. Just us."

He was close enough that she could smell the stink of cattle on him, and whiskey if she wasn't mistaken. He'd been drinking. And cigars. He reeked of cigar smoke.

Her throat felt like it was closing up with each thudding beat of her pulse. "Don't."

"You know what your problem is? You been alone too long." He moved closer and Maggie's backside slammed against the fence rail. "You smell real good, Maggie. How come you always smell like a summer rose, working with these horses all day?"

She slapped him. Hard across the cheek.

Surprise flattened Laird's expression as his head jerked back from the force of the blow, but he didn't give her the chance to duck under his arm. His steely gray eyes went glacial as he caught her by the wrist and jerked her closer to him. "You shouldn't have done that, darlin'. I was just workin' up to another proposal, but now..." His gaze slid over her, as she twisted in his grip, "...now I think I'll just sit back and wait. And watch you go down all by your lonesome."

"Let her go!"

The command came from somewhere behind Laird, who whirled to see Cain striding toward them with a murderous look in his eyes. Laird didn't drop her wrist, he just dragged her with him as he turned on Cain like a bulldog with a bone.

"*Now,*" Cain demanded without breaking stride.

"Who the hell are you?"

Cain walked straight to Maggie and hauled her toward him forcing Laird to drop her wrist.

"Are you okay?" Cain asked as he tucked her behind him.

"Who's this, Maggie?" Laird asked. "Your latest squeeze?"

She gave a growl of frustration before jerking her arm from Cain's grasp. "I'll call Sheriff Winston if you don't leave."

Laird laughed. "You go ahead. Fishhook's finest already knows I'm here. In fact, he advised me to trailer these mares back to you when I told him that you've been letting your fences go."

"You and your *thugs* have been cutting my fences yourselves, you—"

"You're overwrought, Maggie," Laird said, echoing the very words Ernie had used yesterday. "Otherwise you'd show some gratitude for my help."

Cain stepped in front of Maggie before she could launch herself at Laird. "Let me handle this."

"*This* is none of your business, boy," Laird told him.

Cain smiled slowly. "What'd you call me?"

"Why don't you get on back to the barn or wherever it was you crawled out from under, and leave business to me and Maggie?"

Maggie could've sworn she saw the hair bristle on the back of Cain's neck.

"I'm gonna give you to the count of three to get in that truck and get off Mrs. Cortland's land. Or you're gonna leave wondering how those little balls of yours wound up wrapped around your ears."

Laird's face went a dangerous shade of angry. "You know who you're talkin' to, boy?"

"One."

"Don't, Cain," she warned. "He's not worth it."

"Cain?" mimicked Laird. "Like the Bible Cain? The coward who backstabbed his own brother?"

"Two..."

He'd taken enough heat over his name in his lifetime that it shouldn't bother him now. It had been his old man's first mistake, and last laugh, naming his son after a notorious sinner. But coming from this bully who seemed bent on making life hard on the first person to treat him kindly in years, made Cain want to take the arrogant bastard apart, piece by ugly piece. It had been a while since he'd had a good brawl and frankly, he was in the mood. He saw that fact register on the other man's face as he took a step closer.

Laird sent Cain an insolent smile, but backed up as he replaced his hat. "That's highway trash for you, Maggie. Leading with his fists."

Maggie grabbed Cain's arm, or he would've taken the idiot's head off.

"I have more civilized ways of dealing with problems," Laird said. "So call your ape off, Maggie. I'm goin'. I've wasted too much of my busy day already." He touched the brim of his three-hundred-dollar Stetson at Maggie. "We'll be talking."

He didn't hurry back to his truck, but sauntered to it, like he already owned every scrawny blade of grass beneath his feet. Cain watched him go, feeling like he just might explode.

He must be losing his touch, he thought. Inside, he wouldn't have waited for the count of three. He would've jumped him on two, before he had to worry that some hand-made shiv was going to turn up unexpectedly in his back one sunny afternoon on the exercise yard.

He waited until the pickup roared to life and tore out of Maggie's yard, before he slammed the toe of his boot into the steel bucket near his foot, sending it spinning across the yard with a clatter that spooked the horses tied to the rail. He grabbed their reins and settled them down before he noticed Maggie wandering, loose-kneed toward the fence.

He grabbed her before she could fall. "Hey—"

She landed flush against him, curling her fingers into his jacket. Her smallness surprised him, even though he'd held her once before. Maybe because she had such an attitude, he reasoned. Or because she'd managed to make him believe that she'd be fine no matter what. But alarms went off in his head and elsewhere, lower down, despite his best intentions as he took in the feel of her against him.

"I'm all right," she argued, pushing away from him. "I just need to sit." Her face had lost most of its color and she was shaking as she lowered herself to the ground. "I'm sorry you had to see that."

He wasn't. "You okay?"

She nodded.

"He bully everybody like that?"

"Donnelly does what he does because he can," she said, dragging her hair back away from her face.

Cain slumped down in the dirt beside the knapsack he'd dropped earlier. "I should have taken him apart."

"No." Maggie held her head in her hands and closed her eyes. The clouds made way for the sun, warming the chill that had settled around the shadows. "Listen, I appreciate what you did for me. But we both know this isn't your problem. And I don't want you getting in any deeper than you already are. You don't know Donnelly. He's like a timber rattler. The kind that lies on a warm rock in the sun, looking like a piece of the stone. But if you make him mad, he'll come after you. And you've done that. You should go. Now.''

Like hell. "Do I look scared to you?''

She turned to stare at him. "You're angry. That's even more dangerous.''

Cain stared off at the mountains, forcing himself back under control. "What does he want?''

She rubbed her face with both hands, then sighed, staring out across her yard. "My land.''

"I'd say that's not all he wants.''

With a shake of her head, she said, "Yes, but I'm only a side bet.''

He'd been near her for two days now. He wasn't so sure about that. "How long has this been going on?''

She looked away.

"How long?'' he insisted.

"Two years. Give or take a few months. Since before my husband died.''

Cain swivelled a look at her. "Your husband's...*dead?*''

"Yes. What did you think?''

"Moody didn't say. I thought...he left you.''

Her gaze slid away from his. "He did. In a way.''

"Did he know about Donnelly?''

Maggie sighed. "About this? I couldn't tell him. For...a lot of reasons. Look, let's just forget this happened. I was careless. I won't be the next time.'' She got to her feet, brushing off the dust from the seat of her jeans. "You said you were leaving. You should go before it gets dark.''

But Cain didn't move. Instead, he draped his wrists over his knees and leaned back against the rail fence, staring at the two-story house Maggie lived in. Winter-bare rose climbers sprouting mauve-colored leaves ambled up the trellis on either side of the front porch. The paint there and everywhere else was peeling from the Montana weather, and the overhang on the front porch sagged in the middle, bent from the weight of too many snowfalls.

But summer was sneaking up on her valley. The electric sound of a cicadas spun out on the warm afternoon air and overhead, swallows dipped in and out of the barn rafters, feeding their young.

Cain exhaled slowly and got to his feet beside her. "Five hundred acres isn't enough to run a herd."

She swivelled an incredulous look at him. "What?"

"Or form much a barrier between you and Donnelly."

She blinked. Twice.

"That *was* your intention, wasn't it? To put me between you and him?"

She didn't even try to lie. "Yes."

He nodded, still watching her. "A thousand acres on the other hand. A man could start something with a thousand—"

"Done."

Now it was his turn to stare.

"A thousand acres in exchange for a marriage certificate and your promise to stay with me until fall."

He narrowed his eyes against the glare. "Fall sounds vague."

"Six months. October first. I'll have the cutting horses trained by then. Ready for sale. I'll pay off the loan and be back in the black again. And then, the land's all yours. If I fail to do that, the land belongs to the bank. It's as simple as that. That way you have a stake in my success."

Cain didn't answer for a full minute. He was nuts. Psych ward eligible. It was one thing to hold a job that long. Another entirely to play house with a woman who made him hard by simply looking at him with those big brown eyes of hers.

Behind them, Geronimo scraped his hoof in the dirt and whickered softly at the mares Maggie had left tied to the rail. They sniffed each other as the warm May breeze lifted their manes and carried the redolent scent of hay out of the nearby loft.

"I'll need a contract," he began.

"We'll visit my attorney tomorrow. Draw one up. It'll all be legal."

Cain plunged his fingers through his hair, staring off into the distance. "All right," he said at last. "You got yourself a deal. I'll play your husband—"

Maggie launched herself at him, throwing her arms around his neck, nearly knocking him over. "Thank you. Thank you."

The feel of her firm breasts pressed flush against him traveled through him like an electric current. She smelled sweet and fine, and it reminded him with a jolt how long it had been since he'd actually wanted a woman who didn't come with a glass of whiskey in her hand and a trail of bad decisions behind her.

It only lasted the space of three or four heartbeats, though, because Maggie pulled back, embarrassed. The loss of contact almost made him wince.

"Oh, God. I—I'm sorry," she murmured. "I don't know what came over me. I'm very grateful to you. That's all."

Cain gathered his wits and scrubbed a hand over his chin. "Yeah, well," he began, "don't be too grateful yet. I've got a few ground rules of my own."

Maggie lifted her chin. "All right."

"Number one, I won't sleep in the barn. If I'm gonna play your husband, I sleep in the house."

She took a deep breath. "What else?"

"I'm no monk. You should know that up front. Six months is a lot to ask of a man if you don't intend to share his bed."

"Share your—? I hope you don't think that just because I—before...that wasn't—"

"We're both adults, Maggie. We've both been alone a long time. " His eyes darkened as he watched her. "You wouldn't be sorry. I'd make it good for you."

Maggie blinked at him in shock. A vivid, mental picture of just *how* good he could make it skittered through her mind and heated her insides: his hands sliding against her skin, his mouth on her—

"You're totally off base here on this."

"Am I?" He sounded unconvinced.

"Yes. I don't want that," she said unequivocally. "Sex, I mean."

He watched her with a frown, not saying anything.

She longed for a glass of water. "This marriage is strictly a business arrangement."

"Okay." He reached for the knapsack he'd dropped on the ground at her feet. "But you can't expect me to give up sex as part of the deal. So, you have a choice. Either that's part of the bargain—you and me—or I make my own…arrangements on the side."

Maggie gaped at him. "Are you saying that you're not capable of going six short months without—?"

He gave her a look that questioned her sanity. "Yes. Take it or leave it."

Equal measures of relief and disappointment eddied through her as it occurred to her it was simply sex he wanted and not specifically her.

"There's a second bedroom upstairs," she said. "You can sleep there. I lock my bedroom door at night."

A flash of anger crossed his expression. "Rape was never in my repertoire. If anything happened between us, darlin', it would be damn well be by your choice."

Heat traveled up her neck. "I didn't mean—"

"Sure you did. But that doesn't matter. I'll make my own arrangements."

"I'm sorry. You're right. You...do what you have to. But please remember, this is a very small town."

Anger shifted in the set of his shoulders. "I'll be discreet."

"There is no such thing in Fishhook. You'll have to go farther afield for your...extracurricular activities. I'll need your promise."

He touched the brim of his hat in a two-fingered salute. "I'll be the picture of discretion well outside the town limits."

"Fine."

"Fine," he repeated.

The mare beside her stomped her hoof and swished a fly off her back, glancing around at the two of them.

"We'll need blood tests," Maggie said, "and a license."

He stared at the ground with a nod.

"I'll call Harold and make an appointment for tomorrow."

"Harold?"

"Harold Levi," she said. "My attorney."

He shifted the backpack to his other shoulder.

"Cain," she said, watching the shadows cross his face as the reality of what they'd been deciding sank in. "You can still change your mind. If it's not what you want."

He didn't answer immediately and Maggie held her breath, waiting for him to tell her that it had all been a mistake. That he'd agreed too quickly and he'd come to his senses.

But he didn't run. He didn't even move. He just stood there, staring at the ground, his jaw working rhythmically in time to her heartbeat.

"No," he said at last, looking up until his whiskey-colored eyes met hers. "I'm in. But I'm in for the land and that's all I'm in for. Understood?"

There wasn't any one thing about Cain MacCallister that

was particularly perfect. His nose was slightly off center—as if it had been broken once or twice. His blue eyes had flecks of gold in them that made them seem odd and depthless at once. And the small cleft in his chin softened the steely expression he wore most of the time.

No, it wasn't the parts that made Cain what he was, but the sum of them—secrets and all. A package deal. And what he was making clear was that none of it could be hers.

Maggie smiled thinly. ''Don't mistake my need for a husband with my desire for one. I've had what passes for a real marriage. And I have no desire to revisit that particular mistake.'' She ducked under the neck of the nearest mare and started toward the house. ''Come in when you're ready for supper. That is, unless you're concerned about my domestic motives.''

''Should I be?'' he called after her.

She heard a reluctant grin in his voice and glanced back. ''Only if you consider apple pie an extortion tool. In which case, Jigger will happily eat your share.''

''I'd like to think I'm not that easy,'' Cain shouted after her.

Maggie pulled open the screen door and tossed a knowing smile back at him. ''That's because you haven't tasted my pie yet.''

Chapter 5

"If there is anyone here who knows reason that these two people should not be married, speak now or forever hold your peace."

Standing before Judge Kimball in his small, mahogany-paneled chambers, Maggie felt her heart do a little extra ka-thump as the judge glanced around the room. Beside her, Moody Rivers stood, clutching Maggie's small bouquet of violets, looking like she'd just swallowed a chicken bone. Harold Levi hovered to Cain's right, staring at his shoes. And Cain...

She'd noticed that he didn't like crowds and even this small gathering had him itchy and feeling out of place. But if there were ever a man who belonged at the center of attention, it was Cain.

Standing there in the black sports coat, tie and crisp white shirt she'd bought him over in Marysville, and the black jeans that fit him like they were made for him, she guessed he was about the best-looking man in six counties.

But he seemed completely unaware of his looks. In all the hypothesizing she'd done about Cain, about who he was and where he'd come from, cover model/actor was definitely off the list.

"No one?" Judge Kimball prodded with one eyebrow raised.

"Get on with it," Cain told him a little too sharply. Maggie noticed a bead of sweat working its way past his ear.

Judge Kimball nodded tightly. "Then…repeat after me. I, Cain MacCallister, take this woman…"

Maggie felt her throat closing up. Was it hot in here? She glanced up at Cain whose mouth was moving, though she couldn't hear a thing. This was the dumbest thing she'd ever done, a not-so-small voice told her. Marrying an absolute stranger whose best personal outfit included leather biker pants and a white T-shirt without stains.

"To have and to hold…"

She knew absolutely nothing about him. He could be a felon, a Hell's Angel, a polygamist! What was she *thinking?*

"…til death do us part," Cain said, his gaze flicking toward her for the merest instant.

She was definitely going to be sick.

"Maggie?" Judge Kimball's voice penetrated her muzzy brain. "Repeat after me. I, Maggie Cortland, take this man…"

She cleared her throat. Her lips moved obediently, and somehow her voice followed. "…take you, Cain Mac-Callister…for richer or for poorer…" Was it too late to stop this? "…'til—" she hesitated long enough to draw Cain's glare—"'til death do us part."

"The ring?" Judge Kimball asked Cain.

A beat behind, Cain reached into his pocket for the ring

Maggie had given him to use. It had been her grandmother's ring, not the one she'd worn with Ben.

Cain took her hand in his calloused one and fitted the ring gently onto her fourth finger. It fit her perfectly: a simple, slender gold band, etched with flowers. She'd always loved it and was glad there was some small part of this ceremony that felt right. When Cain had finished, he risked a look in her eyes.

She saw a thousand emotions settle there: sadness, fear, hopefulness, regret. The one emotion that should have been there—love—was conspicuously absent.

"I now pronounce you husband and wife." Kimball cleared his throat again. "You may, uh, kiss the bride."

This was, blessedly, the one part of the ceremony she'd been least worried about, because she knew, with absolute certainty that Cain would never even consider—

His fingers tucked against the side of her cheek and he leaned close.

Maggie's eyes widened as she realized what he was about to do. Under the watchful gaze of Judge Kimball, his wife, Harriet, Moody and Harold, Cain planted one on her—a long, healthy, toe-curling kiss that turned whatever was left of her insides instantly to warm mush. His mouth lingered on hers for a handful of heartbeats and in all that time, it never once occurred to her to pull away. In fact, to her horror, she found herself senselessly leaning into the kiss. She felt his arm slide around her back as her knees started to buckle and the intimate press of his well-muscled physique as she moved flush up against him. Her whole being tingled as his words came back to her.

You wouldn't be sorry, Maggie. I'd make it good for you.

He broke the kiss, heaven help her, not her. No, she was too busy trying to get her knees working again.

She was still reeling as he let her go. But before turning toward Harriet Kimball, the judge's wife who was reaching out to shake his hand in congratulations, his eyes went dark with the promise that whatever fantasies she'd entertained about keeping their relationship platonic were exactly that—a fantasy.

Maggie ran a hand over her hair to straighten out the place his hand had ruffled. She was going to have to have a talk with Cain. Reiterate the ground rules. Redraw the line in the—

"Congratulations, honey," Moody said, reaching around her neck to envelop her in a big hug. And in her ear she whispered, "You devil, you. An' I thought you said this was strictly an arrangement between you two."

Maggie cast a look back at Cain who was shaking Helen Kimball's hand. Helen looked a little flushed herself. "It is," she whispered back to Moody. "Believe me. That…kiss was all for show."

"Honey," Moody whispered back, "if that was for show, I'll sell bait at my café."

Maggie looked over at Cain who had moved toward the door, looking as itchy to be out of here as he did uncomfortable in the tie she'd bought him. He was a strong, vital man, as masculine as they come. He wasn't the sort of man who did anything halfway. That, she realized, extended even to his kisses. She'd simply have to be more careful. There was no reason why they would ever have to kiss again, or for that matter, touch. She was in control, after all. Not him.

Judge Kimball stepped up to kiss Maggie on the cheek. "Best wishes to you, Maggie," he said. "Good luck."

"Thank you, Judge," she said, smiling a little too broadly as she searched out Cain, who was watching her from near the door to the judge's chambers, signaling her with a look that he was ready to go.

Moody slipped the violets into her hands. "Don't forget these.

Maggie pressed the flowers back into Moody's hands. "You keep these," she said. "I don't need them. Besides they may bring you luck."

Moody shrugged with a smile. "When you get to my age and the only things nibblin' on your line are a bunch of old catfish, a handful of violets aren't likely to sweeten my chances. But I will sniff 'em every now and then, and dream."

Moody's fiftieth birthday had been just last November and single men ranged in from six counties just to sit at her counters and wait for one of her smiles. But Maggie suspected it would take a special one to get her to readjust the life she'd carved for herself here in this little town.

She gave Moody a kiss on the cheek. "Pooh. You're just too stubborn to get married again. You keep the violets. To remind yourself that luck can sometimes be fickle in your direction."

She took the flowers and buried her nose in them. "All right," she said. "You are comin' by my place for a little celebration? I baked a cake."

Maggie flinched. She'd wanted to keep this day as low-key as possible. "You didn't."

"Sure I did. You think I'd let this excuse for a wingding pass by without a little party? Besides, you can't start a marriage out without a cake to mark the occasion."

Maggie wanted to remind the ever-hopeful matchmaker that this wasn't a real marriage at all and there was no future in hoping for such a thing, but she couldn't bear to spoil the happy look on her friend's face. Besides, how many people would actually show up. One or two?

Maggie glanced at Cain, who was looking as if he'd rather be anywhere else in the world but here. She turned back to Moody and hugged her. "Of course we'll come," she said. "We have to stop at the bank first before it closes.

We'll meet you over at the café. Let me just go and tell Cain.''

The man in question watched Maggie with her friend, looking flushed and beautiful as a spring flower in that dress she'd worn. It was silky and soft, and the same gold color her hair turned in the sunshine. And when he'd kissed her, he'd had trouble remembering that he was only doing it to prove a point and not because he'd spent the last two days and nights wondering what she'd taste like if he did.

Somehow, he'd assumed that once he'd satisfied his curiosity on that account, he could let the idea go. But now, as she moved toward him in that dress of hers with its ladylike slit up the thigh, and her mouth still flushed from his kiss, he realized he'd seriously underestimated the situation. He hadn't expected her to go all soft in his arms, or make that little noise in her throat, somewhere between a protest and a purr as his lips had closed over hers. It made him wonder how long it had been since she'd been kissed—a bend-at-the-knees, take-your-breath-away, kind of kiss. Too long, that was for damn sure. And long enough for him, too, that he'd lost a little bit of control over the situation.

Only a fool would dally with a woman like Maggie, marriage certificate or no. She made him want things he had no business wanting. Things he thought he'd buried so deep they'd lost a pulse. But they were coming to life again inside him.

Something was coming to life inside him. Just watching her walk this way.

"Let's go," he said when she reached his side.

"We can't. Moody's baked us a cake. We have to go and make an appearance after the bank."

The last damned thing he wanted to do was go to some party celebrating this sham of a marriage. His gaze found Moody and he gave her a friendly across-the-room nod.

"You *told* her, didn't you?" he asked Maggie under his breath.

"Of course I told her. But after that little show we gave them, she's probably not the only one who thinks there's more to this than meets the eye. Exactly what did you think you were doing?"

His grin was slow and heated, remembering. "Just doin' what you hired me to do."

She waved goodbye to Moody, Harold and the others and pulled Cain toward the door. "I don't believe *kissing* was anywhere in the job description."

"Husbands," he reminded her, slipping an around her shoulder, "kiss their wives. And if they don't, there's trouble in paradise. And I'm sure the good Mrs. Kimball would be more than happy to spread that little tidbit around town. Is that what you want?"

That took the hot out of her chili. "No," she said as they made their way out into the sunshine dappled street. "But you didn't have to make the kiss so...so authentic."

Cain grinned, enjoying this. "Maybe if you hadn't leaned into me that way—"

She had the gall to look offended. "If you hadn't practically pulled me off my feet—!"

"—or draped yourself around my neck."

"I was *trying* not to fall."

He shook his head and pulled her into the street after a pickup truck loaded down with straw bales passed by. "Yeah, that's what it felt like, all right. Remind me again what it was you had against sex?"

"I have nothing against sex," she retorted to the shocked stares of a handful of passersby.

Cain worked at containing a grin.

"I just have something against having it with a complete stranger," she finished under her breath, tugging her arm from his grip. *"Do-you-mind?"* She stalked ahead of him.

"Hey, I don't mind. But personally, I don't think you're all that strange. I mean except for your habit of forgetting where you're going."

Maggie stopped dead and looked up. They'd passed the bank two buildings back. She refrained from slugging him.

The bank was mostly empty except for a handful of people at the teller windows. An older woman in a button-down suit she'd outgrown several pounds ago, walked briskly past them, giving Cain the evil eye and Maggie, a nod and a disapproving look that could melt down steel. He saw Maggie's composure slip a notch.

Cain suppressed the urge to wring the old bat's neck, but countered it by taking Maggie's elbow as she headed toward a weasely looking desk jockey at the center of the desk area whose nameplate read Ernie Solefield.

Ernie had his head bent at his work but he looked up as they approached his desk. His banker's smile slipped when he saw who it was. Immediately, he pushed to his feet.

"Maggie—I mean, Mrs. Cortland."

"It's MacCallister now."

Ernie blinked, his gaze sliding to Cain and back. "Pardon?"

"I'm surprised you hadn't heard. Everyone else apparently has," Maggie said, pulling an envelope from her purse and sliding onto Ernie's desk. "Ernie Solefield? Meet my husband, Cain MacCallister."

The balding banker looked like he was trying to swallow a really large pill. "Married? But...*married?* Well...congratulations." He held his hand out to Cain and Maggie. Maggie just smiled cooly back. Cain folded his arms.

Ernie pulled his hand back. "So..." He glanced at the envelope Maggie had slid on his desk. "What, uh, what can I do for you today?"

"Approve my loan," she said baldly.

Ernie laughed softly. "Maggie, it's not that simp—"

"Did you or did you not turn me down for being a single woman?"

He shoved his glasses up the bridge of his nose. "There were a number of factors involved with—"

"Don't," she warned, leaning against Ernie's desk with one hand. "I qualify and you know it, Ernie. I've just eliminated the only excuse you had for turning me down. I'm married and Cain is as committed as I am to making my—*our*—place work." She straightened. "Here's the paperwork. I expect to hear from you within two weeks."

"These things take time, Maggie," Ernie said, fingering the envelope she'd left him.

"It seems I'm fresh out of that," she said. "Maybe Harold Levi can move things along faster. Shall I call him?"

Ernie's bank pallor faded another notch. "No. That won't be necessary. You'll be hearing from us shortly. I'll personally see that it gets priority."

"Good." Maggie glanced at Cain, whose gaze was locked with the banker's.

Ernie blinked first. "I'll do what I can for you, Maggie," he said, then nodded at Cain. "Mr. MacCallister."

"Mr. Solefield," Cain replied, and the two of them turned and walked out with every person in the bank watching them go.

True to her word, Moody had baked a cake. Not just any old cake. But a wedding cake, complete with a bride and groom on top. A two-tiered confection not to be outdone in any five-star restaurant. Half of Fishhook had turned out, something that not only surprised, but heartened Maggie. Everyone from old Taylor Green, who sold her feed, to Delilah and Jake Cameron, her neighbors, to a handful of teenage girls who often came out to her place to exercise her mares. The same folks who'd been at Ben's funeral were here now, wishing her well.

Maggie looked at Cain, who was standing beside her with his arm strategically around her back. He was smiling and nodding but looking as if he wished he were anywhere but here. But no one knew that. They all thought he was in love with her. And for a moment, she allowed herself to enjoy that fantasy. Imagine, she thought, a man like Cain actually loving her. Caring about her. It had been so long since a man had put his arm around her waist, stood beside her in a crowd. It was so good to see not pity, but happiness in the eyes of her friends. After Ben, no one had known what to say. After a while, they didn't want to ask how she was doing any more. They knew. She was surviving. Barely. And they knew about Donnelly. Anyone who lived in Fishhook knew he was a bully. Some had even pulled up stakes when the going got too tough.

She gripped the plastic champagne glass tightly and guzzled the last remnants. While she knew almost everyone here, Cain knew no one. He looked antsy as a caged cat, tugging at the tie around his neck while chugging the black coffee Moody had set out. She noticed he hadn't touched the alcohol, not even when Moody made a toast to them. She was grateful that one of them had a clear head to drive home. She rarely drank, but she was working on her third glass and the room was starting to spin.

A dozen well-wishers came up to offer their congratulations and kiss Maggie's cheek. Mary Kate Baxter-Lorenzo, the redheaded, thirty-five-ish owner of Mary Kate's Gifts and Baubles who was a notorious—and now single—husband-hunter, wrapped an arm around Maggie's shoulder and gave her a squeeze.

"I just wanna know your secret," she whispered, slurring her words slightly. "It's so unfair. Here I am, slaving away in the middle of town and there you are on your place in the middle of nowhere and you meet someone like that.'' She shook her head in approval at Cain, who was being buttonholed by Jed Kruener, the local pharmacist. ''Wherever did you find him, Maggie?''

''We're old friends,'' she said, telling the lie they'd agreed on. ''I knew him years ago, before Ben.''

''Oh…Ben…'' Mary Kate said on a sigh. ''So sad about Ben. How long has it been? Five months?''

''Six,'' she corrected. ''If you'll excuse me, I'd better go and see if—''

''Well,'' the redhead interrupted drunkenly, ''nobody's thinkin' less of you for turnin' it around so quickly, I'll tell you that. After all, these days, a girl has to do what a girl has to do. Right?''

Maggie smiled tightly at Mary Kate and handed her another glass of champagne as Moody's tray went by. ''It was sweet of you to come, Mary Kate. Really.''

''Oh. Sure,'' Mary Kate said, taking a slug of champagne and moving her gaze to the next likely victim.

Cain met her gaze with a look so close to desperation she had to smile. She knew exactly how he felt. She sent him a silent signal of commiseration as she shouldered her way through the crowded room toward Moody. Wellwishers gave her hugs of congratulations and stopped her every few feet to ask her about her new husband. She fended off questions as best she could but the lying was beginning to wear on her. She had to get out of here.

Harold Levi stopped her before she could get to Moody. He drew her into a hug, then patted her hand. ''You're all set now?'' he asked. ''Sure you'll be okay?''

''Yes,'' she answered. ''Thanks Harold, for everything.''

''I'll look into that name you gave me. Remus Trimark? Never heard of him, but that doesn't mean he isn't living around here somewhere. You sure it was a man's name?''

''I don't know,'' she admitted. ''He said if I wanted to

know more I should find this Remus Trimark. And that it's not over. Whatever 'it' is."

"All right. I'll let you know what I find out. You sure you don't want Cain to know about this?"

She shook her head. "Not yet. He's got enough on his plate without this, too." Or he might just hop on that bike of his and never be seen again. Not that she'd blame him. He'd driven into a hornet's nest of trouble the day he'd ridden onto her ranch. She didn't want to give him any more reason to leave.

"I'm going to get back to work now," Harold told her. "I can't seem to interest Moody in playing hooky with me." He sent a wistful look over at the coffee-diva behind the counter. "She's really something, isn't she?"

Maggie stared at Harold in surprise. She had no idea he was interested in Moody. Well, well, well… Harold's wife of twenty-seven years had died five years ago. He'd been devoted to her and to their four children. But his wife was gone and his children, too, had moved away to school or new lives in the big city. Life here could be lonely without someone. She knew firsthand. "Yes," she answered, glancing back at Moody. "She is something, all right. Why don't you ask her out? I think she's partial to tulips."

His grin widened as he slid his coat on. "Is she now? I'll surely keep that in mind."

After he left, Maggie found Moody and pulled her into a hug.

"We're gonna go. Thanks for everything, Moody. Especially for not telling me how much I'm going to regret this."

"You're a smart gal, Maggie. You'll figure it out. Just don't let Ben be the one you measure him against. That man's already had his share of you. He doesn't deserve any more."

They walked half a block with Maggie going on about all the people he'd met whose names he'd already forgotten. As she talked, he noticed Donnelly's name was on three buildings in his line of sight: a hardware store, a feed and grain warehouse and a small real estate office. Not to mention the two late model pickup trucks they'd passed on the way in, emblazoned with the Bar ZX insignia—Donnelly's brand.

He had the distinct feeling that Laird Donnelly pretty much owned this little piece of nowhere. And that had the potential of being a very dangerous thing. A bully by any other name was still a bully.

Maggie's truck was parked midway between Hamm's Pharmacy and the Duke Brothers' Ranch Market. He noticed them even before he felt Maggie tense up beside him half way down the block. The three cowhands were a ragged-looking bunch. Just in off some weeklong branding job, he suspected. They lounged against the granite steps of Hamm's, sipping on cans sheathed in brown paper sacks as they watched Maggie and him approach.

''Well, look who's comin'!'' the tallest one yelled out, lifting his brown-paper covered drink in greeting. ''If it ain't Maggie Cortland. Hey, Maggie.''

Maggie tried to ignore them, reaching into her purse for her keys. ''Ignore them,'' she told him under her breath.

''Hey, Maggie,'' the scrawny one with a nose like a scythe and a few day's growth of red beard called out. ''We heard you got yerself hitched.'' They turned their attention to Cain. ''That right?''

Maggie was shaking her purse, searching for the elusive keys. ''Pretend you don't hear them.''

Cain turned to the cowboys who were snorting and grinning and generally having a good ol' time at Maggie's expense. ''You got a problem with that?''

The two who were talking exchanged looks again as if he was the stupidest man alive. "I'd say you're the one with the problem," one of them muttered.

Maggie yanked the keys out of her purse and immediately dropped them. Cain reached for them and shoved them into the lock on the passenger side door. "I'll drive," he told her. She started to argue, but the cowboy was apparently just cranking up.

"Good luck. You'll need it. Right boys?"

The "boys" shared the joke. Except for the brown-haired one who looked barely twenty-five. He just ducked his head and focused on his beer.

Cain opened the car door for Maggie and moved toward the men. "If I didn't know better," he said in a dangerous voice, "I'd think you boys are trying to start something here."

"It's just a little friendly warning," explained the skinnier of the two who got slowly to his feet with a small-town swagger that reminded Cain of a mean little bantam rooster on the Concho he used to know and hate. "We figured it was our civic duty to warn you."

The one who was hanging back shook his head and tossed a look in Maggie's direction. "Let it go, Joe," he muttered almost under his breath.

"You should listen to him, Joe," Cain warned.

"Then I guess she told you right?" Joe said, "about her husband?"

Cain kept his expression carefully blank but the muscles at the back of his neck coiled tighter. "Why don't you boys find something useful to do with your days? Like kicking over parking meters, or treeing cats."

Joe laughed. "I guess she didn't, huh? Yeah, she's easy on the eyes, but she's damned hard on husbands. Her last one hanged hisself."

Chapter 6

The silence that followed that little bombshell was broken at last by the sound of Maggie's car door closing softly. Cain looked around to find her in the truck, staring determinedly out the driver's window, away from them.

Joe was grinning when he looked back at him. "Ol' Ben, he did it right in his own barn. Word is," he confided, "she drove him to it." With a shrill whistle he gestured with his hand like a plane going down. "Right over the edge with her pushin' and naggin'. You could be next. So you better watch yourself, son."

His gut tightened. Suicide? Why hadn't she told him? Not that he gave a damn. He didn't. Her life was her business. But the idea of these clowns cutting her down right here in the middle of town made him want to take each one of them apart, piece by moronic piece, and leave them bleeding on the sidewalks of Fishhook, wondering what hit them. But that wasn't going to happen. Not today. Not with Maggie watching.

Instead, he sent Joe a smile that made his idiotic grin falter and die. "Let me give you a piece of advice," he said so quietly that Joe actually had to lean forward to hear him. "Next time you see my wife coming, walk the other way. Because if I ever hear you've been trash-talking her again, I'll personally make sure that the place where you keep your brains never straddles a horse again. Are we clear?"

Joe's face flamed, and he gave an indifferent shrug. "Don't say I didn't warn you, pal."

"That goes both ways." Cain stared him down for a full five seconds before he turned and headed back to the truck, throwing the keys in the air and catching them hard as they sank past his chest.

Maggie didn't say a word as he started the truck and peeled out of the parking spot, leaving the cowhands and their speculations behind. Dust curled behind them as they tore out of town and she stared out the side window without once looking at him.

The countryside passed by in a blur of browns and greens, but Maggie didn't see any of it. She was remembering that day in the barn, the images that had haunted her for months now and kept her up at night. She was seeing Ben, in that slat of sunshine pouring through the broken barn wood, his lean frame swaying slightly back and forth in the crisp November air. She was seeing the way his hands curled gently at his sides as if he were sleeping instead of gone forever. Those hands that had once loved her. So still.

For months she hadn't been able to think about that morning without being physically ill. Even now, the memory of it tugged at the back of her throat. She thought she had put it behind her. But Joe Johns wouldn't let it rest. He had to taunt her with it. He and the others took their cue from Laird. No one else in town ever even spoke about

Ben. Unless, like Mary Kate, they were drunk and thoughtless. Otherwise, Ben was a taboo subject, his death much too close and uncomfortable for polite conversation. And she preferred it that way. Because to talk about it was to acknowledge that it had nearly killed her, too. And she'd put that behind her. At least she thought she had. Until she saw the look on Cain's face.

"Maggie, you don't owe me any explanations."

Cain's voice broke into her reverie and startled her back to the present. They were almost home. "I never should have let that happen. I should have prepared you."

"Who the hell were they?"

"Laird's men."

He snorted. "At least they're consistent."

"They're not all like that. Joe and a few of the others like Jeb Wrightman were friends of Ben's. Poker buddies. Casino cohorts. They watched him tumble for months and stood by doing nothing to stop it. It's easier for them to blame me."

"He was a gambler, your husband?"

"Only in the last year, when he started losing ground with the ranch. Then he threw away whatever was left."

Cain pulled the truck into the driveway of Maggie's yard. Jigger bounced up from his place under the tree, tail wagging, barking happily. Cain shut off the truck, but made no move to get out.

"You found him, didn't you?" he asked quietly.

"Yes."

He didn't say anything for a long time, just tightened his hands around the steering wheel until his knuckles went white. "It wasn't your fault," he said at last.

"How do you know?" she asked. "Maybe if I'd tried harder. If I'd forced him to stay at home with me instead of going out gambling—"

"Could you have?" he asked.

"Stopped him? Physically? No. But maybe if I'd…done something different. Tried harder…"

"People who are looking for sympathy use pills, or suck on an exhaust pipe at dinnertime. They hope someone finds them. They don't eat a gun or use a rope. There's nothing you could've done. It was his decision."

"You don't know. You didn't know Ben. You don't know me." Maggie yanked open her door and stumbled out.

Cain followed her and caught up with her in a few easy strides. She felt his hand go around her arm and stop her.

"You're right," he said, his voice suddenly soft. "We don't know each other. But that doesn't mean I can't see that you're beating yourself up for something you couldn't have prevented. Ben had his own path and chose to leave you behind on another one. This one's yours. Ours…for now. It's best not to look back at that other one with 'what-if's.' Because it'll kill you, too, if you let it."

"You speaking from experience?" she asked quietly.

He looked away, at the ground, anywhere but into her eyes. "What I'm saying is, I don't want to see that happen to you."

Dammit, she was going to cry now and she didn't want him to see. She hadn't cried in so long, she thought her tears were all dried up. But here he was, touching her, telling her it was all right. And she wasn't sure if she could bear it.

Suddenly, Cain pulled her against him and enfolded her in his arms. Strong arms. Warm arms. Maggie leaned her head against his chest and could hear the steady, strong thud of his heartbeat. How many times in the past six months had she longed for a man to hold her this way, stroke her hair and draw circles on her back with the palm of his hand? Oh, she needed it.

But it wouldn't solve anything and would only make things more complicated.

She gave a nervous laugh as she pushed away from him. "I'm sorry."

"Don't be." He didn't let her go. Not completely.

Her nose was running. She dabbed it with a knuckle. "I'm just tired. That's all," she said in her own defense. "It's been a long week. I wasn't ready for them. I should have been but I wasn't. I'm fine. Really. Thank you for…for everything, Cain. For going through with it today."

He smiled and dropped his fingers into Jigger's fur and gave him a scratch. "My motives were entirely selfish. I'm getting land out of this deal, remember?"

She smiled, watching him pet her dog. Something perverse in him made him want to deny the man she knew lived under that tough exterior he bared to the world. But she suspected that whoever he'd been once—before whatever had happened to him had made him hard—was still there. "I'm glad to know you have your priorities straight."

"Right. So, after a day like this, there's only one thing left to do."

She agreed. "Häagen Dazs?"

"Nope."

He scooped her up in his arms and Maggie gave a shriek of outraged laughter. "Cain!"

He started toward the house with long strides with Jigger trotting along beside them, barking happily.

"This is ridiculous. We're not even really…" But his shoulders felt powerful beneath her hands and she instinctively wrapped her arms more tightly around him.

"Hey," he said. "We can't buck tradition, can we?"

"I hate to remind you, but we've bucked just about every tradition in the book today."

"Oh, yeah." He stooped so she could open the door,

then he pushed it open with his foot and carried her across the threshold. Once inside, he set her gently on the ground. But letting her go took a few seconds longer than strictly necessary. When he finally did, she couldn't miss the darkness that had settled in his blue eyes, or the hunger behind the look.

"Welcome home, Mrs. MacCallister," he said, slipping off his hat.

It was crazy. Absurd, that she liked the sound of that. *Mrs. MacCallister.* Or maybe it was the way it sounded when he said it. Lord, what was wrong with her today? Must be all that champagne she drank at Moody's. Of course it was that. It was making her head spin a little.

The moment of protracted silence stretched uncomfortably between them. What exactly did one say to a stranger who'd just become your spouse?

They spoke at the same time.

"Well, I...uh—"

"I should—"

They laughed uneasily and Cain ducked his head, glancing in the direction of the barn. The afternoon light was already fading. "Why don't you get dinner started?" he suggested. "I'll get those chores finished up."

For reasons she couldn't explain, even to herself, she didn't want him to go yet. "Cain?"

"Yeah?"

He was still close enough that she could smell the clean scent of soap that lingered on his skin. "You were right. We don't know each other," she said. "But I'd like to know you. Do you think that's possible?"

He fingered the hatband on the hat in his hands. "I think," he said, "it's better if we keep it...impersonal. That way, nobody gets disappointed."

She frowned. "What makes you think I'd be disappointed if I got to know you?"

He slid a look out the window. "Look," he said patiently, "you want my muscle, you've got it. My promise? Done. You want me in your bed, you've got that, too. But the rest of me is mine and mine alone. Whatever mistakes I've made, whatever brought me here, that's mine, too."

He started to turn away, but she said, "What is it you're so afraid of, Cain? That someone might actually care about you? It's all right for you to comfort me, but not for me to do the same for you?"

"I'm not looking for comfort," he said, his jaw tightening.

"No, of course not," she said, "It's only third on the list of human needs. Food, shelter, comfort. Oh, well, sex. That's right in there, too."

He didn't smile or even argue. "What is it you want from me, Maggie?"

She let out a long breath and shook her head, unsure. "Friendship?"

His eyes did a long, slow perusal of her, from her mouth down to her toes, considering her offer the way a hungry bird of prey would a nearby sparrow. Maggie felt herself blush, knowing that what he wanted had nothing to do with friendship.

"You actually think," he asked with undisguised amusement, "that's possible?"

"Don't you?"

"Exclusively? No. And especially not when the woman looks like you."

Maggie knew she should feel flattered, but what was going on inside of her was closer to panic. "Let's not complicate things."

"For you? Or me?"

"Obviously, for me," she said. "Casual sex doesn't seem to bother you."

He shifted his stance and grinned at her with a look that

made her want to pull a blanket around herself for protection.

"There's nothing casual about sex, Maggie," he said, his voice husky with promise. "Not the way I do it."

The spring on the screen door screeched as he headed toward the barn with that loose-hipped stroll of his, leaving Maggie behind, to wonder what had happened to all the air in her lungs.

Geronimo pulled tight on the lunge line and balked at the pressure from Maggie's hands, backing away, the way he'd been since she'd started with him two hours ago. The stallion kicked up a mini-dust storm and shrieked a protest at the end of his line.

Cain had been watching her for the past hour, trying to keep his mind on fixing the sagging porch roof, but failing. His eyes kept straying to the way that little white blouse of hers stretched across her breasts when she lifted her arms and to the smallness of her waist.

He shook his head and refocused on the nail he was hammering. She'd made it pretty clear she wasn't interested. He was fighting a losing battle there. But the week was wearing on him. Nights alone in his own bed, listening to Maggie moving around in the room next door. Hearing her tossing and turning in the wee hours of the morning.

They'd run into each other in the hall on the way to the bathroom the other night. She'd been wearing one of those button-up-to-here flannel numbers designed to discourage invasion. They'd done a little dance in the hallway, avoiding each other, brushing each other inevitably despite their attempts to the contrary. Then he'd taken a long, cold shower and thought about Annie.

He slammed the nail home, putting an unintentional dent in the wood. Leaning his head back, he let the sun spill across his face. He wondered sometimes if Annie could see him. Was she watching what he was doing right now? And if she was, would she forgive him for the things he still ached for? Forgive him for being here when she was not? In his heart he knew she would because that's just who she was. It was himself he couldn't forgive—for the first inklings of life he'd felt stir inside him for years. For wanting Maggie in his bed. And most of all, for not having sense enough to walk away from this whole damned situation while he still could. He couldn't afford attachments. He wasn't interested in them. But as he watched Maggie now, struggling to tame a horse that didn't want any part of her world, he found himself wondering what it might have been like if he'd met her years ago. Before his life had stopped moving.

He shoved a four-by-four brace up tighter under the eave and toenailed in a sixteen-penny nail. This roof needed more than a prop. It needed an overhaul. Water and snow had eaten away at some of the understructure and dry-rotted wood needed replacing. He decided to go and forage in the barn for some wood that might work. He tossed the hammer down and started toward the barn.

"He's impossible!" Maggie complained as Cain ambled by the rail. "I don't know what else to try."

She was reeling the animal in, moving in close to touch his tender nose with the palm of her hand. Geronimo's eyes showed white and he snorted loudly.

"Shh—then," she crooned, reaching out to touch his muzzle with a gloved hand. Geronimo stood for it for a full five seconds before pulling back.

Cain climbed up the rail fence and leaned there watching her. "He's afraid to trust you. He wants to, but he's afraid."

"I don't think so. I've tried everything. A potential buyer, Bill Tischman, is coming by to check his progress in three days. I've gotten exactly nowhere with him. I don't know. I may have to admit defeat."

"I thought you were counting on that fee from Tischman."

Maggie sighed heavily. "I am. But I'm beginning to think it's hopeless. I've been working with him for two weeks and we're barely on speaking terms. Forget training him for cutting. I'm honestly not sure he's got it in him."

Cain studied the three-year-old critically. He had good bone structure, a heavy chest and the compact rear quarters that betrayed his championship quarter horse bloodlines. Most important, Cain thought, were the eyes. His eyes were bright and took in everything. Sure he was a hothead. But it was fear, not stubbornness he saw there. And intelligence. He suspected that whatever was keeping him from learning not to hate the rope had nothing to do with his innate ability to understand what it was for.

"Mind if I try?" Cain asked impulsively.

"You?" she said, as if he'd just suggested she should go stand in the middle of the Musselshell River at snowmelt.

"Well, if you're gonna give up anyway," he said. "It's worth a shot."

She looked at Geronimo, then back at Cain and sighed. "All right. You're welcome to it. But I'm warning you. He doesn't like men."

Cain nodded and climbed over the fence. True to form, that bent old Geronimo out of shape all over again and he started prancing around at the end of his tether. "Let him go," he told her. "Undo the lead."

"You're kidding, right?"

"Humor me. Then hand it to me and step out of the pen."

Maggie shrugged and did as he asked, keeping a wary eye on the horse on her way out. She wasn't sure what

Cain had in mind, but she was sure whatever it was wouldn't work.

Cain walked casually to the center of the pen watching Geronimo as he did. The horse cowered at the far end, and Cain walked up to him slowly. Maggie couldn't make out what he was saying to the horse, but she could hear the low vibration of his voice as he moved closer and touched Geronimo's forehead with the flat palm of his hand. Geronimo snorted and tossed his head and Cain backed off, behind the animal, far enough not to be kicked. Giving the line in his hand a snap, he aimed it in Geronimo's general direction. The horse took off like he'd been stung by a bee, even though the rope hadn't even touched him. Cain stayed behind him as the horse tore around the pen, watching him with every pass. Occasionally, he would slow down, but Cain would give the rope a snap to force him to keep going. Around and around they went. Geronimo flat out running, Cain, moving casually yet relentlessly behind.

Maggie frowned. If his intention was to exhaust Geronimo, it might just work. She'd already worked with him for two hours with no success. But she watched Cain work steadily and deliberately like a lion tamer in a circus, never losing eye contact with the horse, nor easing up the pressure he was putting on him.

Cain snapped the line again, forcing the stallion in the other direction. All the while, he kept his gaze fixed on Geronimo's eyes.

"He's tired," Cain told her. "He'd rather stop. But he won't because he knows I won't let him. Horses are flight animals. They'll run from opposition, like me. And this rope." He snapped the line again and Geronimo kept moving.

Resting her chin on her hands, she watched, fascinated as much by what he was doing with the horse as with the man himself.

The midday sun beat down on his dark brown hair, gilding it gold and forcing a small patch of moisture through the spot in his denim shirt between his shoulder blades. Her gaze dropped lower, to the black jeans that hugged his lean hips and his long legs. He could walk into any movie set in Hollywood, she thought, and be the next "it" guy. But he was as unaware of his looks as Geronimo was of her presence here by the rail. He was completely focused on what he was doing. Completely at home here in the training pen.

Geronimo wasn't nearly as happy. He looked like he'd give anything to stop running. But Cain kept up the pressure. The horse started to lick his lips and chew as if he had a mouthful of hay.

"See that?" Cain said, not taking his eyes off the horse. "He's trying to let me know he's not a carnivore. That he's no threat to me. He just wants to graze in peace. He's starting to negotiate."

"Negotiate what?" she asked, watching intently.

"A truce."

Cain let him go on for a few more minutes until the horse began ducking his head down as if he were getting ready to buck. She began to prepare herself for failure when Cain abruptly stopped watching the horse and turned himself away at a forty-five degree angle. When Geronimo noticed this, he stopped as well. Incredibly, after a few tense moments, he began walking toward Cain, who was still virtually ignoring him.

"Watch out," she murmured under her breath.

"He's curious now," Cain told her. "He's tired of running. He's decided he'd rather have me as a friend than an enemy."

Geronimo moved tentatively forward until at last, he touched his nose to Cain's shoulder. Unbelievable, Maggie thought. Cain rubbed his nose and his neck with the flat of his hand and miraculously, the horse let him. It was the first time she'd seen him let anyone but her touch him.

Cain moved away, walking in large circles. The horse watched at first, then tentatively followed. But he stopped after a few steps and simply watched Cain. Uncoiling the line again from his hand, he snapped it, forcing Geronimo back into his run, sending him circling the pen again for five or six revolutions. Then he repeated the procedure he'd done earlier of feigning disinterest. Again, Geronimo moved in toward Cain and nuzzled his shoulder. Cain rubbed him all over again then started the circles. This time, Geronimo followed like an obedient dog.

Maggie watched, stunned. In less than thirty minutes, he practically had the animal eating out of his hand.

"Now we're allies," Cain told her. "He needs one. Horses are herd animals. They're not solitary creatures." He turned to scratch Geronimo's ears.

"Bring me the saddle pad and saddle, Maggie."

In another ten minutes, after touching him all over, Cain had saddled Geronimo up and was sending him back on his way around the pen with the stirrups tied beneath his belly. When the animal had finished that cycle of retreat and follow, he hooked up a lead back to Geronimo's halter and led him to Maggie as if it were something the horse did every day.

"That's enough for today," he said, patting the horse's muscular neck. "He'll use the lead now without a balk and be taking weight on his back within a day or so."

Maggie simply stared at Cain. "Who are you? And what did you do with that guy who rode in here on a Harley?"

He grinned and scratched Geronimo behind the ears.

"Where on earth did you learn that?" she asked, touching Geronimo's nose with the palm of her hand.

"A wise old friend down in California. He's been doing it for years."

A friend in California. So, he had a friend, somewhere. "Will it still work tomorrow?" she asked.

Cain grinned again. "We just had our first date. He's learning to trust me. And you. Long as we don't let him down, he'll return the favor."

"Why didn't you tell me how good you were with horses?"

"You didn't ask." Cain handed her the lead line. His fingers brushed hers for a lingering moment before he let go and started toward the barn.

"That's hardly fair," she said, referring not only to the situation, but the touch. "You don't say anything about yourself."

Cain grinned, shrugging off her protest.

"Hey, does that mean I'm supposed to ask?" she called after him.

"Nobody said you couldn't ask."

"*Huh.* Anyone ever call you abstruse?" she yelled.

He slapped the dust from his thigh with the brim of his hat. "Not to my face," he said, and disappeared into the shadows of the barn.

She patted Geronimo's jaw and gave him a scratch under the chin. "Take it from me," she mused aloud, staring at the barn. "He's abstruse." And no simple drifter. But she intended to figure out him out. If it took a thousand un-answered questions.

Chapter 7

"**I** want to know who he is, where he came from, and what the hell he's doing in Fishhook."

Laird Donnelly stormed around his walnut-paneled office, grinding the fifty-dollar Cuban cigar in his fist into useless powder. He paced to the window and back, ending abruptly ten inches from Gene Fielding's face. "And I want it yesterday."

The attorney leaned back in his seat. "I'll do my best."

"Your best had better be more than good. Because I won't tolerate another screwup like last time. You know that don't you, Gene?"

He was half the size of Laird Donnelly and had little of the other man's personal power, but he had one thing the bigger man did not. Patience. He'd learned long ago that the only way to survive a hell-on-wheels Donnelly was with a full frontal approach.

"You know as well as I do that the last screwup was Butch's, not mine. So if we're going to go around placing blame, let's put it where it belongs. I do what nobody else will do for you, Laird. I've been doing it for almost ten years. If you're not happy with the job I do—''

"This," Laird interrupted, pointing to the 8x10 photo of Cain MacCallister walking down the streets of Fishhook, "is your friggin' job, Gene. You find out what his grandmother ate for breakfast and what kind of goddamn oil he puts in that motorcycle of his. He's standing smack dab in the middle of our future! And I'll be damned if I'm gonna sit idly by and watch while that...*drifter* ruins everything."

"That's the point. He is a drifter, like you said, without two nickels to rub together. We don't know that he'll make any difference at all," Gene argued reasonably.

A bark of laughter escaped from Laird. "Oh, he's trouble, all right. I can smell it on him." He dumped what was left of his cigar into the trash can beside the desk and walked to the chintz-draped window that overlooked his land. A storm was gathering above the mountains. "He's got a past. And I want to know what it is. Ben's widow is too damned scared to think of marrying a stranger like him on her own. Maybe it was Levi's idea. Or maybe Mac-Callister's. Either way, I want him out of the picture. Understand?''

Gene stared at Donnelly's massive back and tried to imagine what his father would say if he could see what his son had become. Robert Donnelly had been a hard man, with a work ethic that would drive most normal men into the ground. It had, in fact, done that very thing to him at the age of fifty-five, ten years ago.

Gene supposed maybe Robert had been hardest on Laird, and the younger Donnelly thought he had a lot to prove. But with Laird it went way beyond ambition. Things tended to move into the radius of obsession with him, whether it was his preoccupation with the young widow, Maggie Cortland, or the scheme he'd cooked up to make his mark on Montana.

If he could have, Gene thought tiredly, he would have walked away from this job years ago. But he was in it up to his neck now. And his only hope of extricating himself was to see this thing through to the end. And try to retain some scrap of integrity in the process.

He got to his feet and brushed the wrinkles from the seam of his trousers. "I'll see what I can dig up on him. Don't do anything foolish, Laird. We've got too much at stake."

Donnelly turned slowly at that. "You, my friend, would be foolish to underestimate exactly how much this deal means to both of us. I'll do whatever it takes to make it happen. And if you're as smart as you think you are, you'll keep that in mind."

"I don't like threats, Laird," Gene said, gathering himself up to his full five feet eight inches. "And I don't like cleaning up after you when things go wrong."

"So see that it doesn't," Laird told him, stalking out of the room. "That's your damned job."

10:50 p.m.
Maggie thunked the clock on her bedside table, sure it was broken. She'd been staring at it for what seemed like hours and it didn't seem to be moving.

The little digital number flipped down. 10:51 p.m.

Okay. It wasn't the clock. It was her. She'd gone to bed at nine when Cain had decided to turn in. It had been a long day and tomorrow would be even longer. She should have fallen asleep when her head hit the pillow. But a thousand thoughts swam through her head. And most of them revolved around the man in the room next door.

All right, so this marriage thing wasn't going at all the way she'd expected. So, it wasn't as simple as she'd naively thought it would be. It wasn't entirely her fault that every time he looked up from whatever he was doing she happened to be watching him. It was...coincidental. And just because they occasionally bumped into one another in the hallway, getting ready for bed, didn't mean she'd planned the encounter. Even if that's how it might look to the impartial observer.

Okay, so maybe she had planned it once. But that was only because she'd forgotten to tell him that one of the mares was off her oats and needed an extra flake of alfalfa in the morning.

Maggie tugged the covers up under her chin, staring at the ceiling. In her own defense, it seemed only natural that since there were only the two of them here, her mind would wander now and again to him. Plenty else occupied her thoughts as well. The horses. Money. And of course, the mysterious Remus Trimark.

She threw the covers off her and headed for the kitchen. Maybe tea would settle her. Padding silently downstairs, she turned the burner on under the kettle and dropped an herbal tea bag into a mug. Sometimes tea helped, she reasoned. Mostly, nothing did.

But that wasn't anything new. She hadn't slept through the night since the day Ben died. Maybe she never would again. In the beginning, his face would wake her and her heart would start pounding erratically. The light would erase his image, but nothing could banish her feelings of guilt. She'd never know the answers to the questions that haunted her in the dark of night. Ben hadn't left a note. No goodbye, no apologies. Just...unanswered questions.

Pulling the phone book from its spot under the counter, she began idly leafing through it.

Tisdale...Trask...Trilburn... she pulled her finger down the column...*Trimble.* No Trimark. And no Remus *anything.*

She flipped to the yellow pages without a clue what she was looking for. *Tribune Printing…Tri-County Plumbing—*

"Good reading?"

Maggie nearly dropped the phone book at the sound of Cain's voice behind her. She whirled to find him leaning carelessly against the kitchen doorjamb in a pair of jeans and an old T-shirt. He looked rumpled and masculine and incredibly sexy.

"Cain," she gasped. "You scared me. What are you doing out there?"

He thumbed a gesture back at the night sky. "Counting stars." He glanced at the phone book. "I have a couple of Clancy novels with me if you've run out of reading material."

She clapped the phone book shut. "I wasn't really reading. I was just…"

"Looking for an electrician?" He flipped on the overhead light.

She laughed and shook her head. "Tea?"

"Sure." He pushed away from the doorjamb, turned a chair around backward and straddled it. "I'm not much good at sleep myself. What's your excuse?"

"I gave excuses up for Lent. Now I just make tea."

The kettle began to whistle and she poured hot water into the two cups and carried them over to the table.

"I think it's kind of a shame most folks miss seeing the world at this time of night," he said, "when everything's dark as pitch and the stars are winking in the sky like fireflies."

She stopped stirring her honey in and looked up at him. "Why Cain. How poetic."

He grinned self-consciously, reaching for his mug. "It's just that you don't really appreciate it until you don't see it for a while."

"I lived in New York City for a few years," she said. "There are no stars there."

"New York? What were you doing there?"

"Going to school. NYU. It's where I met Ben."

"And you ended up here?"

Maggie took a sip of her tea. "He was from here. His father died and left him this place. He'd always thought he didn't want to stay here, but in the end, he loved it and couldn't live in the East. When he came, I came with him."

"That must have been difficult," Cain said, sipping his tea. "Fishhook's no metropolis."

"You're telling me." She toyed with the ring of steam her mug had left on the table. "I fell in love with it, though. It's my home. The only real home I've ever had." When Cain frowned, she explained, "I was an army brat. My parents moved every year, sometimes twice a year."

He nodded. "Where are they now?"

"Gone," she said. "Both of them. My father in a border skirmish in Afghanistan, ten years ago. My mother when I was seventeen."

"Sorry," he said.

"What about you?" she asked. "Are your parents living?"

He took a sip of steaming tea and looked away. "No."

"See? Both orphans," she said. "We have more in common than we thought."

Cain took a final swig of his tea before standing to set it in the sink. "You should get some sleep."

Maggie rubbed the back of her neck absently. At least he was consistently tight-lipped. "You go. I'm too wound up to sleep."

He got to his feet, but instead of heading upstairs, he came around the back of her chair. "I can fix that," he said, sliding his big hands against the taut muscles of her shoulders through the thick, terry cloth of her robe.

"You don't have to—" she began, but forgot what she was going to say as soon as thumbs found the spot between her shoulder blades.

"Relax," he said. "I'm good at this."

He was. The absolute luxury of a shoulder rub was too wonderful to turn down. His fingers dug deeply into the knotted muscles of her neck and upper back and Maggie groaned with pleasure.

"You've done this before," she murmured.

"Once or twice."

His hands found all the right spots on her shoulders as if he knew exactly where she ached. Ben had never had the inclination or the expertise to do this. But Cain did. Slowly, millimeter by millimeter, she began to feel her shoulders relax. His hands slid inside the robe against her bare skin with smooth, deep strokes and his thumbs caressed the muscles bracketing her upper spine. There was no missing the sensuality of it. Because his slow strokes warmed her skin with a building heat.

She should have stopped him, but she didn't have the will. Allowing her head to fall back into the pressure of his hands, she closed her eyes. It had been so long since anyone had touched her. Really *touched* her.

"Cain? Can I ask you something?"

"You can ask."

"What made you come here? This valley, I mean?"

"This is where my money ran out," he said, stroking the sides of her neck with his thumbs.

"But it could have run out a hundred miles south of here. Or east. Or in Missoula." He didn't reply. He just kept rubbing her neck. "Sometimes," she mused, "I think life is odd that way. The things that happen. It seems that there's no rhyme or reason to it. But then here we are. Married, when a couple of weeks ago we didn't even know one another."

"Frightening, huh?" he said with a grin in his voice.

"What's frightening," she said, "is that I feel safe with you. And I don't even know you."

The clock on the kitchen wall ticked loudly. Somewhere in the far off hills, a coyote yipped to its mate. His thumbs found two painful spots between her shoulder blades. "You carry your tension right here," he said. "Annie used to do that, too."

Maggie stilled and opened her eyes. "Annie?"

A long pause stretched between them before he said, "My wife."

Funny how two little words could turn a conversation on its ear. "Your *wife?*" Maggie repeated, pulling away from his hands and turning in his direction. "You were married? As in past tense, right? You *are* divorced?"

"No," he said. "She died a few years ago."

Maggie wanted to bite her tongue. Like her, Cain was much too young to be a widower. "I'm...so sorry. Was she ill?"

"No."

She turned to face him. He was staring out the darkened window, expressionless.

"She was killed buying ice cream at the little store around the corner. In a botched robbery."

She touched the hand that still rested on her shoulder. "Cain. That's awful."

"I don't tell many people that," he said. "It was...it seems like it was a long time ago."

But not long enough, she thought, watching the emotions flicker across his face. Maggie squeezed his hand, then got to her feet, letting the chair stand between them. "Sometimes," she said, "it helps to say those things out loud. Just so you know they don't exist only in your dreams."

His head came up with a start, and for a moment, she

saw it in his face—that he never imagined anyone else would know how that felt. But she did.

"Sometimes," she said quietly, "it seems like my whole life with Ben, and even before all that, never really happened. Except at night. Then it's real." She studied Cain's face, that strong, rugged face that hid everything he felt with such pinpoint skill. "That's my excuse. For why I don't sleep."

He gave her a half smile and brushed a strand of hair from her eyes. He was standing close. So close she could smell the soap on his hands and the scent of mint tea on his breath.

He leaned closer, waiting for her to stop him. But she didn't. Inexplicably, she didn't.

And then he was kissing her, sealing her mouth with his and sweeping aside rational thought. His lips were warm, his jaw, rough. The kiss, at first tentative, grew more urgent as he slanted his mouth in the other direction and cupped the back of her head in his hand.

He took her breath away. And somewhere, in the dim recesses of her mind, she knew she shouldn't be enjoying this. But she forgot to think as he deepened the kiss, brushing the surface of her teeth with his tongue. It weakened her knees along with her resolve. She half clung to him as hunger long ago forgotten tumbled through her. But when he drew her closer still, and she felt his need for her, she cursed her inability to keep a clear head around him.

She broke the kiss, breathing hard and pushing away from him. "I'm sorry," she said. "We can't—"

Taking a step backward, his breath coming a little too fast as well. He turned toward the sink, pulling it together.

"I'm sorry. I shouldn't have—" she began again.

"Don't," he broke in. "That was my fault."

It wasn't, and he knew it. She bore every bit as much of the blame.

"Look," he said, a muscle ticking in his jaw, "I can't...uh...I'm gonna go out for a while. You get some sleep."

"Out?" she echoed, as if the word were foreign. "It's almost midnight."

"Yeah. Don't wait up," he said, reaching for the hat he'd left near the door. He pulled his keys from his hip pocket and left the screen door screeching behind him.

Maggie didn't move. Rather, she stood frozen in place. Out? As in, don't-worry-Maggie-I'll-be-discreet...out?

She heard his bike start up with a roar and listened as it pulled out of her yard and onto the highway. But not toward Fishhook. The other way. Toward Marysville.

She squeezed her eyes shut, still feeling his mouth on hers. "Way to go, Maggie," she said to the empty room. "You show him you've got principles."

She walked to the door and closed it, turning the lock with a final-sounding click. "Now just try to remember what they are."

Chapter 8

The Crazy Eights Bar and Grill was thirty minutes and a million miles away from Fishhook and Maggie. Sitting at the long, mahogany bar, Cain stared into the amber-colored whiskey swirling in the glass in front of him. Above him, the Braves were at bat in the bottom of the fourteenth against the Dodgers on the muted satellite TV and the Judds wailed from the jukebox something about love building a bridge.

But Cain wasn't paying much attention. He was unsuccessfully working on not thinking at all. But Maggie's face kept swirling in his glass of whiskey, and being an idiot made him thirsty.

He signaled the bartender for a water back and tightened his fingers around his glass of booze, contemplating destruction.

One minute he'd been talking about Annie, and the next he was kissing Maggie. That alone would've probably qualified him for some kind of Clod of the Year Award. Forget that he hadn't mentioned Annie's name to anyone in years. Or that Maggie made him forget—on a regular basis—his habit of keeping the details of his life to himself. And, as if that wasn't bad enough...

She was starting to matter to him.

"Aren't you gonna drink it?" asked a female voice beside him.

Cain looked up to find a woman smiling at him from two seats away. At first glance, he guessed thirty, but on second, he figured thirty-five. Her skirt was short enough to reveal a nice, firm pair of legs, and her blouse, tight enough not to hold any secrets. With two fingers, she brushed her sable brown hair behind one ear and tilted her head.

"You've been staring at it for nearly an hour," she said again, indicating his drink. "Aren't you gonna drink it?"

He glanced down at the whiskey. "Haven't decided."

She got up, moved a seat closer and stuck her hand out to him. "I'm Daisy. Daisy Kelleher."

Cain took her hand and shook it. Her nails were long and smooth as the rest of her hand. "Hi, Daisy."

"And you're...?"

"Cain," he answered after a moment. "Just Cain."

"Well, Just Cain, since you can't decide whether or not to drink that whiskey, could I interest you in a dance?"

Cain glanced around at the dark end of the bar where a handful of couples were dancing on a parquet floor beneath some colored lights. He looked back at Daisy, who was still smiling at him behind her plum-colored lipstick.

"I'm not much of a dancer," he said, not really interested in making a bigger fool of himself tonight than he already had.

"Can I just say," she began with a lift of her perfectly plucked brows, "that *that* is totally beside the point?"

Cain smiled. Well, wasn't that the damned truth? "Then I'd be happy to dance with you, Daisy Kelleher."

Daisy smiled and got to her feet, sliding her hand around his bicep. "Where you from, Just Cain?"

"Far away," he said, walking with her toward the colored lights. "No place you'd know."

She'd dreamed about water, the deep caress of a river's current. It flowed over her like Cain's touch, lifting her and guiding her deeper and deeper into the dark eddies. She didn't need air or light to know the danger here wasn't in the water. It was him. Beckoning her. Calling her name.

Maggie.

She rolled toward the sound, feeling the sweet, familiar coolness of it against her skin. She wasn't ready to breathe yet. Not yet.

"Maggie, wake up."

She opened her eyes slowly to find him leaning over her in the dark. With a languid blink, she smiled up at him. He was frowning. And it slowly dawned on her that she was breathing.

Maggie sat up with a start, taking in her surroundings with the muzzy-headedness that came from being awakened from deep sleep. Her fingers closed automatically around the smooth, hard wood of the baseball bat she was clutching in her sleep. "What?"

Cain flinched and stepped back. "Whoa! Put that thing down. It's me."

Maggie lowered it and groaned, rubbing her temple. "I...must have fallen asleep."

"That for me?" he asked, indicating the bat.

"No." She leaned it against the side of the couch beside Jigger, who'd wandered over to nudge himself between the two of them.

"What are you doing up? I told you not to wait."

She shifted on the couch trying to make her voice sound indifferent. "I wasn't waiting. What time is it anyway?"

"Three."

"In the morning?" She blushed there in the dark at the decidedly *un*-indifferent nature of her remark.

He took her elbow and helped her up. "Yeah." He guided her toward the stairs across the dark living room.

Then it hit her. It wasn't booze she smelled on him as she'd expected. It was perfume. Cheap perfume.

She couldn't help it. She stopped stock still and stared at him.

"What?" he asked.

She exhaled sharply and started up the stairs. "Nothing."

"What?" he repeated, following her.

"Forget it."

"Then you wanna tell my what you were doing sleeping on the couch with a bat in your hands?"

"I was practicing my swing."

He grabbed her arm and turned her around. "Imagining my head as your target?"

"Why would I do that?"

He was so close he was practically holding her up. "You tell me."

She hated it that his voice sent a shiver of wanting through her. "I wasn't waiting up for you."

"Are you afraid to be here alone, Maggie?"

Jigger paused on the next step up, watching them both expectantly.

"I'm a big girl, Cain. I can even sleep with the light off." She turned and started up again, only to be stopped again by the pressure of his hand.

He swore softly. "Look, I didn't know. I should have, God knows, after meeting Laird Donnelly, but—"

"Stop, right there. Let's get this straight. I don't need a

keeper, Cain. You're not a prisoner here. We have an arrangement.''

"Nothing happened, Maggie."

"Right. But the next time, nothing happens," she said, heading back up the stairs, "I'd appreciate it if you'd wash off the perfume before you come home."

Cain sent the fly sailing out over the water in a three-four rhythm and set it down precisely where he'd aimed it, the surface of a deep pool under the shade of a bank of red cedar. He flicked the end of his rod, tugging it back. The thigh-high water climbed up the waders he wore, and even through the thick polyurethane, he could feel the glacial cold of the water. It never really warmed up this far north, he suspected. It was as unbearable in August as it was in December. But standing in it was just what he'd needed today, he decided, tossing the line again at a spot where he's seen a speckled brown trout leap minutes before.

The gear had belonged to Ben, Maggie had informed him when she'd handed the stuff over to him this morning and insisted he go. There had been a million chores to do, but she'd reminded him that Sundays were supposed to be a day of rest and that even he needed R and R now and then. She'd instructed him to catch something for dinner, and abruptly abandoned him to it.

More than a week had passed since his botched foray into Marysville. He and Maggie had made a tentative peace, though the topic had been carefully avoided since. It had occurred to him belatedly that jealousy might have inspired the crack about the perfume, but he'd since decided that wasn't possible. She'd been the picture of politeness since that day, with nary a glimmer of the heat from their kiss in the kitchen that night before.

He thought about Daisy Kelleher and the way he'd left her standing at her door wondering what she'd done wrong.

Cain clenched his jaw. Daisy had become his type: pretty, willing and not hung up on goodbyes. Any other night she would have met every criterion he had for a quick roll in the hay.

God knew, he'd gone with that intention. He'd wanted exactly that—a quick, anonymous fix for the tension roiling in his gut. And elsewhere. The woman had invited him up to her place. But before he'd hit the door, he'd changed his mind. Because standing there amidst the fireflies swarming the single bulb above her porch, it hit him. It was Maggie's hands he imagined when Daisy touched him. Maggie's mouth, not Daisy's he'd wanted to taste. Slow and deep and sweet.

He hadn't wanted that with anyone since Annie and it scared the hell out of him. Maggie was right about one thing, though. Sometimes, it felt like he and Annie had only existed in his dreams. The more time passed, the more it seemed true.

It seemed the only way he could fight that was to feel nothing. Anything else seemed…wrong. Because he was still here and Annie wasn't. And where was the justice in that?

But Maggie had a way of sliding beneath the numbness he'd fixed around himself. And all he could think about was holding Maggie against him and pretending that his past wouldn't matter to her.

A sharp tug on his line drew his thoughts away from Maggie as something grabbed his hook and started running. Cain braced his legs against the swift current and tugged back. Whatever it was, it felt big. Big enough, perhaps, for dinner for two. Or maybe he'd just build a little campfire right here and eat it himself.

He worked the line sideways and around following the fish's struggle, reeling it in little by little. He felt along the rocky stream bottom for his footing as the fish hauled him downstream with the strength of a pike. He reeled it closer, and backed onto the bank to reach for the net. The fish jumped and arced in the water. The sun caught the rainbows on its belly. It was a beauty—three and a half pounds if it was an ounce!

He dipped the net into the water to scoop it out and promptly lost his balance. He landed butt first in the shallows, holding the fish aloft like a prize.

The sound of female laughter from the bank behind him drew his humiliated gaze. Maggie was standing in the trees above the river's edge, with her hand clapped over her mouth. He had a face full of dog a second later as Jigger bounded up, mistaking him for a salt lick before splashing into the river for a cool drink.

Perfect.

Cain slogged up out of the water like a wet bear.

"Is that a new netting technique?" she asked when she could almost keep a straight face.

"Yeah," he said. "And did you happen to notice the fish?" He held it aloft.

Containing her mirth, she moved down toward the bank. She wore a day pack and was dressed for hiking. "*Wow.* Where are the others?"

He straightened his shoulders and sent her a thin smile. "It's the only one. But it's a big one."

"Size matters, I suppose," she said dryly.

"Only if you're hungry," he answered with a lift of his brows. She had sun on her nose and the flush of a good walk on her cheeks. She looked so damned pretty. "What are you doing here? I thought you wanted to get rid of me."

She had the good grace to look offended as she took the day pack off and unzipped it. "You went off without food, and I brought you lunch. But you're not very grateful, so maybe I'll just eat it myself."

Cain slid the hook from the fish's mouth and set him back in the water on a stringer he clipped to a fallen pine in the river. He stripped off his waders and sat down beside Maggie. She was already eating her sandwich. Tuna. Cain's stomach growled.

"Did you just come out here to torment me then?" he asked, rolling up his soaked sleeves past his elbows.

"Mmm." She stared out at the hoards of caddis flies darting across the sun-dappled surface of the river.

He kind of liked this playful Maggie. "So if I tell you I'm starving, will that buy me lunch?"

She shrugged coyly but gestured with a little you-can-do-better-than-that wiggle of her fingers.

"Uh...you're a goddess in the kitchen?"

She tilted her head appreciatively. "Warmer."

He braced his elbow on his knee with his palm up for an arm wrestle. "Best two out of three?"

She grinned and reached into the pack for the sandwich. "That's unfair. But I'll give you points for ingenuity."

Cain unwrapped the sandwich, took a bite and sighed. Beside him, Maggie unscrewed the top of a thermos of lemonade and took a swig. Then she passed it to him. "Thirsty?"

It was a small thing. The intimacy of sharing a drink, but it struck him just the same. He took the thermos and drank deeply, then handed it back. Her gaze flicked away.

"I should be doing books," she said, staring out at the water, "but I couldn't face them and decided it was too beautiful to be inside today. Besides, Jigger needed a walk."

The dog was happily splashing through the riverbank, nosing stones out of the mud. "How'd you find me?"

"Jigger found you. This used to be Ben's favorite fishing spot."

Ah. "It's a fine spot."

"Did you used to fish in Texas?" she asked.

"When I was younger. It's been years. But there's nothing in Texas like—" he gestured at the dramatic rock walls fingering up from the river and the scores of pine trees lining the bank "—this. I never imagined a place like this."

She smiled and nodded, listening to the sound of the water. "I love it here. Even in winter when the snow's up to here and the river almost disappears between banks of snow."

He could almost see it as she did. This place was magical and as untouched as anyplace he'd ever seen. It was probably no different than it had been three hundred years ago with trout leaping away at a meal on the surface of the water and the current cutting its way through millenniums of granite. There was a feeling of permanence here. One Maggie desperately wanted to hang on to. It made him all the more determined to save it for her.

The scent of crushed pine needles and the wild river lulled them as they ate. Overhead, a bald eagle drifted on the air currents, watching them. A few months ago, his only view was through the bars of his cell and the scenery was surrounded by barbed wire and high walls. He owed Maggie the truth about himself, he knew, but he could predict how she would react. It was better just to keep things as they were. Friendly, uncomplicated and platonic. That was definitely the best tack.

But when she'd finished, she started to strip off her hiking boots.

With a frown, Cain asked, "What're you doing?"

"Take off your shoes," she said, tugging off one boot and starting on the other.

"My shoes?"

"Yeah. Take 'em off."

He looked at the swift-flowing, glacial water. "I'm not going in there."

"It's great. What are you, chicken?" she challenged.

"*Hey...*"

"Then take 'em off."

He narrowed his eyes, but began undoing the laces on his running shoes. "Okay. Okay. They're coming off."

She grinned as she got to her feet. "See that rock down there?"

He squinted at the hulking slab of granite twenty feet up river that sat poised in the sun ten feet from the bank at the end of a series of precarious-looking stepping stones. He threw off his first shoe. "Why do I think this is going to be painful?"

"Last one on top cooks dinner."

Laughing, she took off at a sprint.

"Hey!" He hopped on one foot, tugging off his other shoe as she splashed into the water up to her knees. A few seconds later, he splashed in after her and she shrieked at the sound.

Rocks stabbed at his feet as he plowed through the current up to his knees. "Ooh! Ow!" he hollered, limping along behind her as she expertly leapt onto the first stepping stone.

"Bwakk-bwaaaw-bwwaak!"she taunted.

He lowered his head and charged. Seconds behind her, he ignored the pain and decided to win. She had the distinct advantage of having navigating this course before. Many times, he suspected.

But brawn won out. He was on her in another five steps when she faltered over a rock. She dove for the slab only a heartbeat before he did, only to lose her footing on the slippery side of the rock. Cain grabbed her and pulled her up with him. Breathless and laughing, they sprawled onto the sunny surface tangled together.

Their clothes were soaked and his skin tingled with the icy cold, but he felt...alive.

She turned her head his way, still laughing. "You cheat. Your legs are longer."

"I *gave* you a head start."

"Okay, okay, I admit defeat."

He rolled onto one elbow, smiling down at her. "So what's for dinner?"

Maggie grinned impishly, watching him slide the moisture off his tanned face with one hand. "Chicken?"

He shook his head, flexing a brawny bicep in a Tarzan pose. "Man catch big fish for woman," he grunted, pointing to the stringer on the bank. "Me clean, you cook."

She couldn't help but laugh at him.

Smiling, he hovered over her, blocking the sunlight. He tucked a wet strand of hair that had fallen across her cheek behind her ear.

Maggie's heart beat faster and the smile faded from her lips. She'd spent the last week thinking about that last kiss, wondering if she'd just imagined how it had made her feel and equal time wondering what would have happened if she hadn't stopped it. She could see the same questions in his eyes now.

But abruptly, he sprawled back onto the rock, away from her.

Maggie waited for a moment before she rolled his way, propping her cheek on her palm. His eyes were closed and he'd tucked one hand beneath his head.

"Cain?"

"Mmm?"

"Were you going to kiss me again?"

He sighed. "Yeah, well, can't blame a guy for thinking, can you?"

"I've been thinking about it for most of the week myself."

He rolled a look at her, but didn't say anything.

"I've missed you," she said simply.

A smile softened his mouth. "Me, too."

"Truce? Let's put last weekend behind us."

"Truce," he agreed.

Jigger splashed up onto the stepping stones, appearing from his foray down river. He leapt on the rock where they lay and began to spin dry. Maggie shrieked and they both lurched up, laughing again. The dog *whoofed* and licked her face. Maggie hugged him and got to her feet.

"Guess we'd better head back," she said reluctantly. She could stay here on this rock all afternoon beside him.

Cain got to his feet and held out a hand to help her down. "Guess so. The real world awaits."

Maggie took his hand with the sudden and unsettling feeling that those four little words were more true than either of them knew.

Chapter 9

Maggie loaded the last of the groceries into the cab of her truck, eyeing the rain in the distance. She'd spent too long at Moody's and now the rain would be catching her on the way home. She hoped Cain was back safely. He'd left early this morning, saying he was going to check the fence line.

How, she wondered, had everything gotten so complicated when it should have been so straightforward?

She almost laughed at her naiveté, imagining she could spend day in and day out with a man like Cain without being affected by him.

Yesterday on that rock, she'd wanted him to kiss her. She supposed it was just as well he hadn't, but if he had, she knew she wouldn't have stopped him this time. Which was crazy, because they both knew where it would lead. He had no intentions of staying. To get emotionally involved with a man like Cain was foolish. But she was afraid it was already too late for regrets. She feared she was falling in love with him.

Walking around to the other side of her truck, she tugged on the door handle.

"Ms. Cortland?" a voice said from beside her.

She whirled to find Brent Hayden, one of Laird's men, standing close to her. She backed against the truck with her hand on her throat.

He held up a hand, gesturing that he meant her no harm. "I didn't mean to scare you."

"Well, you did. And it's MacCallister now."

"Yes ma'am." He glanced up the street and back again. Young, brash looking, and only a few inches taller than her, Brent looked like a hundred other cowboys that drifted through this country. The denim he was wearing from head to foot was as scuffed as the boots on his feet.

Maggie remembered that he'd been one of the boys who'd confronted her and Cain on the street the day of her wedding. Only Brent had been the one hanging back on the step. He hadn't said a word.

"What do you want?" she asked.

He looked nervous and unsure of what he was about to say. "You..." he began, "doin' all right?"

Maggie frowned. "Fine, thank you." She reached for the door handle again, but he moved closer.

"Excuse me," she said pointedly.

"I need to talk to you," he said under his breath.

"About what?"

"Not here."

"On the street, you mean? That never stopped any of you before."

"I'm not part of that." A muscle ticked just under his left eye. "Don't count me into that."

His voice...something about it sounded vaguely familiar...

Her eyes widened. "It was *you*. That night on the phone. You were the one who called me."

"I'm leavin' soon," he said, neither confirming nor denying it. "I just think it ain't right, what happened. I seen what went on. What's still…" He brushed the back of his fist against his jaw. "If they caught me talkin' to you—"

"Who?" she said. "Donnelly? And who's Remus Trimark?"

Brent scowled, shoving his hands in his pockets. "It ain't a who. It's a what."

"Look," she said, impatient now, "if you're going to play cat and mouse with me again—"

She followed Brent's nervous gaze to the two Bar ZX men who'd just come out of the Moody's.

Brent jerked opened the door for Maggie and gestured her inside. "I gotta go. I'll stop by before I leave town. He's out to get you Ms. MacCallister. By God, he'll do it, too."

He slammed the door shut after her and was gone before she could say another word. Maggie rolled down her window, but it was too late. He was already joining up with the others who were casting an inquisitive look her way.

Donnelly again. Damn him! And what did any of this have to do with Remus Trimark?

Maggie turned the ignition over and started down the street.

It ain't a who. It's a what.

Of course. Remus Trimark wasn't a man. It was a company name.

Maggie stepped on the brake, made an illegal U-turn in the middle of town, and headed for Harold Levi's office.

The weather channels had been predicting a weather front since yesterday and Cain could feel it coming in his bones. A cold system moving down from Canada where winter hadn't quite loosed its grip on the land despite the fact that the calender said it was almost summer. He reminded himself that this was Montana, a couple of latitudes and six thousand feet higher than his old stomping grounds.

So he'd decided to get his work done early. Maggie had driven into town for supplies and he'd ridden her favorite gelding, Biscuit, out to the east pasture a mile from the house to check the fence line Donnelly's men seemed inclined to vandalize.

Cold air filtered down from the north as he pushed along the fencing, checking for breaks. But his mind was more on Maggie than on broken wire. He kept thinking about yesterday and the way she'd looked on that rock. All wet and flushed from laughter.

He'd thought about kissing her, but he'd wisely refrained. Their peace was tentative enough without putting sex back into the mix. Somehow, he just had to manage here for another few months without touching her.

He reached down and tugged at the barbed wire with a gloved hand. It was taut and strong here as it had been for the past two miles. One less thing to worry about today, he thought, glancing at the dark clouds gathering above the snow-dusted peaks that circled her valley. He didn't like the look of them. Texas had storms worse than anybody's business, but these clouds looked downright dangerous. When the first, fat droplet hit him, he headed back.

He was cold and soaked through by the time he got home and put Biscuit up in the barn. It wasn't until he went inside and found Jigger waiting expectantly by the door, that he realized Maggie wasn't home yet. He walked into the kitchen and looked at the clock on the kitchen wall—1:40 p.m. A note sat propped up on the table from Maggie telling him she'd be back by noon at the latest.

Cain frowned and glanced at the sky outside and the rain still sleeting against the window. Maybe she'd decided to stay in town and wait it out…get a haircut or have her nails done….

Right. He glanced at her answering machine. The red light was tellingly dark.

Cain frowned. *Would* she have called him? He'd ridden out early, before she was up. And she was used to living on her own, following her own time schedule.

But she had said noon. Cain picked up the phone and dialed.

"Moody's Café," said the woman's voice on the other end.

"Moody, it's Cain. Is Maggie there?"

The sound of china clinking and customers buzzing in the background said the lunch rush was still on. "Maggie? No. She left a couple of hours ago. Isn't she home yet?"

Something tightened his gut. Hours! "What time exactly did she leave?"

In the background she could hear someone calling to Moody for more coffee. "Keep your pants on, Tom," she called with her hand partially over the phone. "Cain? I don't remember exactly, except it was before the lunch rush, so it had to be eleven-thirty at the latest. She had to make a quick stop at the market, but she should have been back an hour and a half ago."

Damn.

"Did she say she was going anywhere else after that?" he asked.

"No, she was going straight home. She was worried because of the weather with you out in it and all…" Moody took a worried pause. "She was in a hurry to get back."

Worried about him? Her face flashed in his mind's eye, looking up from what she was doing, smiling at him with that dazzling smile of hers. He banished the image, forcing himself to think clearly. "Moody, I'm sure she's fine. I'm just gonna go look for her."

"If she doesn't turn up in the next few minutes, will you call me?"

"I will." But that old sense of dread fisted at the back of his throat as he left the safety of the house and headed back out into the weather.

Maggie tightened her hands on the steering wheel, knowing that doing so was as useless as wishing she'd stayed in town in the first place. The water was roaring against the wheels at a furious rate, creeping toward the fender of her truck as the rain rushed down the wash where her truck had been carried by the flash flood. It was stalled.

The sky lit up with a slash of lightning, and thunder rolled right behind it, pounding along the landscape like a big fist.

She should have gotten out before the water rose this high. She should have realized the puddle in this dip in the road was a lake, and turned back. She should have done a lot of things differently, but she hadn't. She felt the truck list sideways slightly as the thigh-high water lifted it off the road.

Maggie tried the ignition again. It whined like a wet dog, then died. She leaned on her horn for the twentieth time in the last ten minutes. The deluge clattering against the metal roof drowned out the sound. Naturally, no one answered. She was in the middle of nowhere, for heaven's sake. There were no ranches even within signal flare distance. If she had a signal flare.

She could climb out on the cab roof and wait for help. But who in their right mind would drive down Old Mill Road if they didn't have to in this kind of weather?

She stared out the rain-streaked window. Maybe the rain would stop. Maybe she could actually ford this rushing river to get to the hillside twenty feet away without being swept into the torrent.

Maybe she should have her head examined for deciding

to stay in Montana long after it had become clear that Montana didn't want her.

The truck moved again with a groan, like a beast nudged from its slumber—slowly at first, then with real conviction. It goosed her already thudding heartbeat. Water began to stream in through the seam in the door at her feet. If she stayed where she was, she risked going over with the truck and getting trapped inside. If she got out, she might at least have a chance if the truck tipped over.

She cranked the window down, angry now, wondering what she'd done in some past life to deserve all of this trouble. Rain instantly soaked her thin jacket and stung her face. Whatever it was, she reasoned, it must have been a doozy.

Climbing up through the window onto the cab's roof, Maggie shivered, then hugged herself, sitting drenched and cross-legged in the rain. It was slippery and freezing cold and she instantly regretted leaving the warmth of the cab. A teeth-chattering chill rolled through her as anger worked its way up her spine. Enough was enough!

"You can t-take my truck," she shouted at the spitting sky. "You c-can take my confidence. You can even take my business. But there's one thing, by God, you can't take!"

She reached into her pocket for the Milky Way bar she'd bought in town, tore off the wrapper and defiantly took a big bite. "And you're just gonna have to learn to live with that!"

In reply, the truck creaked and tipped and slowly, ever so slowly, dumped a defiant Maggie Cortland MacCallister *and* her candy bar into the roiling current.

Cain hauled Biscuit to a stop at the sight of Maggie's truck, lying sideways and half submerged in the swiftly moving flash-flood waters of the wash. And felt his heart move into his throat.

"Maggie!" he shouted at the top of his lungs. But the torrent was loud and the rain, relentless. He vaulted off the horse, already stripping off his jacket, and ran to the edge of the water. Cupping his mouth with his hands, he shouted again. "Maggie!"

Nothing.

There was no sign of her. The driver's side window was open and muddy water was splashing against the inside of the truck's cab. His heart was thudding in his ears.

Don't be dead. Please God—

He yanked the rope from his saddle, tossed it around himself, then attached the other end to Biscuit's saddle horn. She was the best cutting horse Maggie owned and he knew he could count on her to pull him back out if he got in trouble.

He waded into the rushing deluge and immediately knew it was going to be too slippery to navigate. The slick grass underfoot was like ice and the current impossible. He backed up and started upstream to get above it.

That's when he heard it.

The voice was faint, but distinct. And it belonged to Maggie.

Cain slipped on the bank and recovered, dragging Biscuit in the direction of the sound. Forty feet away, he saw her, clinging desperately to a half-submerged chokecherry bush and fighting the current determined to drag her away.

"Maggie!" He sent up a silent prayer of thanks. "Hang on."

"Cain! I'm slipping!" she cried.

Cain ran to the edge of the frigid water and plunged in, feeling the current threaten to take him out into the center of the spreading river. He fought it, stroking hard in her direction.

"Maggie! Don't let go!"

"Cain! Please—"

The current slammed him into the bush near Maggie and she lost her grip. But he caught her wrist just before she flew out of reach and dragged her toward him with one hand. His own grip on the bush was tenuous and he knew he'd have to let go to get them out of here.

"Maggie—" he shouted, "put your arms around me!"

She clung to his neck but she was cold and moving too slowly and her lips were a dangerous shade of blue. "S-so c-cold..."

"The rope, Maggie. Slip under the rope."

Her numb fingers plucked at the rope but the tension kept her from getting any grip on it. And it was impossible to open the loop that held him firmly. The current slapped them in the face and stole Cain's breath. Gulping air, he could feel the cold working on his muscles and knew they had precious little time to get out of here before they were both lost causes.

He threw a look back to the bank where Biscuit waited, braced against the tug of his weight, ears thrust forward. "Biscuit!" he shouted over the roar of the water. "Back! Back up, damn you!"

Slowly, one step at a time, he did. Cain felt the tug of the rope against his chest and felt his grip on the branch of the bush weaken. He tightened his arm around Maggie and transferred his other grip to the rope. Maggie buried her face against his shoulder and Cain focused solely on the approaching bank. One misstep and he could lose her in the blink of an eye.

"Shh!" he hissed at the horse. "Back! Keep going! Back!"

The bottom of the creek rose up beneath his feet and he struggled to stand with Maggie's weight and the current pulling at him. He felt Maggie struggling to do the same and suddenly, they were on the bank, out of the water.

He fell with her onto the cold grass and rolled his weight off her, breathing hard. Maggie lay on her back, arms flung out at her sides, gasping for breath. Cain tore the rope off him and tossed it aside. "Maggie...?"

He brushed the wet strands of hair out of her eyes and off her face. "*Talk* to me."

She muttered something he couldn't understand. He leaned closer. "What?"

Her big brown eyes peered up at him. "What t-t-took you s-so l-long?"

Cain pulled her up against his chest and wrapped his arms around her. "Anybody ever tell you you're a lot of trouble?"

She shivered violently. "All the time."

Cain swallowed hard, his gaze skimming her features, more grateful than he could say to know that he wouldn't have to spend the rest of his life trying to call them to memory. She was here. Alive. And he didn't even think about what he did next.

Her mouth was cold, shaky, as he dropped his rain-slick lips against hers with a heat he didn't even know he still possessed. Her arms came up around his neck and she pulled him against her. There was gratitude in her kiss and fear and the prospect of death between them. He wrapped his arms beneath her and gave her what was left of his heat.

She tasted cold and hungry and sweet. Cain knew he shouldn't be kissing her, but he couldn't stop himself. He needed to feel her mouth against his to reassure himself that they were both alive.

Dimly aware that the rain was still pounding down on them, he eased back, his mouth hovering close, and he looked in her eyes. "Maggie..."

"Don't say anything," she warned, squeezing her eyes shut. "Please, don't say anything."

So he didn't. Instead, he lifted her in his arms and carried her to Biscuit who was patiently waiting nearby, blinking away the rain. Maggie was shivering badly now and he had to get her home. There'd be time to talk later. And maybe, he thought climbing up behind her, talk would be beside the point.

Maggie thought to protest when Cain carried her upstairs to the bathroom and wrenched on the hot water in the shower, but she knew she was too cold to think clearly or even manage to make it up the steps without stumbling.

And she was still staring at the buttons on her blouse, trying to remember how to undo them, when he picked her up again and stepped into the shower with her, fully clothed.

The steaming water hit her cold skin like sharp little needles and she gasped and tried to duck out of it. He lowered her feet to the ground but held her firmly beneath the stream of water. Maggie pressed her face against his chest, feeling the steady thud of his heart beneath her cheek.

She swallowed hard, sighing as the heat began to penetrate her chill. "I didn't think you would come."

"I called Moody when I got back and found you hadn't come home. She said you'd left hours ago."

She brushed her hair back with both hands, remembering. "I tried to stop, but my brakes must have gotten wet. I got caught in a dip in the road. Then I stalled and started moving down the wash with the current."

Cain cupped her chin with his hand. His eyes had gone dark. "You should've stayed in town."

"I should have," she agreed.

"You never should have risked driving on that road."

"You're right."

"You scared the hell out of me."

"I'm sorry," she whispered, meeting his hard gaze.

Then, he closed the distance between them and covered her mouth with his, dragging her up against him. Maggie wrapped her arms around him, knowing how close she'd come to never, ever feeling this again. Never knowing his embrace or hearing the concern in his voice. It made no sense, she thought as his mouth slanted against hers with a need that seemed destined to destroy them both, that she wanted it, too.

His tongue slid past the open seam of her lips and toyed with hers. He tasted of rain and heat and relief. He pulled her flush against him and there was no mistaking where this was going. Her breasts felt full and heavy there against the cool dampness of him and his hand slid upward to cup her there. The sensation nearly stole whatever strength was left in her knees.

"Oh, Cain—" she breathed against his lips.

"Shh—" he said, sliding his fingers into her hair and finding her mouth with his again. It seemed as if she'd always known it would come to this. This awful wanting. This force that wouldn't be stopped.

She was beyond trying to stop it. She needed to feel his skin against hers the way she needed air to breathe. Heat poured down on them from the shower and slid between the chill of her clothes and the warmth of his hands as they slipped beneath her sodden T-shirt and found the cool skin of her belly. His hand skimmed over her, exploring new territory as he kissed her.

Their breath mingled beneath the stream of water, and she tasted his tongue as he discovered hers. Maggie pulled him closer, sliding her fingers into the soaked hair at the nape of his neck. She loved the feel of his strength. The tension hovered there in the muscles of his neck and back and shoulders, radiating heat. Suddenly, he lifted her against him—against the irrefutable evidence of his desire for her—and turned her until her back was flush against the cool wall and his teeth had found her breast through the wet fabric her shirt. He tortured her there for a minute before turning his attention back to her mouth.

A noise came from her throat a ragged sound, not quite a moan and not a cry. But something altogether wanton.

He broke the kiss, sliding his mouth down her throat again until he'd reached the small hollow at the base of her neck. "So beautiful, Maggie," he murmured. "I've wanted to kiss that spot since the first moment I saw you."

She let her head fall sideways to give him better access because what he was doing there had stolen the strength from her muscles and was beginning to coil deep and low at the center of her.

She slid her hands under the sodden black T-shirt that clung to him and followed the twin columns of muscle that ran up his spine. The only part of him that was soft was his skin, like wet silk under her hands. She wanted him closer than he already was. She wanted to feel this strength inside her, be part of it. Their clothes were only in the way and she wanted to be able to look at his chest without pretending she wasn't.

She pushed the soaked fabric upward until he noticed what she was doing and tore it the rest of the way off. Maggie swallowed hard, staring at the sculpted perfection of him. Gone was the sinewy gauntness he'd had when he'd come. The V of hair that dusted his chest was wet and dark and she spread her fingers across his chest testingly, wanting to feel it.

He watched her do it and his chest rose and fell rapidly with his breathing. Then he returned the favor, lifting the hem of her muddy T-shirt and slipping it over her head.

Suddenly, she was standing there with only her pink lace bra and jeans on.

For a moment, he didn't do anything but look, as if taking in what he'd only been imagining. Then his hands slid up from her waist to cup her and test the weight of her breasts in his hands. His eyes rose to meet hers with something close to wonder.

"Pink," he murmured. "I want—"

She pulled one strap until it fell off her shoulder and down her arm.

A shuddering breath escaped him as he followed her movement with his mouth, sliding downward until he'd pushed the fabric aside with his tongue and found her nipple.

Maggie gasped as he took it in his mouth, sucking hard as his free hand found her other breast. She arched toward him, and gave a shuddering sigh as he slid the other strap off her shoulder and let the delicate fabric fall open beneath her breasts. Then he shifted his attention to her other side.

Maggie stared down at the top of his head, the dark silky hair that curled at the nape of his neck and she wondered why it had taken a near death experience to make her realize that she needed this. To feel alive again. Oh, she felt...on fire!

Her skin tingled and a buzzing had started somewhere at the back of her skull. The hum was moving through her like an electric current.

Cain left a trail of hot kisses up her chest as he moved his attention back to her cheek. His lips moved against her ear, "Tell me to stop, Maggie," he whispered. "Tell me now 'cause I'm not sure I can do it on my own."

She moved her head from side to side, breathing heavily. "Don't stop."

Not afraid, she thought. Afraid *not* to, came the next thought. Because his hands, as they slid inside her jeans and shoved them down her legs, made her feel like a woman for the first time in years. And his mouth made her remember what it felt like to be wanted.

She found the metal button at the top of his jeans as well and snapped it open. When she did that, he stopped and looked down at her hands, then slowly lifted his gaze up to her face.

And took her breath away.

Water glistened on his skin and his dark lashes...a sea god, come to shore. All power and grace and surprise, he reached for her, taking her face between his hands.

"No ghosts between us. Not now. Now it's just you—" his mouth taunted hers a heartbeat away "—and me." He teased the corner of her mouth, staying just out of her reach. Then took her hand and guided it down again to the flat plane of his belly. "Touch me, Maggie."

And she did.

Chapter 10

Cain's taut muscles jumped as she dragged her palm across the rippled expanse, then slid upward to find the flat round disks of his nipples nestled in the damp hair of his chest. She rolled the tips of her fingers across them, watching them harden the way hers had at the touch of his tongue. Then she moved her hands downward to the zipper on his jeans and tugged it down.

Beneath the sodden denim, he guided her fingers against him. He was hard for her and Maggie's breath came in a ragged gasps at the intimate touch. And then his hands caught the silky pink fabric around her hips and discarded it somewhere at their feet beneath the hot stream of water.

She felt exposed and raw, every nerve on fire as he drew her closer, sliding his hands down the length of her back until he could cup her against him. He tilted his hips against her and took her mouth with his again, this time without any gentleness. This time, the hunger there was unmasked. His mouth slanted against hers first one way, then the other as if he were searching for a way inside her.

His fingers found a way.

He dipped into her at the apex of her legs and Maggie gasped. Something began to melt inside her, blur any misgivings she might have had into sheer want. He deepened his caress while he kissed her, and Maggie's knees began to buckle.

She wrapped her arms around his neck and buried her face against him. She could feel the thud of his heart against her breast. It was beating fast, like hers. There was no mistaking it this time. The need that pressed against her belly was for her. She needed him, too.

He unlocked her arms from around him, and pushed her back against the wall, pressing wet kisses against the sensitive skin of her inner arm until he reached her breast. He lavished his attentions on it again before moving down the flat curve of her belly and further down. Maggie flung her hands out against the wall for support because she was afraid she would slide down into a little puddle if he didn't stop.

He lifted his head and looked at her, tracing her rib cage with his thumbs and ending at the indentation of her waist. A devilish smile curved the corners of his mouth as he dipped his fingers into her again, torturing her deliciously. She was slick and wet and ready for him and she needed...oh, she needed—!

"Cain—" she whispered with some urgency.

"Mmm?" he murmured against her belly, tracing her hipbone with his tongue.

"Did you notice," she asked breathlessly, "that I'm the only naked one in this shower?"

He moved downward. "Mmm-hmm...Yeah. Nice..."

"I think," she said, clutching at the wall, "I'm going to fall."

"No, you're not." He cupped her backside in his strong

hands and drew her to him, holding her up and stealing whatever strength was left in her knees.

"Oh—!" she gasped, plunging her fingers into his hair as his mouth tormented her. Her breathing had degenerated into something animal-like and she heard a sound that must have come from her. Tension coiled inside her as he drove her to an edge, then stopped just short of pushing her over.

Maybe she would die now, she thought as he got slowly to his feet, following the path of his hands.

"Sweet," he murmured, cradling her breasts in his hands and brushing her aching nipples with his fingers. "So sweet."

Maggie wrapped her arms around him again, her whole being trembling with need. She kissed the side of his neck, nipping him with her teeth as she trailed kisses up to his ear. At the sensitive inside of his ear, she laved him with her tongue. He hissed a breath past his teeth.

"Take off your clothes," she whispered, slipping her wet hands into the waistband of his jeans.

He smiled against her neck and immediately obliged, tugging the wet denims off and sending the cotton briefs after.

She couldn't help it. She looked down. And swallowed hard.

"Better?" he asked, drawing her up against the velvety steel of him.

"Mmm. Did I mention that you're beautiful?" she asked breathlessly.

He laughed, a deep throaty laugh, as his fingers found her again. "No, but that's my line."

"Sorry." Throwing her head back so he could access her throat. "Oh, don't stop doing that."

He growled against her neck. "I've got something better."

"Ohh…yes, please," she begged.

And suddenly he was lifting her up, wrapping her around him and settling her downward until he filled her with an exquisite pressure. Her breath came in shaky gasps in the steamy shower and he turned her under the deluge to warm her even as he began moving inside her. Maggie forgot the cold and the heat and only remembered how much she loved being in his arms and feeling him inside her.

Cain pressed her back against the wall, as he moved with the ageless rhythm of passion. His mouth found hers and she kissed him hungrily. He couldn't get enough of her. He wanted...he needed more, deeper, harder...

She was everything he'd dreamed and more. Her heat fired him and the way she ran her tongue along the inside of his ear nearly made him lose it. She was slick and wet and wanting. He needed to make it good for her, but he was afraid he was going to go too fast, too hard, because she was driving him over the edge and he was barely hanging onto his control. Her fingernails trailed across his back and those small panting sounds she made with each plunge fueled a conflagration that was threatening to consume them both.

"Don't—" she whispered desperately "—stop."

He couldn't if he tried. So he complied, feeling her coiling tighter around him until she bucked in his arms and cried out. Shaking now, Cain followed her blindly over that cliff, driving into her with a hard thrust, spilling himself inside her.

Maggie collapsed against his shoulder, breathing raggedly, and Cain pushed her against the wall, afraid he really would drop her if he wasn't careful. He let her slide down him until her feet touched the floor of the tub, then he buried his face in her hair as he wrapped his shaking arms around her.

Neither of them spoke for long seconds as behind them, the water began to run cool. Cain reached around and shut it off, then tugged a towel off the rack and wrapped it around her. She was trembling. Not from cold. Her skin felt hot to his touch. But from whatever had possessed them. It lingered between them still, but the sharp edge had been blunted for the time being.

Cain rubbed the towel over Maggie's shoulders, tugging the edges together and pulling her toward him for one last kiss. He kept it brief, staring at her and wondering how he'd managed to keep his hands off her until now. It had been a long time since he'd felt like this with a woman. Like he didn't want to leave and find his own bed. He wasn't finished. He wasn't sure he'd ever be finished with Maggie, who was looking suddenly small and uncertain.

She shivered as he dragged another towel off the rack and wrapped it around his hips. "Cold?"

She shook her head, clutching the edges of her towel together in front of her. "Not anymore. You?"

He shook his head, too, tracing her cheekbone with the back of one knuckle. "Scared?"

She gave the barest of nods and closed her eyes against the kiss he pressed against her forehead. So was he, but he wasn't sure why. "C'mon. Let's get outta here."

He pulled her against him and they walked into the bedroom together. Maggie slipped a pink chenille bathrobe on and knotted the belt around her waist. Cain came up behind her, brushed her damp hair aside and kissed the nape of her neck. "You sorry?" he asked.

"No," she murmured, turning toward him to study his face. She didn't ask. She didn't have to.

Outside the rain still beat against the window. He pulled her down onto the bed beside him, folding his arm over her and drawing her near. "You were…incredible."

A disbelieving smile tugged at her mouth. "I bet you say that to all the girls."

There was only one girl he'd ever said that to. But he

couldn't think of Annie now. "It's been a long time for me, Maggie."

She looked away, and he realized she didn't believe him.

"Hey," he said, curling his fingers around hers. "I know you think something happened in Marysville the other night, but nothing did. I won't deny I went there with that intention, but it didn't happen. It was you I wanted, not some stranger. So I came back."

Through a sweep of lashes, she looked up at him. "Our agreement—"

"Screw the agreement," he said softly, brushing her hair off her cheek. "We're both adults. This is where it was headed all along. You knew it and I knew it."

"Maybe so," she admitted, wrapping her arms around herself.

He tucked her against him. "It's not that complicated."

"No?"

He was silent for a few moments. "Is it?"

Maggie brushed back her damp hair with two hands. She knew very well how complicated this would get. "Today. Right now, maybe not. But it will be in October. It won't be simple then."

"October will come," he said, "whether we're... breaking our agreement or not." He rolled onto his back and stared at the ceiling. "I won't lie to you Maggie. I told you how it was with me. Nothing's changed. Don't expect—"

"I don't," she said, not wanting to hear what he felt compelled to remind her. "I don't expect anything from you. That's not why this happened."

He tightened his arms around her, his thumb caressing her breast through the thick chenille fabric. "Maggie," he whispered, "are you sorry you did this? Because if you are—"

She covered his hand before he could move it. "I've

spent too much time being sorry for things I can't control to be sorry about something I could. I wanted to make love to you. I don't want to think about October. I don't want to think about anything right now except how much I want you to hold me.''

Maggie sighed as he pulled her closer and tucked her head beneath his chin. She didn't regret it. But unlike him, she knew someday she would. Someday he would get on that motorcycle of his and ride out of her life the same way he'd ridden into it. And she would stand here and watch him go. But she'd allowed too much of her life to get away from her to let this moment go, as well. She would drink in what he had to offer her now and worry about October then.

"There is one thing though," he began awkwardly. "Like I said, it's been a long time since I've worried about…I should have used something," he said, caressing the back of her head.

"I can't have children."

His hand went still. "What?"

Maggie rolled away from him. "I can't get pregnant."

"You and Ben—?"

"We couldn't conceive. They couldn't find the problem, but Ben was tested. It wasn't him. Finally, we just stopped trying." She pushed away from him. "I don't want to talk about Ben now," she said, sitting up.

"Me either." He followed her to the edge of the bed. "No ghosts. Right?"

"Right."

"So…" He tugged her down into his arms and she gasped with surprise. "Here's my plan."

She relaxed against him with a smile. "What plan?"

"I distract you—" he dropped his mouth down on hers "—until you can only—" and kissed her until the heat began to coil inside her again ''—think about—'' and she felt her will melt away ''—me.''

''Mmm...'' she murmured when he'd finished, ''that *is* distracting. But I'm still not sure I'm completely—''

He slid his hand between her bathrobe and her skin, finding the curve of her breast.

''Oh...'' she sighed. ''Well...''

A slow, sexy smile worked at his mouth. ''Better?'' he asked, nudging her bathrobe open with his wrist. His thumb coaxed her nipple to attention and sent a shiver of pleasure through her.

''Mmm,'' she said with a sigh. ''You're very good at this.''

''I'm just getting started,'' he promised, moving south and finding the damp warmth he'd left only minutes ago.

Maggie sucked in a breath and shuddered. He watched her the way a hungry man watched for a pot to boil as he dipped his fingers in and out of her. She arched against his hand. He was a magician, and with each stroke, he drew her out like a long, colorful ribbon and wrapped her around him.

She glided her hands over him and followed her touch with her mouth. His skin felt hot and damp, his muscles hard and coiled. And the rest of him, lower down, that was hard and coiled, too. She urged him closer and he nudged her legs apart until he was inside her again. Sprawled together, wrapped around each other, they moved with the frantic pace of lovers. He sent her spinning out of control and plunged into the whirlpool with her. Maggie held him until he collapsed on top of her, as full and as spent as she.

Afterward, she held him close, painfully aware of how short life could be. She loved feeling him inside her, holding her. She knew she had fallen in love with this man whose past haunted him the way her own still did. Was it a mistake? Undoubtedly. But she didn't care. She would walk through this door, just as she had the rest and see what was on the other side. And somehow, when it was over, she'd find a way to let him go. But until then, she would let him hold her and forget about how much she wanted him to stay.

The other day's rain had left the sky scoured and blue and the pasture sprouting with new spring shoots of green. Gene Fielding steered his Jeep Wrangler over the rutted pasture toward the collection of cattle and men milling around the branding fire in the north pasture. He could see a pair of men straddling a bawling newborn in the mud, pressing the ZX brand into the animal's smoking hide while another pair of ranch hands chased down the next victim.

Donnelly sat astride his prize gelding, Lazarus, overseeing the operation, directing traffic. Gene pulled to a stop near the branding truck and shut off the engine. What he was about to do was as distasteful as anything he'd ever done, but he had no other choice. The information he'd dug up on MacCallister was explosive and could very well save both his and Donnelly's necks. But at what cost? What was the price of a man's future? What had happened to that damned line he'd sworn long ago not to cross? He couldn't seem to locate it anymore. The damned thing kept moving.

What the hell, he thought. Chrissy was starting at Stanford in the fall and his son, Kyle, would follow two years later. Gene couldn't afford the luxury of conscience or regret. It was too late for that. His children looked at him as if he could do no wrong. And he'd be damned if they'd find out differently.

He reached for the dossier and climbed out of the Jeep. Donnelly saw him coming and eased Lazarus over to meet him.

"Well?" Donnelly asked.

"It's all there," Gene told him, handing him the paper-work. "I think you'll be satisfied."

Donnelly stared at the dossier in his hands and gave a long, slow whistle. "You sure about this?"

"As sure as I am that his old man owns the biggest spread east of the King Ranch," Gene Fielding told him, lighting a cigarette with the engraved silver lighter Laird had given him for Christmas. "They don't speak. Haven't for years."

"Resources?"

"Disinherited. Six years ago when he married that gal from upstate New York. His father, Judd MacCallister, kept a pretty tight rein on his boy and didn't take it too well that some girl from the wrong side of the tracks was going to mother his future heirs."

Laird looked up, a smug smile beginning to curve his mouth. "And the rest?"

"...is on the public record. If he'd thought to use an alias, it would have made my job harder. But I found a booking photo. It's him all right."

"You think she knows?" Laird asked.

"Doubtful." Gene inhaled deeply and blew out a ring of bluish smoke that drifted to the bright, cerulean sky like a dented halo. "No mention of it on the marriage license application. And I asked around. He plays his cards close to the vest. Nobody knows anything about him. Not even Moody."

"Moody talked to you about him?" Laird said, surprised.

"Not intentionally. We were just...passing the time, you know? Over a cup of coffee."

"So..." Donnelly scanned the contents, "Santa Fe, Boulder, Orem...Boise. He's worked all over the damn country. Where's he heading?"

"I plotted out his last few months. It seems random to

me. Looks like it was dumb luck he landed here at Maggie's.''

Donnelly closed the file folder and fingered the sharp edges. "Nothin' lucky about that," he said with an ugly smile. "Nothin' lucky at all. You're sure he's not a hired gun?"

"Maggie can't afford one and I don't think he's in the market for another stint behind bars. I think he can be handled.''

"Anyone can be handled for the right price. If this deal isn't closed by the fifteenth of July, we lose everything. Make this happen, Gene. Call Kipling," Donnelly told him. "Set up a meeting. Then call Solefield. We'll bury this son of a bitch." He hauled back on his reins and urged Lazarus into a sharp pivot, leaving Gene behind, eating mud.

"Will do. Sure thing," Gene muttered to himself as he walked back to his Jeep, brushing the specks of mud off his coat jacket and kicking a dirt clod out of his way. "It's been my pleasure to conspire with you to destroy a man's life."

Bill Tischman, the owner of the Lazy H spread over in Helena, slipped his black Stetson off and slid his hand down Geronimo's foreleg, then patted the animal's muscular chest.

"Sound. He looks in top form, Maggie," Bill said, "and I like the way he's settled down." He smoothed a hand down Geronimo's muzzle. "I'd like to see him work."

"Absolutely. Cain? Bill, this is my husband, Cain MacCallister."

Cain, who'd spent the morning getting Maggie's truck up and running again, wiped the grease off his hands and took Bill's proffered one. "Pleasure. Maggie's told me about your place."

Bill smiled proudly. "It's just a little spread, but it suits me. Maggie says you've worked wonders with this crazy horse of hers. You gonna show me what he can do?''

Cain nodded. ''I think you'll see his potential.''

Cain mounted Geronimo and put him through his paces with the cows. Her chest tightened, watching Cain work. He rode as if he were born on the back of a horse, his movements so in tune with the horse's that Maggie herself couldn't see the signals he was giving. It made her wonder again where he'd learned to ride like that.

Since that first time two days ago in the shower, they'd barely been able to keep their hands off one another. Even now, as she watched his shoulders strain the seams of his denim shirt and the strong muscles of his thighs guide Geronimo through his paces, an illicit thrill stole through her at the prospect of what might happen between them later.

As if he could read her thoughts, Cain caught her eye, giving her a secret wink as Geronimo successfully cut a steer from the herd and cornered it against the fence.

Maggie felt heat bloom on her cheeks and she prayed Bill's attention was on the horse, not on the raw sexual tension between her and Cain.

Geronimo missed a cue, a common mistake for a green horse, and Cain patiently corrected him and moved ahead.

''He's come a long way,'' she told Bill, stepping up on the rail and wrapping her arms around the rough pine pole. ''He needs another couple of weeks. Maybe a month. He'll be ready to cut in the futurity over in Boise by late August if you're going to enter.''

Bill nodded, his expert gaze missing nothing. ''Your new husband's quite a talented trainer. You say he's the one who's been working Geronimo?''

''Yes. And he's not just talented. He's gifted. We both know Geronimo had a less than even chance of coming around.''

Bill regarded her with a smile. They'd known each other

for four years and they respected each other. Bill had known Ben, but he'd mostly worked with her.

"Frankly," he said, sliding his hat back on, "when I saw you bid on that horse at the auction that day, I didn't think you had a prayer. I wouldn't have taken that chance. That horse had more problems than three of my worst cutting horses combined. But you've turned him around. I like what I see. I think we can safely say that if he's everything you promise by the end of July, I'll be payin' you another visit. This time with my checkbook."

Maggie had to work to contain her elation. His checkbook! They'd already talked about price. Geronimo would be well worth more than ten times what she'd paid for him. And with that amount, she could pull herself out of this hole she'd been in for the past few months and get back on top.

Cain guided Geronimo up to the fence and leaned over to shake Tischman's hand.

"Nice work, Mr. MacCallister. If Maggie hadn't snagged you first with a wedding ring, I'd have been tempted to hire you away from her."

Cain's smile gave little away, but he met Maggie's eyes briefly before he said, "That mean you're interested in Geronimo?"

"I certainly am. Your wife can fill you in on the details." He touched the brim of his hat to Maggie. "I'm gonna head back. I've got a million things to do before the sun goes down. But I sure am glad I stopped by today. You take care, Maggie. I'll see you in a few weeks."

Maggie smiled broadly. "I will. Thanks, Bill."

Cain dismounted and they watched the rancher pull out of her yard and onto the highway. Maggie couldn't contain her whoop of joy as she flung herself into Cain's arms. He laughed and spun her around.

"You did it!" she shrieked. "You *did* it!"

"*We* did it," he said, twirling her to a stop and staring down at her. "I couldn't have done it without you."

"Do you know what this means? It means I can pay back my debt. Get back in the black again. Back on my feet. I'll be able to repay those old debts, and with the yearlings due for sale this year…"

"Whoa!" he said, setting her down. "He's not sold yet."

"But as good as…" she said, throwing her head back and spinning around. "Oh, I feel a thousand pounds lighter!"

He drew her back to him and curled his arms around her. "Any news on the loan yet?"

"Not yet. But if I don't hear by tomorrow, I'm going to have Harold call. Once we get the loan, it'll tide us through the next few months. But Geronimo's sale will put this place back on the map." She beamed up at him. "Thank you, Cain."

He hesitated, as if he'd been about to tell her something, but changed his mind. "I think," he said, reaching for Geronimo's reins, "this calls for a night off."

She tipped her head up with a grin. "A night in, you mean?"

"Hmm. That, too," he said, kissing her nose. "But I had something else in mind."

"What?"

He smiled down at her, his eyes full of mystery. "How do you feel about cotton candy?"

The carnival came to Fishhook only once a year and drew crowds from every nearby town—Marysburg, Wolf Creek, and Craig to name a few. Banners in town had been proclaiming it for weeks. Next to the rodeo in Helena, it was the highlight of most folks' year. The Ferris wheel and the other rides were set up on the high school field, with colored lights strung from light pole to light pole. Barkers shouted over the din of the fluid crowd, hawking people in to their game booths. It brought back old memories to Cain of when he was a kid and his old man used to take him to carnivals like this one. The whole town would turn out and stay up late to ride the Tilt-o-Wheel and the Electric Serpent.

Cain actually smiled at the memory. It was the only time he'd ever seen ol' Judd green around the gills. He'd always believed his old man had toughed it out because that's what MacCallisters did. But it occurred to him, as he watched the fathers brave the carnival with their children, that maybe Judd had toughed it out for him.

He couldn't imagine where such a generous thought had come from, so he steered Maggie toward a ball toss game where a brawny teenager had just missed the three cement bottles entirely and was taking a ribbing from his friends.

"You play baseball, too?" she asked with a grin.

"That remains to be seen," he said, handing the barker a dollar. The barker handed him three balls.

Cain pointed up to the stuffed Kewpie dolls, snakes and huge stuffed elephant hanging above the game. "Which one?" he asked her.

Maggie laughed. "I have my choice?"

"Yeah. Pick one. Three hits for the elephant."

"Well, that's the one I want then." She laughed again, shaking her head, sure he wouldn't do it.

Cain pointed to the three bottles poised on the small circular stand ten feet away like Babe Ruth pointing at the destination of a home run.

The high school boys who were lingering nearby let out hoots of disbelief as Cain did an exaggerated windup. And let the ball fly.

Three bottles exploded off the stand dead center!

The brawny one who'd missed moments before, got

shoved good humoredly by his compatriots who couldn't help but point out Cain's advanced age. Feeling elderly, he knocked down the next three and the three after that. Beside him Maggie and the rest of the crowd *whooped*.

"Winnah, winnah, we got a winnah!" the barker announced, pulling the huge gray elephant from near the ceiling of the tent.

Maggie shrieked, hugging the stuffed animal to her as if it were the best present she'd ever recieved.

Cain felt a tug in his chest, watching the excitement in Maggie's eyes. He loved watching her smile. He loved that something as dumb as a stuffed elephant could make her happy.

It had been a long time...longer than he cared to remember since he'd given himself permission to feel that way. But with Maggie at his side, smiling up at him like he was sliced bread for winning that stupid elephant, he felt alive.

He'd dreamed of Annie the other night. He dreamed he'd woken up as he lay beside Maggie and Annie was standing there, smiling down at him. The strangest part was she was holding the hand of a child. A beautiful little blond girl he'd never seen. Annie didn't talk or say a word, but he'd heard the other sound, the child's laughter. It was the sound of Maggie's laugh. That same sound.

He didn't understand it then. And he wasn't sure he did now. Except that he hadn't been able to dredge up the guilt he knew he should feel over allowing himself to make love to Maggie since that night. She was the first good thing to happen to him in years. He'd never intended to let her in, but somehow she'd worked her way inside him. And he wasn't sure what to do about it.

"Why didn't you tell me you were a closet jock?" Maggie asked as they walked away with their prize.

"What? I don't look like a jock?" he asked, feigning offense.

"Don't try to tell me you never played. With that arm?"

Cain shrugged. "I played some college ball."

"College?" Surprise widened her eyes. "Where?"

"A small school back East," he hedged.

"Which one?" she pressed.

Cain sighed. "Cornell."

Maggie stopped dead in her tracks and stared at him. "Excuse me? *Cornell?*"

He kept walking. A bunch of teenaged girls bumped into Maggie, catching her in their current and she had to fight her way back to him. *"Cornell University."*

"It's not a big deal, Maggie."

"Cornell is…well…it's *Ivy League.*"

"Mmm…not much Ivy. Lakes and lots of grass."

She stared at him in shock.

"It was a long time ago," he said, wishing he hadn't told her. It made what had happened since seem even worse.

Maggie started walking again, clutching her elephant. The candied apple/cotton candy truck appeared as the crowd parted. He grinned. He hadn't had cotton candy in years. "Want some?" he asked. She nodded, and after they'd fought their way to it, he paid the vendor and settled a cone of spun pink cotton candy in her hand.

"Mmm…" she murmured wickedly, diving in. "Don't make me eat all this."

He flicked a tuft of pink off her nose with a smile and accepted a spun-sugar wisp from her fingertips.

"So…" she began again, "this drifter-on-a-motorcycle thing is a relatively new pastime?"

He glanced around the fairgrounds. He didn't want to talk about this. "You wanna ride the Ferris wheel?"

"Cain…?"

"Or are you afraid of heights?"

"I'm not afraid of heights."

"Atta girl." He took her by the arm and dragged her toward the giant wheel, that lit up the evening sky with colored wonder. They walked right onto the ride. The operator held onto the elephant and Maggie and Cain were soon winding upward toward the top of the wheel as they loaded on more passengers.

"Oh, my," she whispered when they'd reached the apex of the loop. "It's looks so different from up here. Beautiful."

Cain slid his arm around her against the chill in the air. The breeze blew against their faces and tugged at their hair as they went around and around. Maggie's ranch and the others in the valley spread out like lush green quilts. The sunset cast the jagged stony mountains in purples and grays and one could almost imagine that this place didn't exist in a world of cities and crowds and dark corners.

Couples dangled their feet above and below them, snuggling in the illusion of privacy that surrounded the revolving wheel. Real couples, he mused, who intended to spend the rest of their lives together, or at least had every intention of trying.

He knew it was past time to tell her the truth about himself. But he didn't want to spoil tonight. Not when she was feeling on top of the world for the first time in God knew how long. Because truth was a risk and he figured once he told it, the odds against her ever being able to look at him the same way were slim to none.

So he'd wait, he thought, pulling her against him. Tomorrow. He'd tell her tomorrow.

Above them, the stars were coming out against the deepening violet. Maggie snuggled against him, eating her cotton candy.

"Pink decadence," she said with a moan of pleasure. She offered some to him but he shook his head with a smile. "You're going to force me to eat the rest, aren't you?" she said.

"Yup."

"I can't tempt you?"

"Nope." His gaze slid down her face.

"Don't feel like talking?"

"Nope." He dropped his mouth on hers, tasting the sweet cotton candy on her lips and the hunger in her kiss. Their seat began to rock gently and Maggie laughed against his mouth.

"Maggie! Cain!" came a shout from below.

They split apart guiltily and looked down to find Moody waving at them from below. Harold was standing beside her, scowling up at them. They waved back, but Cain felt heat move up his neck at the look on Maggie's lawyer's face.

When the wheel had stopped and they'd gathered up their elephant, he and Maggie walked to where Moody and Harold waited. Moody, who hadn't seen Maggie since the day after the truck accident, made a fuss over her and the elephant Cain had won, then dragged Maggie to the food booth where they were judging her brownies and chocolate sauce. Cain sauntered along behind with Harold, the tension between them thick enough to cut.

Harold spoke first. "She looks…happy."

The observation definitely lacked conviction. "She found a buyer for Geronimo today," he replied, checking out the dozens of gaming booths as they walked.

"Ah, that must be it," Harold said unconvincingly.

Cain slowed to a stop. "You have something to say, Harold?"

The older man clasped his hands behind his back. "Only that Maggie's like a daughter to me. And I don't want to see her hurt."

"That's not my intention."

"Is it still your intention to leave at the end of that contract I drew up for you?" he asked bluntly.

Jaw tightening, Cain stared off into the crowd, aware that he was being backed into a corner. "Yes."

Harold started walking. It took Cain a moment to follow. "You'd never think of Maggie as fragile," Harold said carefully. He stopped in front of Atlas's Hammer where younger men were testing their testosterone levels by trying to ring the bell for a dollar a shot. "I haven't thanked you yet for saving her life."

"You would've done the same."

Harold threw two dollars down and picked up the huge wooden mallet. "Or I would've died trying," Harold agreed, as he swung the hammer down on the small metal target. The little red ball rose halfway up the scale to "Ninety Pound Weakling." With a sigh, he handed Cain the mallet. "Try your hand?"

He took it, centering himself over the target. In the distance he could see the food judging booths and caught sight of Maggie and Moody under the tent. He smashed the mallet down hard, and forcing the little red ball satisfyingly all the way to the top. The buzzer sounded and lights flashed. The carny working the booth handed Cain a stuffed chartreuse unicorn. At least that's what he figured it was supposed to be. He and Harold moved toward the food booth.

"My granddaughter's got one of those," Harold said. "Thinks Sedgewick's all that with a cherry on top. Funny what little girls get attached to."

Cain just kept walking.

"Wanted Sedgewick's to come for her fifth birthday party. Her father told her that Sedgewick's was just a television character and not a real unicorn. But she didn't listen. She just loved him the way little girls do. She was so sure he'd come.''

Harold glanced up at Cain. ''So her father found a Sedgewick costume and rented it. Showed up and played the part. He made the party and he thought everything was going well until it was time to go. Seems Katie thought Sedgewick had come to stay. She cried all night long.''

Cain shook his head sympathetically. ''That's a real sad story, Harold. I'll try to remember it next time I plan a five-year-old's birthday party.''

Harold smiled and started to walk again.

''Maggie's a grown-up,'' Cain said. ''And party games and innocent Ferris wheel kisses are the least of her worries.''

With a frown, he asked, ''What do you mean?''

''Somebody tampered with the brake line on Maggie's truck.''

Harold stopped dead. *''What?''*

''I haven't told Maggie yet. We had the truck towed back to her place and it took me two days to get the carburetor and the fuel pump dried out. So I didn't notice the brake line until yesterday. It was punctured with some kind of tool for a nice slow leak. Any idea who might've done that?''

As if the question had conjured him, Laird Donnelly turned up twenty feet away, heading right toward them. He had his hands in the pockets of his leather jacket and a smile Cain didn't like at all on his face.

''Well, now, if it isn't the newlywed groom and his lawyer.''

Cain's fists tightened of their own accord. He wanted to beat that stupid grin right off of Donnelly's face.

''Isn't that strange,'' Harold said wonderingly to Cain. ''And we were just talking about you.''

"You were?" Laird folded his arms across his chest. "I'm real flattered, boys."

"Yeah," Cain said, "We were just saying that the sheriff might be interested to know you've expanded your ranching skills to brake jobs."

He laughed. "Brake jobs? 'Fraid I don't know the first thing about brakes unless they've got four legs and a set of reins."

"That so?" Cain asked moving closer, but Harold put his hand on his arm.

"Now you, on the other hand," Laird said to Cain, "you must've learned all kinds of practical skills while you were behind bars. Let's see…license plates? Manhole covers…"

Cain felt the blood leave his face. Felt Harold's gaze turn to shock. Saw Maggie walking toward him looking happy and excited.

And his only coherent thought was *Not yet*.

"Course I suppose Maggie's the one who'd know more about your…special skills." Laird said as she moved beside Cain.

He lunged at Donnelly, but Harold grabbed his arm and held him back.

"Leave her out of this, Donnelly," Cain warned with low menace.

"What is this?" she asked, her panicked gaze moving between him and Donnelly.

"'Course Maggie knows all about this, doesn't she? I mean, surely you told her before you said your 'I-do's.' Didn't you?"

Confused, she turned to Cain. "What's he talking about?

His throat felt like cotton and he couldn't seem to swallow. Dammit, dammit!

Laird clucked his tongue. "Aw, you *didn't* tell her, did

you? Shame on you, MacCallister.'' He turned to Maggie. ''By rights, he should've told you.''

Her voice sounded small, as if she really didn't want to know. ''Told me what?''

''Well, about the state of Texas's hospitality he enjoyed for the past three years. In a federal penitentiary, Maggie. Your husband's a cold-blooded killer.''

Chapter 11

Shock fingered down her spine, cold and awful. Maggie turned back to Cain, whose tight-jawed expression made the hair on the back of her neck prickle. "Cain?" she said, curling her hand around his arm. That same arm that just moments ago had been holding her. "He's lying. Tell him he's lying."

Cain didn't say a word. White as the plates catching pennies behind him, he stared at the ground, unable to even meet her eye. Maggie jerked a look at Harold, whose horrified expression probably mirrored her own.

"Oh, my God," she whispered.

Moody, who'd stayed behind at the food tables to pick up her ribbon came hurrying up, waving the thing.

"Didn't I say I made the best chocolate—" her confused gaze traveled between her and Cain and Harold "—sauce? What?"

Maggie shoved away from him. Impossible. *Impossible.* Not Cain. He would've told her. He would've warned her. "*Cain?*"

Slowly, his gaze—devastating in its hollowness—rose to meet hers. His blue, blue guilty eyes.

Maggie reeled away from him, plunging into the crowds and running blindly away. She heard Harold call after her and the sound of Moody's voice. She wanted to disappear. Be sucked down into the ground and disappear. Would she *never* learn?

All around her crowds of people were laughing and talking as if the world hadn't just been thrown off-kilter. Her head throbbed and her cheeks were suddenly wet and she needed to—what? Hide? Run? There was nowhere to go.

She stopped and looked up at the House of Mirrors entrance directly in front of her.

"Maggie!"

This time it was Cain's voice she heard. She whirled around to see him shoving through the crowds after her. She tugged some tickets from her pocket and stumbled into the mirrored entrance to the fun house. Behind her she heard Cain curse and argue with the ticket taker outside. She hurried in, following the maze of mirrored glass until she'd lost herself. Then, pressing her forehead against a mirrored wall, she flattened her palms against it and wept.

Somewhere at the far end of the maze, she heard children shrieking with laughter as they tried to find their way out while her insides tumbled around like bits of broken glass.

How could he have lied to her that way? Not tell her something so huge? A murderer. A cold-blooded murderer? She'd made love to him. Cared about him. A shudder went through her.

"Maggie?"

She jerked her head up at the sound of his voice. He was inside, working his way through the maze. She moved backward and a thousand Maggie's moved with her. "Leave me alone!" she shouted.

"Maggie, just let me explain."

She started to blunder her way along the glass, moving away from the sound of his voice. "There's nothing to explain. You lied to me."

"I didn't lie. I just didn't tell you."

She felt her way along. "Oh, is that it? Well, I guess it never occurred to me to *ask* if you'd killed anyone lately."

"I didn't think you needed to know."

She saw him behind her in the mirrors, but she couldn't tell where he was.

"Really," she said, her voice like chipped ice. She could see dozens of Cain's behind her somewhere in the mirrors but she couldn't tell which one was real. "You didn't think I'd want to know I was sharing a house with a—" She faltered. She couldn't even say it.

"It didn't seem to matter to you who I was," he said, "as long as I married you and got you your loan."

Silence fell over the mirrored room as Maggie contemplated his words. Damn him. He was right. She hadn't asked and she hadn't cared. She'd been desperate and he'd said yes. She'd trusted her gut and this is where it had gotten her.

Cain took a step closer. "The man I killed was the man who murdered my wife."

His words seemed to ricochet around the glass room. Maggie stopped moving and looked back. He was still there watching her from a hundred different angles.

"*What?*"

"I did kill him, Maggie. Donnelly was right about that part. And I was in prison."

"What part wasn't he right about?" she asked in a small voice.

Cain sighed tiredly. "The cold-blooded part. At least that's what the state of Texas decided when they overturned my verdict four months ago and let me go."

She waited, not saying a word.

Cain closed his eyes and tipped his head back. "I went there to kill him. To rip his life away from him the way he had Annie's. I went with a gun and an intention and I waited for him. When he came out from that seedy, back alley bar, I pointed that gun at him so he'd know how she'd felt at the end. I wanted him to beg me to not to kill him and then I wanted him to feel his life slowly leaking out of him the way that goddamned technicality had punched a hole in the case against him."

A hard smile crossed his mouth. "And he begged me. On his knees, he begged me not to kill him. And as my finger tightened on the trigger...I realized Annie would hate what I was doing. Killing him wouldn't bring her back. So, I broke his jaw and left him moaning on the ground. I turned around to leave but I heard him slide a gun from somewhere and cock it behind me. I dove for the ground. His bullet missed. Mine didn't."

Maggie had forgotten to breathe. She felt the cold glass under her palms and could hear the thud of her heart in the empty room.

"Naturally," he went on, "the jury didn't see things that way. I mean...there I was with a gun, waiting for him in an alley. My court-appointed lawyer was too busy trying to figure out how to shave to defend me and the whole witness process seemed to baffle him. Even my old man was convinced."

"Your father?" she asked. "I thought you said he was dead."

Cain gave a sharp, humorless laugh. "To me he was. He'd disowned me years before for marrying Annie. I wasn't about to go to him when I lost her. So I got fifteen to life."

He looked up at her in the mirrors and scrubbed his fingers against his skull. "Six months later, some lawyer bent on righting wrongs came and filed an appeal for me based on incompetent representation and found new evidence and a witness who'd never been called. After three years, a jury figured maybe the first one had been wrong. Or maybe they just figured I'd paid the debt for ridding the world of a scum like him. The state of Texas overturned my conviction four months ago.''

A handful of children spilled into the maze, squealing with laughter, barreling past Cain and finally her. Maggie got spun around and when she looked back, Cain was gone.

She turned and started back, feeling her way along the walls and bumping into a few. ''Cain?''

Suddenly he was there again, moving and reflected in a thousand places. ''Still wish I'd told you before?''

''You should have trusted me,'' she said, inching toward his reflection only to have him disappear again.

''Your reaction was,'' his voice said from somewhere nearby, ''predictable.''

''That's not fair!'' Maggie moved farther down the mirrored aisle and bumped into his reflection. She looked around her. ''You can't know that, because you decided I couldn't be trusted with the truth.'' She shook her head. ''Because it was safer for you to lie. What is that? Some genetically linked trait in men?''

''Don't compare me to Ben.''

Her eyes stung as she searched the mirrors for him. ''Why shouldn't I? How is what you did different?''

Suddenly he was right beside her in the flesh. She could feel the damp heat of his skin and the vibrating tension his closeness always brought. His gaze moved over her with unrelenting intensity.

''I never asked you to believe in me,'' he said.

Maggie's lips parted, feeling the crush of that truth against her chest. He hadn't. But she'd done so recklessly anyway. And heaven help her, she still did.

He didn't touch her. He just stood there like a coiled spring ready to explode.

"I'm sorry, Cain. I was wrong."

His expression was unreadable as he stared down at her. "It doesn't matter now. It'll be all over town tomorrow. It'd be better for you if I left."

She fisted the material of his shirt in her hands. "*No.* That's exactly what he wants. Don't you see that? He'll win if you go."

Cain cursed under his breath as he took her shoulders between his hands. "Don't you get it? He'll use me against you now, Maggie."

"It was self-defense."

"It's a small town. It's not about the truth, but what the truth looks like." He let go of her, but he was still close enough that she could see the muscle twitching his jaw and feel the damp heat radiating from him. "It'll go better for you if they think you didn't know and sent me packing, than if you do know and let me stay."

"Nothing will be better for me if you leave."

"Dammit, Maggie, I'm not the kind of man you should count on. I've been places you wouldn't want to know about. And I've done things—" He sighed, squeezing his eyes shut. "Dammit, we both knew this was only temporary."

She reached for his hand and felt it quake at her touch. "I don't care about those things. I only care about the man standing in front of me. The one who held me last night in his arms…"

"That was sex, Maggie. Don't confuse me with another kind of man. One who could love you the way you deserve to be loved. I can't be what you want me to be. Maybe once, but that part of me died a long time ago."

She knew he was wrong about that. "I won't ask you to love me, Cain. Stay because you promised you would," she said quietly. "Stay because if you go, Laird Donnelly will have everything he wants. And we'll have nothing. Stay because I'm asking you to."

His gaze was on her mouth and she pulled him closer until her breasts brushed against his chest. Despite his claims to the contrary, she saw in his eyes what he didn't want her to see—an eddy of those damned emotions he was so good at denying.

He cupped the back of her head in his hand and dropped his mouth down on hers. He kissed her hard and deep with an urgency that stole the strength from her knees. She wanted to drag him inside her and keep him there, safe from all the forces bent on his destruction. But she couldn't protect him, any more than he could protect her.

"Take me home, Cain. Make love to me. I don't want you to go."

They didn't make it all the way home. Cain pulled the motorcycle off the highway onto a side road a few miles south of Maggie's place because she was doing things to him with her hands that made driving any farther suicidal. She had his shirt nearly off before he'd lifted the bike up onto its kickstand. He ripped off the rest and returned the favor with her blouse.

Slanting his mouth against her hers, he dragged her up against him until close wasn't close enough. So, he lifted her in his arms and headed for the cattle crossing grate that separated the road from the pasture beyond.

It was dark with only the moon and the stars overhead for light, but he took her there in the thick, soft grass. They tore at each other's clothes until the night air washed over their bare skin. The tall grass and the pines nearby rustled in the evening breeze.

Kneeling above her, Cain stared down at her pale beauty, knowing it wasn't his to possess and never truly could be.

She deserved so much more than him. But she was like a drug. She made him do things he shouldn't do. Want things he couldn't have. Believe things about himself that were patently untrue.

And none of that mattered. Because the wanting was more powerful than anything else. He cupped her breasts in his hands, lifting and caressing, brushing his thumbs against the pale dusky pink of her nipples. Maggie arched against him, then pulled him down to her, impatient and needing him nearer.

She wrapped her legs around him and he drove into her. Their union was hard and fast and raw. Everything this night had been and more. Somewhere in the still functioning part of his brain he knew that staying was a terrible mistake. Because someday soon, when trouble came—and it would—she'd hate him for staying every bit as much as she'd hate him now if he left her. But then he forgot to think at all as she moved underneath him, urging him to let all of that go.

They found release together there. And for a long time afterward, they didn't talk. He simply held her, watching the stars wink above them. And when, at last they rode home, Cain knew he would stay. Not for any of the reasons she'd offered. He'd stay because he was too selfish to give her up just yet.

The sound of Jigger whining downstairs woke Maggie the next morning as sunshine spilled through the east-facing window of her bedroom. He had to go out, but Maggie couldn't drag herself up just yet. She turned to look at Cain, who was sprawled on his stomach beside her with his arm across her belly and one knee draped over her leg. She blinked languidly and smiled. Last night was something of a blur, but she remembered coming home after the adventure in the meadow and not making it to the bedroom before he had her in his arms again.

A delicious smile curved her mouth. Like bread crumbs leading into the forest, pieces of her clothing still lay where he'd discarded them on their way to the bed. She'd never known that kind of passion before. When Cain made love to her, she forgot everything else, but him.

He claimed it was only about sex. Perhaps, she thought, that was true. After all, men as a breed, seemed to be able to separate sex from the emotional aspects of lovemaking— a skill she'd never been much interested in perfecting. And there were moments last night when she could have sworn Cain hadn't perfected them yet, either. She suspected that underneath all that armor he wore, there was still a spark of the man who had once loved so intensely.

Her gaze traveled over his sleeping form, from the dark hair that curled against his nape to the muscular drape of his arm across her belly. And his face...

It was rare to catch his rugged handsomeness in its raw and unguarded form. Awake, the tension in his expression rarely left him. But now, with his dark lashes so still against his cheekbones, and the strong angles of his face relaxed with sleep, his appeal, she saw, was not in the perfection of any one feature, but in the sheer artistic composition of all of them. She had yet to find his bad angle because from any side his face was fascinating.

Maggie couldn't resist the impulse to reach out with one finger and skim it down his jawline, to feel the rough morning stubble of his beard.

A smile curved Cain's lips. "Awake already?"

"It's seven," she said, sliding down under the covers, closer to him.

"Impossible," he muttered, pulling her toward him with his arm still around her waist. "We just went to sleep."

"For the third time," she murmured as he wrapped himself around her. "But who's counting?"

"Mmm…" He tucked his face against her shoulder with a grin. "Are you always this insatiable?"

"Only recently."

"That's good." He pulled her closer, tucking her against the welcoming curve of his body.

"Hungry?" she asked.

"Is that a leading question?" he answered, sliding his hands over her breasts and stomach.

"One-track mind," she murmured, closing her fingers over his.

"Yeah…I like this track." He pressed a kiss on her neck and nuzzled the spot below her ear.

She felt happy and safe here in his arms. It was almost as if last night had never happened. Maybe it would work, she thought languidly. Maybe when Laird understood that she didn't care about Cain's past…maybe when the town understood what really happened…

Without warning, Jigger jumped up on the bed and bounded between them whining. Cain covered her protectively from the dog's plowing feet. "Aw, geez, Jigger!" he said.

Jigger *whoofed,* prancing restlessly around them.

"D'ya think he's gotta go?" he asked blandly.

Maggie frowned. "He's not usually this pushy." She got up, pulling on the robe near her bed. The dog bounded down the stairs and back up again twice before she could make it to the door.

"All right, all right…" she said, pulling open the front door. Jigger was out like a shot. But he didn't pause to answer the call of nature. He made a beeline toward the north pasture at full tilt.

"Hey!" she called after him. "Where you going?"

She frowned again. It was unlike Jigger to—

The barn door.

It was open. They'd definitely closed it last night. Closed it and latched it. Her heart started a heavy, fearful thudding.

"Cain!"

Maggie didn't even bother with her shoes. She ran out across the yard, half dressed, praying it wasn't what she thought it was. But when she got inside the dim barn, her heart sank. She stared disbelievingly.

Geronimo's stall was open and empty.

Chapter 12

Wearing only his half-buttoned jeans, Cain appeared at the barn door seconds behind her. He cursed viciously. "I latched it," he said. "Last night I know I latched it."

"I know you did. Some one else opened it," she said, turning on her heel and heading back to the house. Tears were threatening, but it was anger that clogged her throat. "Jigger headed for the north pasture. We'll start there. I'm going to get dressed, then I'll get the truck started."

"Is it running?"

"It'll run." Cain was matching her stride for angry stride. "We'll find him, Maggie I promise you that."

Twenty minutes later they did find him, tangled in a vicious twist of loose barbed wire at the far end of the north pasture. Squeals of terror erupted from the fallen, exhausted horse. Jigger was crouched loyally by Geronimo, waiting for them. He whined and thumped his tail against the ground. Cain cursed viciously as jumped out of the truck and dropped down beside Geronimo. The animal's high-pitched squeals of pain seemed to echo across the valley.

"Oh, God," Maggie gasped, joining him at Geronimo's side. It was bad. Very bad.

With his hand on Geronimo's neck, Cain surveyed the damage. It was considerable. His legs and chest were streaked with blood and there were cuts everywhere. Some were bone deep. Foamy white sweat glistened on his coat and his eyes were white with terror.

"Shh—boy," Cain soothed, his words hitched with emotion. "It's gonna be all right." But he turned back to her and said, "Maggie, go back and get the gun."

Maggie shook her head pleadingly. "No. We can save him."

Cain stared back down at the horse. "Maggie, *look* at him. He's in terrible pain. Even if he makes it, he'll be scarred. Maybe lame for life." He didn't say that they'd already lost the sale to Tischman, but they both knew that was true. "It's not fair to him not to do it."

"But is it fair to put him down before we know for sure? If nothing's broken…?" she said. "He's got a strong heart. He can survive this. Let him try. Please, Cain—"

Cain shook his head and stared down at the fallen horse. "We'll let the vet make the decision. Go back and call him. Tell him to bring his truck and trailer up here."

Tears were streaming down Maggie's face, but she didn't even hesitate to follow Cain's orders. She was on Biscuit and heading back to the house almost before he could finish.

"Then come back with wire cutters and Betadine solution," he shouted after her. He stroked Geronimo's neck. "And hurry."

"It'll be touch and go for a while." Kip Ridlinger, the handsome thirty-something local vet stood and stretched his back, then bent to help Cain gather up the refuse of the battle to save Geronimo. Used sterile pads, bandages, empty bottles and strands of suture thread littered the barn hallway.

Standing near Geronimo, who was lying in his stall covered in a blanket on a fresh bed of clean straw, Maggie's gaze was fixed on Cain. He'd hardly said a word the whole time Kip had been working on the animal, his barely leashed anger over the fiasco plain as the cuts on Geronimo's legs. Laird had stepped way over the line this time and she was afraid of what Cain might do.

"He has an even chance," Kip went on, shoving his dark hair out of his eyes with the back of his sleeve, "considering the severity of the lacerations. It's going to depend on him. But you should know there'll be scarring. The tendon on his left rear fetlock was injured most severely. It may heal well, it may not. We'll just have to wait and see." He reached into his bag and handed Maggie a handful of medicine. "Apply this Nolvasan ointment on all the cuts twice a day. Betadine solution and Furacin ointment at bedtime on all the sutured areas. I'll come back in a day or two to check on him. If there's any change, call me immediately. Get him on his feet by tonight if you can. Tomorrow at the latest."

Cain reached a hand out to him and Kip took it. "Thanks, Doc," he said tightly.

"You're welcome. Good luck," Kip said. "He's a beautiful animal. It's a crime, is what it is. You think this was a prank of some kind?"

Cain and Maggie exchanged glances. "That wire in the pasture was no prank," Cain said grimly. "I checked that whole fence line myself three days ago. It wasn't there. Someone put it there then deliberately ran Geronimo into it."

Kip shook his head in disgust. "Any idea who might have a bone to pick with you?"

Cain threw the refuse into a trash can. "I have more than an idea."

"We don't know that for sure," Maggie argued.

"Like hell we don't."

"Why don't you let the sheriff handle it?" Kip said.

"Yeah? And what do I give him?" Cain asked, a muscle working in his jaw. "An open barn door? A stray coil of fencing? No, the sheriff's gonna take one look at this and decide we were careless. I intend to take care of this personally."

Maggie's heart took an elevator drop. "Cain...no—"

"Somebody's got to stand up to him," he said. "It might as well be me." He turned to Kip. "Thanks for everything, Doc. Let us know what we owe you."

The vet shook Cain's hand regretfully, then watched Cain storm out of the barn toward the house. Maggie let out a shaky sigh. "I'd better go try to talk some sense into him."

"If he's going where I think he's going," Kip warned, "you'd better do more than that. Hog-tie him if you have to. He's walking into a world of trouble over at the Bar ZX."

Stunned, she said, "How would you know who he was talking about?"

Kip smiled thinly getting into his truck and starting the engine. "I haven't lived here my whole life for nothing, Maggie. Let me know if you need anything."

When he'd gone, Maggie hurried into the house to find Cain searching for the keys to his motorcycle. God only knew what had happened to them when they'd gotten in the door last night. And she prayed he wouldn't find them.

Cain yanked the seat cushion up on the chair in the living room, muttering to himself.

"Cain, you can't just go over there and accuse him with no proof."

"Like hell I can't." He stalked across the room to the jacket he'd left hanging over a chair back. He rifled the pockets and threw it back down again. "Where the hell are my keys?"

"I don't know. Listen to me," she said. "We can't fight him that way. We have to come at him legally."

"You mean use Sheriff Winston?" He laughed out loud. "Don't you see what Donnelly's doing, Maggie? He's got the dam nearly eaten away. Pretty soon that floodwater's gonna come pourin' over your side of the dike and there won't be any stopping it."

"And you think you can stop him by going over there and using your fists?"

"I sure as hell am not gonna sit here and take—"

The phone rang and they both scowled at it. Cain took up his search again as Maggie answered the phone. He knew the damned keys had to be here somewhere. They'd gotten home, hadn't they? Opened the door?

He stalked over to the table and saw Maggie's truck keys and decided to settle. Then he heard a tone in Maggie's voice that sent a chill through him and made him stop on his way to the door.

"Unanimous?" she was saying, her back rigid as a fencepost. "Really. Yes, I understand perfectly...Mmm-hmm....Oh, and Ernie? I hope you die soon." She slammed the receiver down and stood there shaking.

He didn't really have to ask. "The loan?"

She nodded. "They turned me down."

He wanted to break something. Specifically Laird Donnelly's face.

So that was it. Everything he'd feared was coming to pass. His life, it seemed, was just a series of backfires set to try to stop the coming conflagration. But he should have known that this particular one had been doomed from the get go. It was too good to be true. Now Maggie had been caught in the burn and the only thing he could think to do was to walk straight into the oncoming flames.

He tightened his fist around the keys until they dug into his palm and he headed for the door.

"Cain—" The word was a plea. "Don't go."

He turned back to her, his hand on the door handle. "You know I have no choice, Maggie."

The Bar ZX was a sprawling operation that covered ten times the land Maggie's did. Thousands of head of cattle ranged on surrounding pastures and the landscape was punctuated with signs of prosperity, from the newly built state-of-the-art stables to the indoor training ring the size of an Olympic skating rink. The main house was practically part of the land, situated at the top of a knoll, massively built of Montana pine logs and river rock from the nearby Musselshell.

None of which impressed Cain as much as the sheer numbers of cowhands whose presence he felt from the moment he drove onto Donnelly land. He felt their stares as he pulled the truck to a grinding stop in front of the main house and slammed it into park. He got the distinct feeling he'd been expected.

It was the cowhand who'd given Maggie such a hard time in town, Joe Johns, who happened to be lounging on the railroad tie steps that led to Donnelly's front door.

"Do something for you?" he asked with a grin, standing to prevent Cain access to the stairs.

"Where is he?" Cain demanded.

"Who?"

Cain started to shove past him, but Joe grabbed his arm. "He ain't here."

"Like hell." He started to shove the man aside when a voice from somewhere behind him stopped him.

"Looking for me?"

Cain turned to find Donnelly and several of his men striding toward him. Cain shoved Joe out of his way and moved in Donnelly's direction.

"You son of a bitch," he growled, diving at Donnelly. The rancher dodged him as the three nearby men intercepted Cain's lunge and dragged him back by the arms.

"Well, well…" Laird said with a surprised laugh. "The dog has teeth."

"Call off your gorillas, Donnelly, and fight me like a man."

"I don't need to fight you, MacCallister. I just have to watch you sink yourself."

Cain jerked at the hold of the men who held him fast. "You're a real piece of work. It's bad enough that you can't keep your filthy hands off a woman like Maggie who wants no part of you. That you have to resort to pulling her loans and scaring the hell out of her at every turn. Now you've stooped to breaking and entering…ambushing defenseless animals. Well, Geronimo is gonna live, in spite of you."

The other man laughed, but a few of the cowhands looked around uneasily. "I don't know what you're talkin' about. Geronimo who?"

"What is it, Donnelly?" He shot a furious look in the direction of his grazing cattle. "All this land isn't enough for you? You need to suck the heart out of her place, too?" Cain jerked at the hold of the men. They held him fast. There were three of them and one of him.

"I think Maggie's been workin' you too hard over there, MacCallister. You need to calm down. Now," he said, "You gonna behave? If you are, I'll let you go."

"Screw you."

His cocky smile widened. "Let him go, boys."

They did, and Cain shrugged off their hands, snapping

his shirt back into place again. He looked around, gauging his odds. They weren't good.

"I think," Donnelly continued, "all that prison time made you a little paranoid, MacCallister. You're misinformed. I got no designs on Maggie or her place. I'd say if anyone had designs, it's you. Exactly what did she promise you in exchange for a roll in her hay?"

His fist connected with Donnelly's jaw with a satisfying crack before anyone could stop him and the two of them were on the ground, rolling in the dirt. The rancher had him by the shirt but that didn't prevent Cain from connecting with Donnelly's soft belly twice before he was dragged off him by a pair of his men who threw a couple of quick punches, knocking the wind out of him. He doubled over and coughed.

On an oath, Donnelly wiped the blood from his lip with the back of one hand as Cain straightened and blew out a breath. "That was a mistake," the rancher said, staring at the blood on his wrist.

"You leave Maggie alone." Cain snarled, "I'll kill you or any one of your men who touches her again, you son of a bitch."

Donnelly rubbed his aching jaw and got slowly to his feet. Unbelievably, the smile was back, and Cain had the sinking feeling that somehow he'd played directly into his hands.

"Well, that sounds like a threat. You heard it boys." He nodded to the men holding Cain as he brushed the dirt off the sleeve of his two-hundred-dollar shirt. They let him go and shoved him toward the truck.

"Get off my land, MacCallister. If I see you back here, I'll see you in jail."

It was Cain's turn to smile now. He opened the truck door and slid into the driver's seat. "You forget. I've been inside, Donnelly. It ain't pretty, but I'd survive." He turned over the ignition. "A man like you…a rich piece o' white meat who needs his hired hands to fight his battles for him? Well," he said, "they'd spread you with jam and eat you for breakfast. You think about that the next time you consider coming over to my place."

Jamming the truck into reverse, he made a sharp three-point turn and left Donnelly and his men staring after him as he tore off the Bar ZX.

There was no choice now. He knew what he had to do.

There was only one bar in Fishhook worth calling a bar. Mahoney's was a small, hole-in-the-wall that doubled as a bingo parlor on Wednesday nights and sported Naugahyde covered bar stools and whiskey worth drinking.

But this was a Monday and the place was empty except for a lone drinker in the back, the bartender and Cain. For the second time in as many weeks, Cain sat staring at a shot of whiskey. He'd gone to First Federal. Set up the account. All that was left was to work up his nerve to finish what he'd started.

"Hey, aren't you Maggie Cortland's new husband?" the bartender asked, swiping around Cain's still full shot with a bar towel.

Cain looked up at him. The kid couldn't be more than twenty-three with a thick head of blond curls and eyes the color of an ocean. He looked like he belonged on the California coast with a surfboard instead of a seedy little nowhere bar.

"You're him, aren't you?" he pressed. "You're the one."

"I guess I am," he answered, hunkering over his whiskey like a dog with a bone.

"I'm Bruce Winslow, Moody River's nephew." He grinned. "My dad was Moody's older brother. You know Moody, right?"

Cain nodded. "Listen kid, I'm not in the mood to—"

"Yeah," the kid went on, not hearing him. "My aunt Moody, she kind of adopted Maggie and me, you know when my dad passed on, and after Maggie's husband...well..." His voice trailed off as Cain lifted the whiskey, turning the glass in the light.

The kid leaned closer. "Hey," he said, glancing around the empty bar, "is it true?"

"Is what true?"

"That you were in prison for murder."

Well, that didn't take long, Cain thought, sliding a look up at the kid who was looking at him with something close to awe. "Yeah," he said, realizing the news was all over town by now. After all, how often did a town like Fishhook have a real live murderer in their midst?

Bruce leaned closer. "What'd you do it for? I mean... why'd you kill him?"

Narrowing his eyes, Cain knocked back the shot of courage in one long gulp and felt it burn all the way down. "Because," he told Bruce, "he talked too much."

"Oh. Hey," Bruce said with a frown, "I'm...I'm sorry, man. I shouldn't have—"

"You're not the first and you won't be the last," Cain told him. "Don't worry about it, kid. Just don't be impressed. Nothing good came of it."

Lowering his eyes, Bruce let his gaze settle on the towel in his hand. Cain suddenly wished he had a second chance to be as young as Bruce and know what he knew today. To have his whole life ahead of him instead of behind. But what the hell?

He pulled out a handful of bills, tossed them on the bar. "You know where the nearest pay phone is?"

"Sure." Bruce pointed eagerly up the street. "Half a block up, next to the pharmacy. Need some change?" He pulled a handful of quarters from the register and held them out to Cain. "Drink's on me. Just call it an apology."

"Thanks," Cain said. Pouring the change into his pocket he left Mahoney's and went in search of the phone.

Judd MacCallister had just come in from outside when he heard the phone ring. He had half a mind to let it go. He wasn't in the mood to hear bad news from that damned private eye, Goehner again. Besides, the crew was right in the middle of castrating the young bulls and he had to get back.

He passed by the phone, on the way to the sink. Thirst had brought him in from the oppressive Texas heat outside, he thought with a grumble. The older he got, the less he could keep up with the young bucks he employed. He'd made up some excuse about needing to take care of some business, but the truth was, he was getting old.

The phone rang for the third time and he narrowed a look at it. The caller ID listed an area code he was unfamiliar with. Definitely Goehner. What the hell, he thought. Might as well hear bad news today as tomorrow.

He lifted the receiver. "If you've called to give me bad news, Goehner—" he began.

"Only for your wallet," said a voice that made his heart stutter and do a little sommersault. Judd swallowed hard. It…it couldn't be.

"*Cain?*" There was a long pause, "Is that you?"

"I should feel flattered you still remember my voice."

Judd's backside collided with the kitchen counter and he let it hold him up. For a long moment, he couldn't talk. Couldn't get his throat to open up. Finally he said, "Cain. God. It's so—"

"I didn't call to chat."

Judd checked the hurt in his voice. "Why did you call?"

Cain cleared his throat. "I've never asked you for anything. But I'm asking now."

Judd waited, feeling his heart thudding against his ribs. He'd kept his room the way he'd left it. With his baseball glove and his bat and the trophies he'd earned for gymkhana still lined up on the shelf above his bed. He'd never even changed the color of his walls.

"I need some money," Cain said.

He remembered to breathe. Seven years and he'd called for money. Well, he supposed it served him right. He pressed his palm against the table to get his fingers to stop shaking. "How much money?"

"Sixty-thousand dollars."

Judd didn't even blink. "All right."

There was a long pause at the other end of the line. "I don't want it for me," Cain said. "I wouldn't touch it for me."

Of course. Judd sighed. "Who then?"

There was a long pause. "Her name is Maggie Cortland."

Closing his eyes, Judd closed his fingers around the phone. Of course. A woman. "Are you in some kind of trouble, Cain?"

He heard the soft, unpleasant laughter coming from the other end of the line. "Some things never change, right, Father?"

Oh, hell. He'd done it again. "Listen to me, son, if you need anything. Help or anything…I—"

"I *need* you," Cain said through clenched teeth, "to wire the money. That's all. The rest you can—" He paused again as if trying to rein in his temper. "Just wire the money, Father. I won't bother you again."

"That's not what I—"

"Are you going to send the money or not?"

Defeated, Judd picked up the pen and pad of paper near the phone. "Yes. I'll wire it. Give me an account number."

Cain dictated the account number and he wrote it down. Judd had imagined this conversation a thousand times, but it had never gone this badly.

"It'll be in by the close of business today," Judd told him. Cain didn't say a word, but he didn't hang up either. "Cain? I know there's been a lot of water under our bridge. But if we could just—"

"Thank you for the money," his son said abruptly. "I'll pay you back when I can."

"You don't have to—" The dial tone rang in Judd MacCallister's ear and he pulled the receiver away from his ear with a scowl. A sinking feeling stole the strength from his legs and he sat down hard on one of the kitchen chairs.

Damn.

He'd sounded...different. Older. Harder. But what did he expect? That he would be the same boy who'd once ridden to please him? Who had hoped that just once his father would give him the credit he'd deserved for being who he was?

Judd rubbed his forehead, watching the kitchen table blur. He'd spent the last five years of his life regretting what he'd done to his son, and the last three doing whatever it took to make up for it. And dammit, after all that, he wasn't about to let this phone call be the end of it. He looked at the phone number again, then lifted the receiver.

"Goehner?" he said when the connection was made, "Where does the 406 area code originate?" He listened to the answer, then looked at the phone number again. "Find the closest airport to the city that has this prefix and book me a flight on the next plane there."

It was nearly 4:00 p.m. by the time Cain headed back to Maggie's. He'd waited until the money had appeared in the account he'd set up for her at the bank. It had appeared just before the bank closed and Cain breathed a sigh of relief. His old man may be a son of a bitch, but at least he'd kept his word.

The phone call kept turning in his mind as he steered the truck. His father had sounded older. That surprised him. And more than that, he'd sounded almost entreating. Not that Cain gave a damn. He didn't. He was just glad it was over.

He rubbed the back of his neck. It had been a long day, starting with Geronimo. He should have called Maggie, he supposed. Let her know he was on his way back. Knowing her, she'd be worried about him. But he didn't—

An explosion jolted the truck and the wheel jerked in Cain's hands. He gripped it tighter, trying to hang onto the road and felt the telltale thump-thump-thump of a flat.

Dammit, dammit, dammit!

Pulling over to the side of the road, Cain got out and inspected the tire. Rather, the place where the tire had been. There was little left but rim, with the rest scattered to kingdom come behind him. Another aftermath of the dip in the river, no doubt, he thought, digging into the box at the back of the truck for the tire iron and jack. Thank God there was a decent spare tucked under the truck bed, he thought, even though the last damned thing he wanted to do right now was change a tire.

He got the blown wheel off and nearly had the spare unbolted from under the truck bed when he heard another car coming. He didn't think much about it until he heard the vehicle roll to a stop right there in the road opposite him.

Cain looked up. It was a red truck, he noted absently from his vantage point under Maggie's truck. New. He heard doors open and it wasn't until he saw four pairs of boots hit the ground on either side of the truck that the first inklings of trouble began to work their way up the back of his neck.

Oh, hell.

He rolled under the truck and came up the other side, only to be grabbed by two thugs who strong armed him hard up against the truck bed. From somewhere, a fist plowed into his kidney. A crippling pain stole his breath. He tried to jerk free but that earned him an elbow in the mouth rattling his teeth. A foul oath slid through his clenched teeth.

"Where you goin', MacCallister?" the giant wearing a green plaid shirt asked, lifting his arm to the point of real pain. "Looks like you got a tire to change."

"Gee," he said trying to catch his breath. "That's nice of you to offer, but I can do it myself."

By now, the other two were rounding the truck, intent on some serious bodily harm. He hadn't spent three years in prison for nothing. He shoved the heel of his boot into the knee of the man on his left, sending him down with a howl and took the Jolly Green giant out with a quick hard jab to the throat and a left to the gut. The man gagged and grabbed his neck and belly. Cain ran around to the other side of the truck and snatched up the tire iron he'd left there.

The other two men had split up and came at him now from both directions. The giant was struggling to his feet on the other side of the truck. Cain brandished the iron knowing he could take one of them, but probably not the other one if Jolly got here first. Running would have been his best option, but they had wheels.

"Drop it, MacCallister," said the one who looked like he was in charge. His greying Pancho Villa mustache twitched as he reached into the front pocket of his coat and withdrew a handgun. "Or we can do this the hard way."

He cocked the gun and pointed the barrel precisely between Cain's legs.

That was one alternative he wasn't particularly interested in exploring. If they intended to kill him, he thought as a trickle of sweat cut a path through the dirt on the side of his face, he'd damn well prefer to go intact.

It occurred to him only then that the flat tire had been no accident. That they'd probably shot it out from under him and waited until he had nowhere to go. These men weren't any he'd seen today at Donnelly's but without question they were working for him.

He had no choice. He swore under his breath and dropped the tire iron. It hit the ground with a hollow, metallic clang.

Instantly, Jolly had him again, pinning his arms behind his back and dragging him toward the open ground near the back of the truck. "You boys hire out for parties, too?" he asked the others following in the giant's wake.

"Shut up," said Pancho, swinging his handgun across Cain's cheek with stunning force.

Pain exploded in his head and stars blotted his vision out for a few long, intakes of air. When the world merged back into one, he spit blood out at Pancho's feet and smiled thinly. "Wow, you know... I knew a guy in prison...Lido Martinez...who mugged old men for their social security checks?" Cain swallowed hard. "He would've admired that move."

The man's expression didn't even change, but his knee came up hard and accurately between Cain's legs. Cain doubled over, gagging for air. Nausea clawed at his throat and for a minute he thought he would pass out. The Green Giant dropped him to the ground where he curled in a tight ball.

Though he couldn't open his eyes yet, it was Pancho Villa, he decided, who leaned over him. "See, we were sent to give you a message, MacCallister. You ain't welcome around here. Hear me?''

Cain mouthed a two word obscenity, though no sound came out.

''I don't think he heard you, Leon.''

Someone kicked him in the stomach, half-lifting him off the ground. Cain groaned and rolled to protect himself, his ability to breathe gone. But he was hauled up again and held between two of them while the other two took turns pounding on him. He felt his jaw crack and through a haze of red, saw the guy with the mustache smile as he tried to put his fist through Cain's gut.

Pain crashed him down like a rogue wave until he couldn't stand or fight against it. His last rational thought was of Maggie. He'd forgotten to tell her—

Something knocked his head back hard and blackness dropped over him like a curtain.

And then, there was nothing.

Chapter 13

Maggie clutched the phone as she paced near Geronimo's stall and listened to the concern in Harold's voice on the other end of the line.

"I've been all over town," he said, "And I even went by the Bar ZX. A few hands confirmed that he'd been out there earlier today, and that there had been some kind of a confrontation, but that no one had seen him since. There's no sign of him, Maggie."

She exhaled a shaky breath and tightened her hand on the portable phone. "He wouldn't leave, Harold. I know he wouldn't. Something has happened to him."

Harold was silent for a minute. "Maggie, I hate to be the one to point this out, but the man has a criminal record."

"His conviction was overturned," she reminded him impatiently. "He wouldn't leave. You don't know him the way I do. What if he's had an accident?"

"I checked the highway all the way out to your place and back. No sign of him."

"Did you try the back way?"

"Maggie—"

"Something bad has happened to him, Harold, or he'd be here."

She could almost hear Harold wrestling with the conviction in her voice and the logic that made him such a good attorney. But it was instinct she was following. And her heart.

"All right. I'm heading your way now," he said. "I'll try the back road. I should be there in about twenty minutes."

A sigh of relief escaped her. "Thank you, Harold. See you soon."

Maggie clicked off the phone and sat holding it in her lap, listening to the labored sounds of Geronimo's breathing. There was no possibility in her mind that he could have simply left without a word. He had to be all right, she told herself. She'd know it if he was dead. Wouldn't she?

The sound of crickets somewhere nearby woke him. The noise became one with the pounding at the back of his skull. He moved his head fractionally, but froze as pain shot through his neck and jaw. He groaned and eased back down.

Damn.

He risked a few quick, shallow breaths and swallowed. Everything hurt. His teeth, his jaw, his fingertips…and some elephant had apparently stepped on his chest.

Maybe he was dead. Maybe this was hell, he reasoned. Because it wasn't possible for every inch of him to hurt like this and still be alive.

He pried his eyes open and blinked several times. Okay. He was on the ground. There was the truck. But he couldn't remember how he'd—

Oh, yeah, he remembered woozily. Pancho Villa and his merry men. He moaned again as he rolled gingerly onto his side. He touched a knuckle to the painful cut on his lip. His face felt sticky and bruised. And his left eye felt like a mountain.

Rolling onto his back, he stared up at the moon just rising over the mountains. He wondered where Maggie was and if she was worried about him. He wished she'd appear right now and help him get up because he wasn't sure he could do it on his own. But night was rolling over him and he felt the dampness of it chilling him to the bone. He had to get up or whatever Pancho hadn't accomplished, the Montana night would.

He rolled back to his side and pushed himself up until he was sitting. The movement stole his breath and made the world spin. At least one, maybe two ribs were cracked, he decided. Dammit.

Slowly, at about the speed of grass growing, he crawled toward the truck, only then remembering that there was a tire off. A low oath slid past his lips. No way he'd change it in his condition. But to his shock, as he made it to the other side of the truck, the tire was on as if it had never blown off.

"Well..." he muttered, "that's real...considerate of you boys." Grabbing hold of the back bumper, he hauled himself up using it for leverage. An involuntary groan escaped him as the darkness got punctuated by stars again. He waited until it passed before he moved again. "I'll have to remember to thank you next time we meet."

Hand over hand, he made his way to the cab and lowered himself into the seat behind the steering wheel. He felt sick and horrifyingly weak. He wasn't sure he could even handle the wheel. Turning the key in the ignition, the engine turned over—the only thing that seemed to be working well tonight—and he reached out slowly to pull the door shut.

The sight of headlights screaming up behind him in the rearview mirror temporarily blinded him and the expletive that leapt to mind was low and foul. They'd have to kill him this time, he thought.

But it wasn't a truck, he decided in the next instant as the vehicle pulled to a stop opposite him. And the voice shouting his name didn't sound like Pancho's.

Thank God for that, Cain thought, forgetting about his door. Forgetting about everything but breathing as the blackness circled in on him again. Peripherally, he heard the man get out of his car and mutter *God Almighty,* but everything else slid away as blackness swooped back down on him like a crow's wing.

The truck's headlights pulled down her lane and Maggie ran out to meet it. But it was Harold behind the wheel. Her heart staggered to a stop.

On the passenger side, propped against the window, was Cain. At least, she *thought* it was Cain.

"Oh, my God."

"I found him on the back road, just like you said," Harold said, pulling to a stop and shoving the truck into Park. "Get in. We're taking him to Emergency down in Helena."

"No," Cain groaned from the other side of the cab. "Just…get me inside."

She and Harold exchanged looks. She wanted to cry. His cheek was swollen and his left eye looked like he'd gone ten rounds with a heavyweight. And there was blood everywhere. "Cain, don't be an idiot. You're hurt."

He tugged on the door handle and shoved open the door, having none of it. "Nothing that won't heal," he said. "I think they broke a few ribs. Got tape?"

"Yes, I've got tape. But—"

He shot her a silencing look and moved to get out of the

truck. Maggie was at his side before he could tumble out of the cab. She threaded her arm beneath his shoulder. "Look at you. Who did this?"

"Three guesses," he mumbled, allowing Harold to slip his shoulder under his. "And they're all...correct."

"Donnelly himself?" Harold asked.

"Hell," Cain said, swaying on his feet. "He can't...zip his own fly. Not stupid enough to use his own men. Hired thugs. Professionals. From outside."

Maggie didn't care right now who they were. She was more concerned with seeing what kind of damage they'd done. He'd been worked over like a punching bag. It was hard to imagine how anyone could get the jump on Cain MacCallister. But someone had. In the morning she'd call the sheriff. Right now, she had more important things to worry about.

In spite of Cain's arguments, they'd called Doc Henson, the local family practitioner who was older than God, to come over and look Cain over. He'd been right about the ribs. Doc Henson guessed at least two fractures. He wrapped Cain's ribs tightly with tape and left him resting.

"He should be in the hospital," he said, "but he's not having any of it. He may have a fracture in that cheek and most certainly a concussion. I don't think he's got any internal injuries but you call me should he start having tenderness in his belly. Wake him up every hour or so tonight. He'll be a bear, but ignore that. Don't let him sleep too deeply. I'll come back tomorrow to check on him. Time'll heal the rest."

He left Maggie some painkillers for Cain and promised he'd check back in a day or two.

Maggie drove Harold back to his car around ten then checked on Geronimo. Her other patient was still off his feet, but resting more easily, she thought. She decided to try to roust him up again in the morning.

Maggie walked back to the house in the moonlight, trying to shove down the anger that was clouding her thinking. She had decisions to make. Plans to form. It was over here, she'd realized earlier in the day. She'd lost and Laird had won. He'd managed it all without leaving a single scrap of proof she could pin on him. He'd outmaneuvered her and almost killed Cain in the process. And if Brent Hayden was to be believed, he'd had something to do with Ben's death as well.

The screen door sang on its hinges as Maggie jerked it open. He wasn't going to get away with it, she vowed. She didn't know how, but she'd find a way to stop him.

Cain's eyes were closed when she ducked her head inside the door of his room a few minutes later. She moved back, intending to quietly close his door, but his voice stopped her.

"Don't go." His voice was rough but just the sound of it made her feel infinitely better.

She eased back into the room. "Did you take those pills?"

"I don't do pills," he said, watching her sit down on the edge of his bed.

"Stubborn," she murmured, touching his jaw tenderly with the back of her hand.

His smiled faded. "We need to talk."

"Tomorrow. I'm calling the sheriff in the morning. He won't get away with this, Cain."

He gingerly tongued the cut at the side of his mouth as he shook his head. "Not about that," he said. "About this place."

"Talking won't change anything. It's over. The loan was my last hope. I've lost." She looked at his bruised hand and willed her voice not to crack. "I'm sorry about the land. I wanted you to have it. I'm sorry for all of it, for getting you involved.'' Her gaze skimmed over the angry purplish bruise on his cheek and the way he was looking at her. ''I was angry that you hadn't told me about your past, but the truth is, I was no better. I had no right to drag you into this. I'm so sorry.''

His bruised hand closed over hers. ''I stayed because I wanted to. I knew you were in over your head. So don't go there.''

''It doesn't matter now,'' she said, trying not to cry. ''It's over. Geronimo won't even get up. What am I going to do with him once I lose this place? The other horses I can sell. But I'll have to put him down.''

Cain eased up on the pillow, wincing with the effort. ''You don't have to sell him. And you don't need that loan.''

She gave an teary laugh. ''Right. And maybe I can teach Jigger to rob banks.''

''I set up an account for you today at the First Federal Bank in Marysville.''

She stared at him blankly. ''What?''

''It'll take care of everything you need. Put you back on your feet.''

Maybe she was going crazy. ''An account? You mean…money?''

''Sixty thousand.''

She blinked. *''Dollars?''*

''The paperwork is…in my pocket.''

''Where would you get that kind of money? You…you were *penniless* when I met you. *Hungry.*''

''It doesn't matter,'' he said, wincing as he looking away from her. ''Take it.''

She laughed. ''No. I can't. I can't possibly take it.''

''Sure you can,'' he said tiredly.

She stared at him, dumbfounded. "Cain, where did you get this money?"

He closed his eyes and mumbled something.

"What?"

"Feeling kinda...punk," he said. "I'm...just gonna rest...now."

She blinked at him in disbelief as his breathing almost instantly fell into the deep rhythm of sleep.

She moved off the bed and stumbled toward the chair where she'd dropped his bloody clothes.

Sixty-thousand dollars!

She searched his pockets until her fingers closed around paper. Pulling the bank statement open, she read it. A long numbered account in the name of Maggie Cortland. And there it was. Sixty-thousand dollars. Three times what she'd asked for in her loan. Where had he gotten that kind of money?

She looked back over at Cain, whose battered face made her want to cry. Whatever this was about, she decided, she'd talk to him again in the morning. He needed sleep and she...well, she wasn't sure what she needed anymore.

By some miracle, Geronimo had gotten to his feet during the night and was standing with his head hanging over his stall door when Maggie came out the next morning. She sent up a quiet prayer of thanks and patted the animal's velvety nose.

"Good boy," she murmured. "You're a fighter. I knew you were." She scratched him under his chin. "You hungry? I've got some oats with your name on them."

She filled a bucket with a scoop of oats and held it while Geronimo indulged himself. She finished a half-dozen chores and, exhausted, she was leaning against the weathered barn wood of his stall door when the realization that she wasn't alone struck her. She opened her eyes to find Cain filling the doorway, limping toward her.

"What on God's green earth are you doing out of bed?" she asked, moving to intercept him.

"Figured since you were determined to keep waking me up every hour I might as well get up," he said, moving as if he had a bent piece of steel up his spine. And his color, except for the purples and blues of his bruised cheek, looked downright peaked.

"You go right back to bed, Cain. You're no good to me out here today."

"How's Geronimo?" he asked, ignoring her and moving toward the horse.

This man was a stubborn as the day was long. "See for yourself. He got up during the night sometime. I think he's going to make it."

A slow smile tugged at Cain's mouth as he ran a hand down the blaze on Geronimo's nose. "Tough cookie, huh, boy?"

"Must be something in the water around here." She smiled. "How are your ribs?"

"Sore. But it looks like I'll live."

Joining him at Geronimo's side, she touched his arm. "You want to tell me what happened?"

He summarized the encounter on the road last night and about what had happened at Donnelly's before. "It was an ambush. Premeditated. And it didn't happen on the back road. I was on the main road. Somehow, I ended up on the old mill road."

Maggie frowned. "They moved you? Maybe you're confused."

He turned to look at her. "They fixed the tire and then they moved me. I suppose they didn't want anybody finding me right away." He moved away from Geronimo and walked toward the morning sunshine spilling through the door. "But there's something I'm missing. Something off."

"Aside from the fact that they nearly beat you to death?" she asked.

The sound of a car coming down her drive made Cain look up. What he saw made a line form between his eyes.

"Who is it?" she asked, moving toward the doorway.

"Did you call the sheriff?"

"Not yet. I was going to when I went inside."

"Well," he said. "Looks like he saved you the trouble."

Sheriff Joe Winston pulled his patrol car up beside the barn and got slowly out of his car. In his fifties, and already in the third term of his office, Winston moved with the slow deliberateness of authority. He was barrel-chested and beginning to gray around the temples and Maggie had never cared for him. Laird Donnelly had supported him through all three elections and the two were thick as molasses in December.

Right behind him was Ken Chernoff, his deputy, who lacked Winston's authority, but had managed somehow to retain his dignity, despite the fact that he was a mere footnote on Winston's staff. Nobody did anything in the Fishhook sheriff's department without Winston's say-so. The fact that they were here at all made Maggie's already frayed nerves unravel even further.

"Hi, Maggie," Joe said, tipping his hat to her.

"Joe. Did Harold call you?" she asked, moving beside Cain.

"Harold Levi? No. Afraid not." He regarded Cain with a scowl. "You expecting me, Maggie?"

"I was going to call you as soon as I went inside. About what happened last night to Cain."

Winston slid his sunglasses down his nose and squinted at Cain, taking in the damage on his face. "Looks like you had you a little trouble."

"I guess you could call it that."

"Which brings me to why I'm here."

"Why are you here?" Cain asked bluntly. Ken Chernoff walked up beside Joe and glanced at Maggie.

"Well, sir," Winston began, "seems one of Laird Donnelly's men, a young fellow named Brent Hayden, got his head bashed in last night."

Maggie inhaled sharply. Oh, no. She'd just spoken to Brent Hayden days ago. She remembered he'd been afraid of something even then.

"He was found dead out along the old mill road this morning," Joe continued. Maggie looked up at Cain.

"What has that got to do with us?" he asked.

"Funny you should ask," Winston said. "I got an anonymous call at the station this morning about the murder. Seems someone saw your truck out that road last night about the same time the coroner put the time of death for Hayden."

Maggie tightened her mouth. "Cain was jumped last night and beaten nearly to death on the way home last night, Sheriff. He had nothing to do with Brent's death."

"Somebody jumped you, you say?" Winston said. "In your truck?"

"I had a blowout," Cain said. "I was changing the tire when they jumped me."

"Well, maybe you can show me your tools then," Winston said. "You know, jack…tire iron."

"You're welcome to search the truck," Maggie said. "He's telling you the truth."

Joe sent Ken over to Maggie's truck to search for the tools.

Winston hitched up his gun belt. "That's quite a shiner you got, MacCallister."

Cain ignored him, watching Ken. The radio in his car erupted with static and Joe went to answer it as the deputy crawled under the truck. In a moment, he reappeared, carrying the car jack in his hand. "This is it," he said, holding up the jack to Winston, who was ambling back. "Tire iron's missing."

Tightening his jaw, Cain glanced at Maggie, who was looking at him now with a worried expression. He turned to Winston. "Look," he said, "I don't know where the tire iron is because they moved my truck after I passed out. They changed the tire and moved my truck."

Winston sent him an incredulous look. "The boys who beat you up changed your tire for you?"

"I know it sounds—"

"There's a good spare in the wheel well," Ken interrupted, not looking at Maggie.

Cain's expression flattened. "That's impossible. The spare is on the truck. They shot out my other tire."

"Brent Hayden was killed with a tire iron, Mr. MacCallister. You're missin' one. The one we found has blood evidence on it and some clear prints. I called down to Texas where I understand you've had a run in or two with the law and asked them for a match on those prints. They belong to you, Mr. MacCallister."

Maggie grabbed Cain's arm. "Of course his prints are on it. He was changing the tire!"

"Yes, ma'am. But if any of the blood on it matches yours," Winston continued, "well, I have to say things aren't looking in your favor. You see, I have several witnesses who will swear that you made threats against Donnelly's men yesterday."

For one awful instant, Maggie wondered, horrified, if it was possible. Cain chose that moment to look in her eyes. Maggie's lips parted, trying to erase the doubt from her expression but it was too late. He'd seen it. He looked away.

Winston was still talking. "Now, clearly, you were in

some kind of a fight last night. Brent fought off his attacker. These could be defensive wounds. And the other facts, well, they just don't add up. Maybe you're telling me the truth, maybe not. I'm sorry, but I'm afraid I'll have to take you down to the station for questioning.''

Winston pulled a set of handcuffs from his back belt and reached for Cain's wrist. Tight-jawed, he submitted, his abject gaze meeting Maggie's.

"You're *arresting* him?" Maggie watched in horror as Winston clapped the cuffs around Cain's wrists and snapped them shut.

"He's a suspect in a homicide, ma'am."

"Are handcuffs necessary?" she asked, outraged.

Cain winced as Winston tugged him by the arm toward the patrol car. Maggie called his name, but Cain didn't turn around.

"You have the right to remain silent," Ken recited. "Anything you say can and will be used against you in a court of law. You have the right to an attorney. If you do not have an attorney or cannot afford one…"

The words blurred in Maggie's mind as she watched in disbelief. This couldn't be happening. She was staring at Cain, who had just checked out emotionally and was staring straight ahead, not at her, not at anyone else. Maggie's heart sank.

He couldn't have killed Brent. They'd nearly killed him. Couldn't Winston see that?

"Sheriff, this is crazy," she told him, crowding the three of them. "You know he didn't do this. He had no reason to want to murder—"

Winston used his chest to block her way and he took her by the arm. "I'm really sorry about this, Maggie. I know he's your husband, but he's got a history and he's our prime suspect. Now you just calm yourself down and call your friend Harold Levi. He's gonna need a good lawyer."

Ken was guiding Cain down into the back of the car with one hand on his head. "Don't hurt him—" she shouted at Ken. "His ribs are—" he winced and inhaled sharply as Ken pushed him down into the car "—fractured."

Joe walked around to his side of the car and Maggie moved to Cain's window. "Cain?"

He didn't look at her. He just burned a hole in the floor with his stare. The car began to pull away and she pounded on the window. "Cain! I'm calling Harold. Don't worry. I'll get you out."

His expression had shut down like a slammed door but he looked at her one last time as the patrol car pulled out of her yard. The bleakness in his eyes staggered her.

And then he was gone.

Maggie was pacing in the postage stamp-sized waiting room when Harold Levi walked out of the interrogation room, looking grim. She'd been rehearsing what she'd say when it was her turn to talk to Cain. But every pathetic justification for the look he'd seen on her face in that moment sounded lamer than the next. She met Harold at the door.

"He doesn't want to see you, Maggie," he told her. "He doesn't want to see anyone right now."

Disappointment and more than that, hurt, rifled through her. "I need to see him, Harold."

"He doesn't want you to see him behind bars. He's a proud man."

That she knew. "He denied it all, didn't he? You believe him, don't you?"

"He denies it. But beyond that he's not saying much of anything. He's been through all this before. It's his frame of mind I'm concerned about. As far as believing him? I was there last night, Maggie. I saw what they left behind and Cain didn't win that fight. I'll testify to that."

"Can you, as his attorney?"

"I'm not a criminal attorney, Maggie. My specialty is contracts law. But I'll do the preliminaries. The first hurdle will be bail. He's a flight risk. And his bail will be substantial. You don't have that kind of money."

Maggie turned around and paced to the other side of the room, pressing her hands together.

Behind her, Harold set his briefcase down and walked closer. "Is there something you're not telling me, Maggie?"

She stared down at the industrial brown couch shoved against the wall. "Yes. It could be bad for him."

Harold turned her toward him. "Tell me."

Tears started down her cheeks. "He…" she began, then started over when her voice cracked. "He put sixty-thousand dollars in an account for me yesterday. To save my ranch. He just gave it to me. I don't know where it came from. As far as I knew he had no money. Where would he get that kind of money, Harold?"

"Sixty-thousand dollars?" Harold let out a low whistle, then frowned thoughtfully. "That's a helluva lot of cash." Naturally, the same scenarios played across his expression that had run through her mind. "Don't mention that to anyone, Maggie. I'll find out about it."

"I need to see him, Harold. You've got to convince him." The smell of this place, the sterile awfulness of it was beginning to get to her.

"Give him a little time. He's a little raw right now. Go home. Get some rest." He took her elbow and began guiding her out.

"What are you going to do?" she asked.

"My job," he answered with a grim smile.

Outside, Maggie moved mechanically to her car. The sun was brilliant and the breeze carried with it the scent of every nearby ponderosa pine. The good people of Fishhook were moving about their daily lives as if nothing was wrong. But everything was. Her life was coming undone like a pulled thread on a cardigan. And Cain's...

She slammed her eyes shut as she reached the car Harold had rented for her. They'd impounded her truck as evidence and she had to get back home to Moody, who'd come out to look after Geronimo.

Opening the door to the Toyota, something caught her eye on the van parked across the street. She squinted and shaded her eyes with her hand to read the writing on the side of door. Her heart stuttered. It said, Remus/Trimark Development Corp., Denver, Colorado.

Chapter 14

Forty minutes later, Maggie watched from the driver's seat of her rental as three men—strangers in business suits—and Laird Donnelly walked out of the professional building on the corner of Main and Crescent that housed a dental office, the local Bureau of Land Management offices and Nelson, Kramer and Associates, a construction firm. They headed toward the parked van.

Of course Donnelly was with them, she thought with a sinking feeling.

She slumped down in her seat, staying out of view. The three men were still engaged in conversation with Donnelly and he was pointing toward the road that led out of town. The three men nodded and Donnelly shook their hands, then headed to the tan Range Rover parked half a block down.

Maggie turned the key in her ignition and followed them as they pulled out and headed in the direction of Maggie's ranch. She kept a quarter of a mile between their little caravan so that they wouldn't notice her, feeling ironically fortunate she wasn't in her more recognizable truck.

The Range Rover and the van pulled off the road halfway between Laird's property and hers and the men got out. She pulled over, too, waiting.

Laird pointed to his land, the upper third of his property that hugged the Musselshell River and forked into hers. Here, along this stretch of the river, was the only level playing field in the whole valley. Then he gestured at her land, encompassing it in the same conversation. One of the men went back to the van and pulled out a tube of some sort and withdrew a rolled up set of papers.

Maggie opened her door and got half way out, squinting into the glaring sun at the men. Blueprints? Pieces began to fall into place like puzzle bricks. Blueprints involving her land, Remus/Trimark Development Corp., Kramer Construction...

For a long time, the town of Fishhook had talked about ways to increase revenue and tourism. Besides the quaintness of the town itself, there were only two real selling points: the Musselshell, with its incredible fly fishing, and the local game hunting. Other towns had exploited these assets. Built tourism and brought in jobs. But Fishhook, as a whole, remained staunchly opposed to commercialism, seeing what it had done to other towns. Prime forests had been trampled, traffic had increased exponentially and the reason residents loved living where they did disappeared with the invasion. This was a small ranching community and most wanted to keep it that way.

But she suspected Laird Donnelly had other plans. He had enough land to develop whatever he wanted. What he didn't have, what Fishhook had always opposed, was access. The nearest airport was eighty-five miles away in Helena.

Maggie blinked. And the only piece of land flat enough

to accommodate a landing strip was the piece of land adjacent to his. Her land. And nothing could prevent him from putting a private landing strip on it once he owned it.

She suddenly remembered the morning Ben had come home drunk from a casino, pouring himself in the door at 3:00 a.m. He'd been angry about something one of Donnelly's men had said to him. He'd muttered something about not trading horses for Cessnas. It made no sense to her at the time. But it did now.

She thought about Brent Hayden's phone call and what he'd said about Ben's death. If Laird Donnelly had wanted their land that badly, and Ben was the only thing standing in his way, then the slow ruination of a man—a man with weaknesses like Bens—would not have been hard to orchestrate. It would have taken merely the opportunity and the will. Laird had both. And Ben had been an unwitting accomplice.

The men were still talking, but Maggie jumped back in her car and turned back toward town. While his destruction of Ben had been slow and deliberate, his plot against Cain seemed almost desperate. If time was running out for him, he was desperate enough to make mistakes. She only needed one. And she intended to force him into making it.

"Why don't you let me make you up some soup?" Moody asked, watching Maggie rifle through a box of old papers she'd brought up from the garage.

"I don't have time to eat," Maggie answered, pulling a receipt for baling wire out of the stack of papers in the box. She tossed it aside and dug into the pile again.

"You have to eat," Moody reminded her. "You're not going to be any good to him if you make yourself sick."

"I'm not going to be any good to him at all if I can't find something to help him," she said without looking up. Ben's copy of a gelding sale fluttered into the discard pile and she sighed hopelessly. "This is impossible. I don't even know if there's anything here."

"You've been at this for two hours. Let me fix you something to eat."

"I can make a sandwich later." She looked up at Moody, who was hovering over her like a sweet old hen. "You should get back. Dinner rush is almost here."

Moody waved a hand. "That's why I hire help, darlin'. They can handle the dinner rush without me once. You're more important right now."

Her kindness almost undid Maggie. It wasn't as if Moody wasn't always good to her. But she felt horribly alone today and having the older woman stay with her made her almost feel like she could tackle this impossible task. She squeezed Moody's hand.

The sound of a car crunching gravel on the driveway drew Maggie's gaze to the window. She couldn't see the car, but was sure it must be Harold with news. Jumping up, she rushed outside. But the car wasn't Harold's. It was a Lincoln Town Car. And the silver-haired gentleman getting out of the driver's seat was no country lawyer. He could have been a banker or an oilman, she thought, the way he was dressed, but he walked like he'd been sitting a horse most of his life. More than that, there was something familiar about him.

"Maggie Cortland? he asked, nearing the steps of her porch.

"It's MacCallister," she corrected. "Maggie Mac-Callister. And you're—?"

His lips fell open. A thousand emotions flickered through his sky-blue eyes as his gaze swept over her. "I see," he said gruffly. He held out his hand. "My name is Mac-Callister, too. Judd MacCallister. And I'm looking for my son."

* * *

Cain eased back on the lumpy cot in the holding cell, clenching his jaw against the ache in his ribs and the ache everywhere else and trying to ignore the snoring coming from the other side of the room. He'd spent the last eight hours cooling his heels in this cell with Sleeping Beauty over there—a drunk named Charlie Grinow, who hadn't moved in the last four hours—while Donnelly's men hightailed it out of Montana. They'd never find them now.

He squeezed his eyes shut wishing he'd never laid eyes on this damned town. In the next breath, he knew that was a lie.

There was one part of it he wouldn't trade for another fifty years of freedom.

Maggie.

She was probably the only reason he was still alive. A month ago, before he'd met her, he wouldn't have thought twice about swinging that crowbar and trying to take out as many as he could before they killed him. He'd been at the end of his rope a month ago and somehow, she'd given him back a reason to live. But he'd failed her. And now she doubted him.

He'd seen it in her eyes this morning. There would always be doubt with a man like him. A man with his past. It would follow him the rest of his life. So what the hell? He should just resign himself to the fact that his life was headed in the same meaningless direction as Charlie's over there.

But that wasn't the hard part. The hard part wasn't giving up on himself. It was losing Maggie.

The guard appeared at his cell door. "You got a visitor, MacCallister."

"I don't want to see her," he said, turning his head. He couldn't stand for her to see him in here.

"It's not a her. It's a him."

"My attorney?" Cain asked with a frown.

"Says his name is Judd MacCallister."

Shock rifled through him as he rolled to a sitting position. His father? Here? He glanced around the cell, the crashing awfulness of this kind of a reunion more than he could face. "I don't want to see him."

"Well, you're going to see me," a voice boomed behind the guard. Judd appeared at Cain's cell door in all his silver-haired glory, strong-arming the help as usual. He got his first good look at Cain and his expression lost its edge. He swallowed thickly. "Because," he said more softly, "I didn't drive all the way to this godforsaken wilderness to be turned away now."

Cain thought he'd rather have glass shards shoved under his fingernails than sit in this stinking cell with his old man, but he gestured to the guard to let him in.

The door clanged shut behind him and Judd hovered just inside. Cain stretched out indolently on the cot and put his hands beneath his head, ignoring the throb in his ribs.

His father looked older, he thought, and less certain of himself than he once had. It gave Cain some small measure of satisfaction that he looked uncomfortable as hell. This was, after all, Cain's turf. Not the old man's.

Judd stood there awkwardly with his hat in his hands. "It's good to see you again, son."

"What are you doing here?"

"Looking for you. I've been looking for a long time."

Charlie gave a snort from the far corner, and Cain gestured grandly at the accommodations. "You always know where to find me, right?"

Judd leaned back against the metal bars of the door. "I met your wife. Maggie."

The careless grin slipped off his face. "I don't want to talk to you about her."

Fingering the brim of his Stetson, the old man said, "She's outside...wanting to see you."

"You didn't come all the way from the Concho to tell me that, did you?"

"No." Judd's gaze took in the bruises on Cain's face. "Are you all right, son?"

"I'll live."

"Say the word and I'll bring Douglas Fleming up from Dallas Memorial to look at your—"

"No."

Wiping his hands against the fabric of his coat, Judd glanced around the cell. "I know you're angry."

Cain snorted. "I'm not angry. I hardly think of you at all anymore." The lie sat between them like the wall it was supposed to be.

"You're not going to make this easy for me, are you?"

"Should I? You want absolution?" He made the sign of the cross. "You're absolved. Now if you don't mind, I'd like you to get the hell out."

Judd sat down on the end of Cain's cot. "I've come to say what I need to say. When I'm finished, if you still want me to go, I will."

Cain dragged two hands through his hair. "Then say it."

"All right." Judd paused, collecting himself. "I was wrong. About Annie. About you and what happened after Annie.... I want you to know, I'm deeply sorry for it. More than you can know. For everything that happened. Most of all for turning away from you when you needed me most."

Cain stared at the old man in shock. Never in his entire life had he heard him apologize for anything. But it was too damned little, too damned late.

"I'm sure Annie would have given you a nice warm hug and invited you over for dinner for that little speech, because that's just how she was. But she's dead now. It's a little late for apologies."

"I know." Judd stood and paced to the other side of the cell, looking older and frailer than Cain could ever remember him. "I won't make excuses for it," Judd continued. "I was bullheaded and thought I knew what was best for you. I was dead wrong. She made you happy. Something I was never able to do. I suppose I resented that a little.

"In the beginning I thought she was just your way of getting back at me. Too late, I realized that wasn't the case. And by then, the hole I'd dug for myself was too deep. So when she was...when it happened, and you wouldn't let me help you..."

"You sent your *lawyer* to see me. Not even a *word* of regret for Annie."

Judd's deep sigh was full of that emotion. "Did you know I came to her service?"

Cain hadn't known. It shocked the hell out of him.

"I was, of course, uninvited. I...was at the back of the church. I wanted to see you. To tell you how sorry I was. But I lost my nerve. Imagine that. Me? Judd MacCallister. Unnerved by his son's grief. I hoped that by my offering you help, we could somehow... Oh, hell. It doesn't matter what I thought." He went quiet for a minute, then looked up at his son. "It might comfort you to know that her name's on a new wing at Dallas Memorial."

That brought Cain's head around. *"What?"*

"The Annie MacCallister Pediatric Wing. I donated it in her name. I think she would've liked it."

Shaken, Cain looked away, rubbing a thumb beneath his nose. "Thank you."

"If I could've brought her back for you with all that money, I would have."

The silence stretched between them now like the chasm that yawned between their two lives. There was no going back, Cain thought. No matter what. But the idea that her name would be remembered for something good instead of for the awful way she'd died took some of the sting out of the years of bitterness.

"Your phone call yesterday," Judd continued, "the one that brought me here, was too brief to say the things I've wanted you to know and the letters I'd sent you in prison were returned unopened. You should know that my threat to disinherit you when you married Annie was an empty one. Your trust is still there. It always has been. It's yours, Cain. I want you to have it."

Cain rubbed an aching spot between his eyes. "Do you think a hospital wing changes everything? Do you really think I want your money? That it will solve anything between us?"

Judd stood and shoved his hands in his pockets. "Do you see that man over there? Your snoring friend? Is that what you want for the rest of your life? Is that what you want for Maggie?"

"Maggie and I have an agreement—"

"I *know* all about the agreement," Judd said. "And I know about the look in her eyes when she told me you were innocent. She's in love with you. Surely this whole mess hasn't blinded you to that."

Cain shook his head. "She's lonely. That's all. And scared. Besides, it's a bit of a moot point, isn't it? I mean, I'm going to spend the rest of my life in prison."

"Self-pity doesn't suit you."

Cain bowed his head as he dropped down on the cot again. "Get out."

"Son, I know you're innocent. I won't let this happen again. I promise you that. But you've got to fight for what's out in that hallway, waiting for you. Hang on to her, dammit. Or you're not the man I think you are."

"The perennial convict?"

"No," Judd said carefully. "A man who's not too proud to grab a second chance when it comes around. And one who's wise enough to know how lucky he is to get one. Most of us never do." He rapped on the cell door and called for the guard, then turned back to Cain. "Greg Janeson's on his way here. He should be here within the hour."

Cain frowned. Greg Janeson was the attorney who had single-handedly masterminded his appeal. "You know my attorney?"

Judd didn't reply. He just waited for Cain to catch up. It only took him another moment. "Oh my God. You *hired* him. You hired him for the appeal. He wasn't some altruistic do-gooder, pro-bono—"

"He's all that and more. But we did just so happen to go to Yale together. If he'd told you the truth, that I'd convinced him to take your case on, would you have let him help you?"

He knew very well that he wouldn't have and today he'd still be sitting in... Hell, he *was* still sitting in jail.

"We'll get bail set," Judd said, "and have you out of here by sundown. Hang in there, Cain."

The jailer came and opened up the metal door and Judd disappeared down the hallway, leaving Cain to wonder after him. He'd set the appeal in motion? After everything that had happened? He couldn't get his mind around it. He'd spent too many years hating him to feel anything else. Now, he didn't know what to think.

"Your wife's still out there. You want to see her now?" the jailer asked.

He tightened his jaw. Maggie was another story. His father was wrong about that. Cain knew how that one would end. "Yes. Send her in."

The swelling on his cheek had gone down a little, Maggie noticed as the guard let her in, but the bruise there had changed to an angry purple. And when he got to his feet, his movements were slow and stiff. But those were just the obvious changes. The ones she was more concerned about were the changes she saw in his eyes when he looked at her. He'd gone somewhere, far away from her emotionally. The last few days between them, all but erased.

Maggie moved toward him, awkwardly touching his arm. "Are you all right?" She lifted her hand to touch his cheek, but he moved away from her.

"Just fine. Great bed—" he gestured at Charlie "—great company. All the amenities…"

"We'll get you out of here. I promise you that." He didn't say anything and she took a step nearer. "I know you think I doubted you this morning—"

He wouldn't meet her eye. "Who could blame you?"

"But I didn't," she whispered. "I *know* who you are. And I've fallen in love with you, Cain. Did you hear me? I'm in *love* with you."

His gaze went dark as if she'd struck him. "Don't say that. Don't even think it. This is who I am. Take a good look at it. Is this what you want?"

"This isn't who you are. This is what Laird Donnelly's done to you." She reached out and touched his chest, felt the muscles there quake beneath her fingertips. "It's you I love. The man I've come to know. The man who pulled me out of that wash and held me all night long. The man who has stood by me through things most men would've run from. I never should have asked it of you, but if I hadn't, think what we would have missed."

Angry now, he turned away from her. "Maggie, I'm going back to prison. Hell, there's an open-and-shut case against me."

"It's all a lie and we both know it."

"They had less evidence in my last trial and they sent me up for fifteen to life."

"That's not going to happen. Cain. *I'm* not going to let it happen."

He rounded on her now. "You stay the hell out of it,

Maggie. You hear me? You leave this alone. Donnelly will—"

"You can bluster at me all you want Cain, but I'm going to prove that Laird Donnelly set you up."

He took her by the arms and bodily moved her against the cell door. "You listen to me. You stay away from him. He's dangerous. He had Brent Hayden murdered and only left me breathing to take the fall for him."

"And then there's Ben," she said in a small voice.

"What about Ben?"

"He had a hand in Ben's death. Not in his actual suicide. But I believe it was Laird who pushed him against the wall until he felt suicide was his only way out. Brent told me as much. And now, I think I know why."

Cain frowned at her. "What are you talking about?"

She told him about the Remus Trimark van and her suspicions about why he wanted the land. When she'd finished, Cain released her and paced to the other side of the cell.

"It makes sense," he said. "If he's got blueprints that means he's already in deep financially. He may be running out of time, which explains why he's moved out onto that limb."

"Yes," she said. "And he's about to find out just how fragile that limb is." Maggie rapped on the cell door. "Guard?"

Cain turned back to her with a scowl. "Maggie, you give this to Harold. You let him handle this. Don't go anywhere near Donnelly. Do you understand?"

She smiled and pressed a kiss against his mouth. The memory of having his arms around her stoked her determination. "He won't get away with it," she told him. "Not this time."

The guard unlocked the door and she pulled away from him, leaving his cell without a backward glance.

"Maggie?" he shouted after her. *"Maggie!"*

It was seven forty-five before the paperwork was finished and Judd and Greg Janeson appeared at Cain's cell door announcing they'd posted bail for him. By then, Cain was nearly jumping out of his skin.

"Where's Maggie?" was the first question Cain barked at them.

Judd exchanged a look with Greg. "I sent her home to wait for us."

"Alone? When?" He brushed past them out the cell door and into the hallway. The two men hurried to catch up.

"After she saw you," Judd told him. "Harold might have gone with her. What's wrong?"

"Why didn't you go with her? Dammit. Give me your cell phone, Greg."

Greg grinned, handing him the phone as they passed the front desk. "Nice to see you, too, Cain."

"You, I'll deal with later," he said narrowing a censuring look at his attorney. He dialed home and listened while the number rang. No answer. Dammit. He clicked off, pushing out the front door of the small sheriff's office. "Do you have Harold's home number?"

Greg produced it from a scrap of paper in his pocket. Cain punched in the number as they headed out into the cool Montana evening. Harold picked up on the second ring. "Hello?"

"It's Cain," he said. "Is Maggie with you?"

"No," he answered. "She went home by herself. I offered to stay with her but she told me I was being overprotective and that she needed time alone."

Cain swore foully.

"Why? Isn't she there?" Harold asked, the worry beginning to grow in his voice.

"If she is, she's not answering. Maybe she's out with Geronimo. I made bail. I'm heading there now."

"You know something I don't know?" Harold asked.

Cain gripped the phone more tightly. "Only that she's even more bullheaded than me. And she thinks she can save me."

"She's in love with you."

Cain had no intelligent response to that. The idea that she could die because she cared about him was almost more than he could take. He'd been through this once and sworn never to do it again. Judd opened the door to the Lincoln and Cain slid gingerly into the back seat, wincing at the movement. He slammed the backside of the front seat with his fist.

"Call me when you get there on my cell. I'm on my way," Harold said, then clicked off.

Judd got behind the wheel and started it up.

"Step on it, old man," Cain said. "Let's see if you've still got the stuff."

"I've still got it. And I'm not that old yet."

The Town Car took off with a grind of tires down the highway toward Maggie's house.

Gene Fielding handed the giant of a man a brown paper sack with the twenty thousand in it, anxious to be out of this smoky bar and out of this town.

"You won't need to count it, Dusette. It's all there."

Dusette regarded him with an uneven smile and opened the sack. He scraped his thumbnail against the stack of bills, fanning them out. "I'm sure it is," he said in a gravelly voice. "But there is a problem."

Here it comes, Gene thought. "What that?"

"Well, see Leon thinks twenty's a little shy of what the job was worth. After all, the guy busted Everett's knee and nearly took out my voice box. Not to mention the fact that your friend can identify us."

"That's not our problem," Gene said reasonably. "You should have worn masks or hoods or…whatever it is you people wear. Besides, you'll be out of the state by tonight. Out of harm's way."

"That kinda puts us outta the runnin' for jobs in these parts, though, don't it? And us havin' to look over our shoulder and all. I mean, we figure that's worth a little something extra."

Gene despised Laird for making him come here tonight. He got to his feet, withdrawing a handful of bills from his pocket and throwing them on the table. "That's worth exactly nothing. You were hired to do a job. You did the job. It's not without its risks. You can tell Leon he should choose a safer line of work next time if he's not happy with the arrangements. It's more than equitable."

Dussett stood too, towering over Gene like a redwood. "Oh, I think Leon will have somethin' to say about that," he said, tossing back the last of his tequila with a hiss as the burn went down. "See, I figure you and your boss ain't considered the implications of our unhappiness. Fact is, my friend, you and your boss? You got a lot more to lose than any of us. And in the end, another twenty thousand will do more than make us happy. It'll buy you peace of mind, if you catch my meaning."

He slid his Yankee's baseball cap on over his thinning hair and tugged at the brim. "We'll be in touch, Mr. Fielding. You have a real nice night now, y'hear?"

Gene watched Dusette disappear out of the bar before he pulled his cell phone from the breast pocket of his coat. He hit speed dial and waited. "Where are you?" he asked when the number connected. He turned away from the couple necking in the next booth and leaned into the phone. "I don't give a damn what you just ordered, get in your friggin' car and drive home. We've got a problem and we need to talk. Yes, now!''

Gene punched the end button furiously. Damn, damn, damn. He hadn't been in this business twenty years without knowing how this sort of thing went down. Blackmail by any other name was still blackmail. And by forcing him to make the drop, Laird had upped the ante for him as well. Well, dammit, he'd *had* it with this whole fiasco and with Laird Donnelly's blind ambition. No piece of land was worth all this trouble. After tonight, he'd be out of it. Or he'd be dead. Either way, he figured, he was screwed.

Chapter 15

"Her car's still here." The tightness in his chest eased when he saw Maggie's rental parked in the yard as they pulled in. He was out of the Lincoln the minute it stopped, limping toward the lighted kitchen.

Be there, he begged silently.

He pictured her standing at the stove, stirring some savory dish that made the whole house smell amazing...turning her head as he walked in from outside...seeing the sunset in her eyes over a cup of coffee. Holding her in his arms in her bed.

Ruthlessly, he shoved those images from his mind as he pushed open the kitchen door. He had no right to inflict himself on her, no matter how damned comfortable she made it. She deserved better than him.

The kitchen was empty except for Jigger who, met him at the door, planting two feet squarely on his chest. Cain hissed and grabbed for his ribs, shoving the dog away. "Dammit, dog," he groaned, folding in the middle. Jigger's ears fell and his tail drooped miserably between his legs. Cain half straightened as Judd and Greg walked in the door.

"Take it easy, Cain," his father warned, grabbing Jigger by the collar. "You've got broken bones still moving around in there."

Pale and still struggling for air, Cain forced himself upright, shoving past the pain. "She's not here."

There was no stew in the pot. Just the lingering scent of Maggie and a tightening in his gut at the thought that she was already in trouble.

He headed into the other downstairs rooms, banging open doors to empty rooms. "Maggie!"

Starting up the stairs, one awkward step at a time, Judd stopped him before he'd gone two steps. "You go check the barn. I'll look upstairs."

Nodding tightly, Cain headed out the back door. Greg followed him.

The barn was full of horses, but no sign of Maggie. Geronimo stood in his stall watching them over his stall door, snorting for attention. Cain ran a clammy hand down the horse's muzzle with an oath.

"Her car's here," Greg said. "Where could she be?"

Cain's gaze drifted a stall or two down from Geronimo's. Biscuit was missing. Oh, Maggie...

He headed out of the barn with Greg on his heels. Judd was just coming out the back door. "Where are you going now?" Greg demanded.

"Give me the keys, Greg."

"Like hell."

"Then you drive."

"Okay. Where are we going?"

Cain shook his head. "Into the lion's mouth."

Breaking and entering.

Add that to the list, Maggie thought, contemplating the

unlocked window on the downstairs floor of Laird Donnelly's sprawling estate house.

She glanced behind her. Darkness enshrouded the expanse of lawn behind her. Somewhere, two hundred yards back, she'd left Biscuit tied to a hedge of red cedar, hidden from view. The bunkhouse was quiet with a few dim lights still glowing. But mornings came early on a cattle ranch and most of them had already turned in. The house, on the other hand, was completely dark. Fortunately, Laird was gone. She knew he would be. She'd called Elena Madrigal, his housekeeper, an hour ago asking for Laird, only to be told he was out for the evening. A business dinner, Elena had said. He'd be back very late.

Which suited her purposes just fine, she thought, standing on the gas meter that sat below the window. She shoved it open and smiled. She hoped Laird had a nice leisurely dinner, sure his plans for her demise were well on their way to completion. She hoped he choked on those plans, because she meant to find a way to stop him.

She hoisted herself up through the window and stopped halfway through, halting her fall with her hands on the tiled bathroom floor. She froze, listening for sounds in the house. Elena had a small cottage of her own on the property that she used at night and Maggie prayed the housekeeper was already gone.

Flicking on the small flashlight she pulled from her pocket, Maggie headed into the hallway. She'd only been in Laird's house once before, the night she'd come looking for Ben. Though Laird had sworn Ben wasn't there, he'd come stumbling through the doorway drunk only moments later with his gambling pal, Butch.

It had been only one in a string of such incidents where Laird was somehow involved with Ben's call toward the dark side. Laird had fed Ben's gambling sickness. And he'd done it intentionally. When Brent had said that Ben had had help, he hadn't meant that anyone had helped him tie that noose around his neck. He'd meant that Laird and Butch had pushed him and pushed him until Ben was in so deep the only way out he could see was to throw a rope over that rafter and end it.

And it had all been about the land.

Her flashlight illuminated a guest bedroom, a spacious bit of luxury with a canopied timber bed and Flathead antiquities on the wall: a hand-painted buffalo skin shield, a lance, a quiver of arrows. They hung on the wall like trophies and sent a shiver through her. It seemed almost appropriate that he decorated his house with violent things. It suited him.

She moved down the hallway. The fourth room she shone her flashlight into was his office. Relief poured through her. It had to be here, she told herself. The proof against Laird had to be here among his things.

Maggie illuminated the room, getting her bearings. The walnut paneled room was elegantly masculine. The massive desk that sat opposite the door was bracketed by two chairs on the opposite side and a comfortable leather desk chair that fitted neatly into the kneehole under it. The walls on either side were occupied by file cabinets and bookshelves. Maggie ran her finger down the labels on the front of the file cabinets until she came to the one marked ''R-W.''

She gave the handle a tug. Locked. Turning, she reached for the letter opener on his desk and shoved it into the lock at the top of the cabinet. After some prodding, it popped open. Maggie smiled. She was good at this, she thought. But a few minutes later, she realized her quest was going to prove harder than she thought. There was no file on Remus/Trimark.

She looked under T. Nothing. Then she moved to his desk and tried the drawers. Locked again. Damn, but he was cautious. She reached for the letter opener again, this time sliding it between the lock and the edge of the drawer. Feeling for the latch, she wrenched it sideways until it clicked free.

She wrenched open the drawers one at a time, searching through the papers and miscellaneous files. Nothing. In the top drawer, however, she found a key. She frowned and tried it in the lock to the desk. It didn't fit. She glanced around the office and tried it in the file cabinet. Not that.

Her gaze fell to a door to the right of the file cabinets. She tried the handle. Locked. She sighed. He was very careful. She inserted the key. It turned in the lock like butter.

Inside the small closet of a room, Maggie found a wall safe and another set of file cabinets. These were unlocked, presumably because they were not accessible without the key in her hand. She opened the first drawer and let her gaze slide over the file names until it stopped at Cortland, Ben.

Her hand trembled as she lifted it and she opened it up. Inside were photographs of Ben with another woman draped over him at a blackjack table, one of Ben kissing that woman, and a series of closed circuit photos of him, awkwardly attempting to cheat at cards.

And there were photos of her. Surveillance photos that sent a shiver of fear through her. He'd been watching her.

"I knew I hated you, you bastard. I just didn't know how much," she muttered to herself as she stuffed the file into the back waistband of her jeans. Then she looked for Cain's file.

Of course it was there. It was complete, with booking photos and a complete history of his checkered past with the law. It was exactly as he'd said it was. And this report noted the overturning of his conviction four months ago.

Maggie swallowed thickly. She didn't need to see this

proof to convince her that he had told her the truth, but it made everything that had happened to him seem all the worse. Here was a man who'd simply wanted a fresh start but wouldn't get one because Laird had deemed it so.

He'd played god with so many people's lives. Including hers. But nothing she'd found so far could implicate him in any crime, though she was convinced he'd committed several. But how could she prove that he was blackmailing Ben, or that he'd had Cain attacked. She needed receipts, records. And Laird wasn't likely to be foolish enough to keep either one.

She closed the file cabinet, her flashlight beam crossing something on the shelf behind the cabinets. It was a model. An architect's model labeled Musselshell Resort, Donnelly Enterprises and Remus/Trimark Development Corp., John Remus, Architect.

And there it was. The reason Ben died. The reason Cain had been framed for murder. The reason her ranch was sinking like the Titanic. A resort perched on the banks of the Musselshell River tucked into the shoal that curved into her property. And there, squarely on her land, was a runway strip with miniature planes coming in for a landing.

She'd known, but seeing it in three dimensions made her throat tighten with rage. All for this. For Laird Donnelly's bid for power. Why at the expense of so many? And obviously, he'd already spent copious amounts of money on the premise that he would eventually get that piece of her land so essential to his project. Without that landing strip, his whole project would be in jeopardy.

Maggie shoved the model back into its place and swept the area with her flashlight. *Think!* She needed more. Something solid, tangible.

She locked the door to the closet and went back to the desk to put the keys away. That's when she saw it.

The palm-sized tape recorder was tucked under some papers, hidden from view. She picked it up and pushed the play button.

Donnelly's voice erupted from the small black recorder. *"...looking a little pale, Gene. Sit down."*

Gene Fielding, Laird's attorney?

The sound of furniture rustling and a shaky sigh coming from Gene. *"It's over."*

"What's over?" Donnelly asked.

"Cortland's dead. Hung himself this morning in his own barn. It's what we wanted, isn't it? I mean, it was inevitable, right?"

Donnelly's voice sounded shocked. *"I never wanted that, Gene. Good God, I never wanted the man dead."*

"What did you think would happen if you pushed him that hard? The guy was sick. The gambling was a sickness. We had no right to play with a man's life that way—"

"As I recall that was your idea."

Gene cursed. *"I only said to find his weakness. To drive him out of business. Not to push him to the edge of reason."*

Maggie shivered, listening to the cold-blooded dissection of a plot to destroy her husband.

There was a long pause. *"What about Maggie?"* Laird asked.

"What do you think? She's a wreck. She'll fold inside a month without him. God, I hate this."

"Ben made his own choice," Laird said sagely. *"You can't blame yourself for this. I'll send her some flowers. Something nice. What a shame. You know, I really did like Ben."*

Maggie punched the button viciously and swore out loud. The tape had been made without Gene's knowledge, she was certain. It was, she guessed, a safety net for Laird. In case anything ever happened. It was thin, but it was enough to interest the—

The sound of the front door opening made her nearly drop the tape recorder. She fumbled it, but caught it before it hit the desk. Maggie froze, listening. Someone—make that two someones—were coming inside the house. They were arguing.

She ran to the office door, but realized it was too late. They were coming this way. Fast.

Scanning the room, she looked for a place to hide. The closet! She crossed the room in four steps and jerked on the door. Damn! She'd locked it!

The voices were getting closer.

Oh, God!

Maggie rushed back to the desk and shoved the desk chair out of the way, ducking into the kneehole just as the office door opened. She held her breath and braced herself flush against the inside of the desk.

Laird stalked into the room, banging the door against the wall behind him. "Dusette is bluffing," he told the other man.

"You want to take that chance? I'm telling you, Laird, these guys aren't guys you want to mess with. Leon Bridger makes Butch Capwell look like a choirboy. They could hurt us. They could hurt us badly."

Maggie frowned. Butch Capwell? And what men were they talking about? The men who'd beaten Cain? Maybe they weren't gone after all. Her fingers tightened anxiously around the tape recorder, and she noticed she was still holding it.

Laird swore foully and she heard the clink of crystal against glass as he poured himself something to drink. "I'm not giving them another dime. This was the price we agreed on. They did the job, I paid them."

"You're a fool then," the other man said.

Maggie recognized his voice then. It was Gene Fielding.

"Do you think this will be the end of it?" Laird asked.

"They'll keep coming back for more if we give in to their demands now. Let them go to the sheriff. Who do you think will believe four ex-cons? No one will believe I paid them to hit Brent, or have MacCallister jumped. They can talk until they're blue. That drifter is in so deep he won't see the night sky for another fifty years."

Maggie's eyes widened.

"I'm finished with this, Laird. You hear me?" Gene said. "I'm out. This has gone too far. First Ben. Now Brent and this drifter. Who's next? Where will it stop?"

"You're in just as deep as I am and don't forget it, Gene. Don't even think about jumping ship on me, or so help me I'll find a way to make you sorry."

"Threats won't work anymore. You can't implicate me without implicating yourself. I'm personally two hundred grand in debt over this Musselshell deal and I don't give a damn. I'll gladly give up my house, what little honor I have left and whatever else it takes to be out of this whole damned mess. Because I don't want any more part of it. You've gone too far. I never signed on for murder."

"You pathetic whiner," Laird sneered. "What did you think? That this was some playground game? You don't get the team you want so you run home? Well, guess what, Gene? I'm half a mil into this game and so are my partners. If I don't come up with the land we need they're going to plant me in some field somewhere. So don't tell me about honor or mortgage payments. You're not going anywhere. If you think they can't plant you in that same field, you're sadly mistaken!"

Something crashed and shattered against the desk next to her ear. A frightened gasp escaped her mouth before she could clap her hand over it. Dead silence descended on the room. Maggie's eyes widened and she held her breath, waiting.

Oh, God. She'd done it now.

Footsteps moved slowly around to her side of the desk. Oh, no. Please.

The desk chair jerked out of place and Laird's face appeared in the kneehole. "Maggie." His nostrils flared in anger. "Really, you should have knocked."

It had started to rain. A slow, soaking drizzle that slicked the roads and made driving perilous. Greg Janeson didn't let that slow him down. He tore down the country highway like he'd been driving Indy cars his whole life. Cain was impressed.

But up ahead, the flashing red lights of a patrol car and ambulance had a line of cars backed up twenty deep. There had been an accident. A car was on its roof smack dab in the middle of the road and traffic was at a standstill.

Cain swore. "Go around," he told Greg.

"I can't go around. There are ditches on either side."

Cain pounded the back of the seat with his fists.

"It should clear up any minute," Greg assured him. A cop with flares was standing dead center on the road. Nobody was going anywhere for a long time.

"We don't have a minute," Cain said, jerking open the handle on the passenger door. "I'm going."

"On foot?" Judd demanded. "How far is it?"

"Half a mile down the next turn off. Meet me there when you get out of this."

"I think not," Greg said, throwing the car into park. "Judd, meet us there. I'm going to go back him up. He's liable to do something crazy." He jerked the car door open and took off after Cain.

"Well, hell," Judd muttered, glancing at the mess up ahead, imagining his fifty-four-year body doing a mile at a dead run. Then again, he thought, why not?

He got out and hit the remote lock on the keys and took off after the others. He'd waited a long time for the chance to stand behind his son. There was, he decided, no time like the present.

Laird jerked Maggie out from under the desk and yanked her toward the center of the room. "Look what I found," he told Gene, dragging her up against him.

"Ah, Maggie." Gene gave a miserable shake of his head. "What the hell have you done?"

"That's a question you should be answering, isn't it?" she said, ignoring the hammering of her heart. "In front of a jury."

Laird gave a humorless chuckle and jerked her arm up behind her until she gasped in pain. "Not in this lifetime, sweetheart. And I believe breaking and entering is still a crime in this state. What did you think you'd find here, Maggie? A smoking gun maybe? A dead body or two?"

"I found exactly what I expected to find. A man whose ambition has gotten the better of him."

"Laird—" Gene warned.

"So…you got yourself an earful, did you?" Laird said to her. "That's really a shame."

She just glared at him, fighting the stinging in her eyes. How on God's green earth she was going to get out of this now? She could feel Gene's stare burning into her and almost hear the gears turning in Laird's brain as he contemplated what to do with her now.

She'd blown it. She'd taken a chance and she'd blown her chance to help Cain and to save herself. He was going to have to kill her now, too. What else could he do? He certainly couldn't risk letting her tell what she'd overheard. She glanced at Gene. He looked like a man who'd just swallowed a hook and was contemplating pulling it back out.

"I saw the model," she told him, stopping him dead in his tracks. He glared at her.

"A landing strip?" she said. "That's what this was all about? That's why Ben had to die? That's why Cain is in jail now for maybe the rest of his life? So you could land planes here?"

A slow smile tugged at Laird's mouth. "Ben was a necessary casualty. His own weakness is what killed him. Nobody put that noose around his neck."

"You didn't have to, did you? You put him in the ground long before he could do it himself." Maggie shrugged against his painful hold on her. "He never hurt you, Laird. He never lifted one hand against anyone but himself. And this…" She gestured with a jerk of her head around the room. "This is all about a piece of land? You killed him for dirt? That was all his life was worth to you?"

"I didn't kill him," he said tightly.

"You pushed him and pushed him until he broke."

"He broke because he was weak. I did you a favor."

She jerked against his hands at that, wanting to spit in his face. He wrenched her arm again until she curled toward it in pain.

"Dammit, Laird," Gene said, "let her go."

"And what? What would you have me do, Gene? Let her go to Winston?"

"It'll be her word against ours."

"He's right," Maggie said. "You're not afraid of one little woman are you, Laird?"

He put his mouth right beside her ear. His breath smelled like whiskey and felt hot against her skin. "You've been a lot of trouble, Maggie. But this time you've gone too far."

"So…what? You gonna kill me the way you did Brent? Was he too much trouble, too? That's what you do when people get in your way, isn't it? You just…remove them from the equation. Or, like Cain, you set them up to take the fall for you."

"Oh, your new husband walked into that one on his own.

I just opened the door. And Brent? Well, if we hadn't caught him having a little cozy talk with you in town we might never have known about his little attack of conscience. He just couldn't leave it alone. Just like you.''

She felt dizzy and sick, remembering Brent and that day in the street. How frightened he'd looked. He'd tried to warn her.

"See, the way I see it," Laird hypothosized, "I came home from dinner and heard a prowler. I got my gun and—'' He shrugged. "See? It's all very legal."

Laird started dragging her toward the door.

"No," Gene said, blocking his way.

Laird shoved him aside and Maggie reached out for his sleeve. "Is this what you want? For Ruth? For your kids?"

Sweat was beading above Gene's lip. "Let her go, Laird."

"Get the hell out of my way, Gene." He shouldered past him, only to have the lawyer move in front of him again, shaking now.

"No, dammit, this has gone too far. I'm not going to let you do this."

Laird stopped and regarded his attorney. "Yeah?" Then, his fist shot out and he coldcocked the man with a sickening smack of bone and flesh before he could react. Gene's head slammed back against the door frame and his eyelids fluttered. He slid down the casing like hot candledip and landed, unconscious, at their feet.

A shocked breath jangled out of her. He dragged her backward, wrenching open a little box on the table near the desk. Inside was a little forty-five caliber gun that fit neatly in his left hand. He was going to kill her. Of course he was going to kill her. And she had no one to rely on but herself.

Laird dragged her into the hallway with an arm around her waist and another still holding her aching right arm up behind her. She tried to kick at him, but he evaded her every attempt.

An animal-like sound of rage tore from her throat and she stumbled along down the hallway beside him. He fitted the gun against her side and said, "Don't make me do it here, Maggie. It would be so messy."

She stopped struggling. Think. Think! She couldn't let him get her out the door. He dragged her toward the foyer.

"You just had to stick your nose in it," he muttered through clenched teeth. "You couldn't give up."

Maggie scratched at his hold on her but it did no good. "People knew I was coming here tonight. They'll figure it out, Laird. If you hurt me, they'll know it was you."

He shoved the gun harder against her ribs. "Shut up."

They approached the front door and he rearranged her in his arms to reach for the elegant brass knob. But a violent bang reverberated against the thick slab of wood as he touched the handle. Wide-eyed, Laird stared at it, frozen for a heartbeat before it exploded open and smacked them backward.

Together, they sprawled on the slate floor. She heard the gun fall, too, and saw the shadow of the man who'd kicked the door in stumble into the room.

Cain!

He was on Laird before the rancher could defend himself, dragging him up and off of Maggie. He slugged Laird hard in the jaw, sending him flying backward against the hallway table.

The table splintered under the assault. Laird rolled to avoid Cain, who threw himself at him again. This time, it was Laird whose fist connected, coming up hard under Cain's already damaged jaw. Cain landed backward on the splintered wood, stunned for a moment.

Maggie screamed his name as Laird moved in on him. Blinking, Cain rolled to the side before Laird's foot could connect with his ribs. Cain kicked Laird's legs out from under him and the other man went down like a felled ponderosa. Cain rolled away, reaching for the gun a few feet away.

Still on her knees, Maggie saw it too, and crawled for it. Her hand closed around it just as Laird was reaching for the back of Cain's jacket to haul him backward.

"Don't move, Laird," she told him. Her arms were shaking and the gun tip wavered wildly.

The sound of the men's labored breathing filled the suddenly quiet foyer. Laird eased back from Cain and wiped the back of one hand across his mouth. "You won't shoot me," he said, watching her. "Look at you. You're shaking. You don't have the nerve."

She blinked. Oh, she was tempted. So tempted.

With his eyes on Donnelly, Cain crawled over to her and put his hand on the gun. "Give me the gun, Maggie."

She shook her head. Cain couldn't be anywhere near the gun. "No."

He insisted, tightening his hand around it. "Give me the goddamned gun, Maggie." He pried it out of her hands and pointed it at Laird whose expression flattened now with something she'd never seen on him before. Fear.

"I'm not shaking," Cain said, moving toward the rancher. "Do I look scared to you, Donnelly?"

"Cain—" Maggie warned, struggling to her feet. "I'm calling the sheriff."

"Call him," Laird blustered. "I'll have you both arrested for breaking and entering. You'll both be behind bars before you can—"

Cain's lawyer, Greg Janeson, stumbled into the foyer, breathing hard, and he braced his hand against the doorway. He swore colorfully. But Cain kept moving toward Laird, who'd plastered himself against the wall, watching him come.

"Don't bother to call," he told Maggie. "He's not gonna live long enough to press charges."

Laird's face went a couple of shades paler as the reality of his situation began to sink in.

"How's it feel, Donnelly? Being outgunned. Watching your life pass before you as you realize someone's gonna end it for you?"

Laird blinked, and sent a pleading look at Janeson. "They...they b-broke into my...house. This man is a murderer."

Cain smiled. "That's right, Laird. I am. I've killed before. And you know what they say inside? 'First time's hard time. Second time's my time.'" He pressed the gun up against Donnelly's temple. Both men were sweating profusely.

"Cain—don't—" Maggie pleaded. She pulled the tape recorder from her pocket. "Look, I tape recorded them talking. They admitted everything."

"Inadmissible," Cain said, shifting the gun to fit just underneath Laird's jaw.

Greg took a step toward him. "Cain, for crissakes, give me the gun. We'll get a search warrant. They won't get away with this."

But Maggie could see the hard muscles of Cain's arm tighten as he contemplated the justice found in the federal judicial system. Grim resolve slicked his skin with sweat. He leaned closer to Donnelly. "Maybe this is how Brent felt before he died, you think?" he said in a low voice. "Wondering how many breaths he had left? Did that make you feel powerful, Laird? To control the minutes in a man's life? Or how about the hours? The *years* like you tried to do to mine? That make you feel like a real man?"

"I did what it took. Just like you," Laird said.

"That's right," Cain said, forcing Laird's head back with the gun. "Just like me."

"So what are you made of, MacCallister? You have the guts to pull that trigger a second time? Go ahead then. Do it. Go on. *Shoot me.*"

"Cain, please—" Maggie begged, moving next to him. "Think about what you're throwing away."

"What are you waiting for?" Donnelly taunted. "*Do it.* Do it, damn you!"

Cain's finger tightened on the trigger. Judd stumbled through the door, red-faced and breathing like a blown racehorse. It only took him a heartbeat to realize what his son was about to do. His horrified glance went from Maggie to Greg then back to Cain. "No, Cain. Give me the gun. Do you hear me? Give me the gun."

Cain's mouth twisted and he shook his head.

"You're not a cold-blooded killer." Judd took a desperate step toward him. "Don't you let him tell you different. You hear me? You're worth ten of that piece of slime."

Cain swallowed thickly and Maggie dared hope Judd's words were getting through.

Judd went on. "I know you don't give a damn how I feel, so don't do it for me. Do it for her. Do it for, Maggie."

Long seconds ticked away. Finally, Cain took a breath and lifted the gun away from Donnelly's head. He handed Judd the gun.

Maggie wasn't sure her legs would hold her, but she got to her feet and walked to Cain. She put her hand on his shoulder and urged him up and away from Laird. Greg pulled out his cell phone and dialed the sheriff's office.

Cain looked down at her and started to say something, but at that moment Gene Fielding staggered down the hallway, rubbing his jaw and taking in the situation. He rolled his eyes and pressed his back against the wall with a low curse. "I didn't mean for any of this to happen, Maggie," he said. "You have to know I didn't."

"But it did, didn't it?" she asked. "Ben's still dead. And so is Brent."

He closed his eyes as Judd ordered him to get over beside Donnelly. She knew he was thinking about his wife, Ruth, and their two children. But she couldn't work up an ounce of sympathy. They'd nearly succeeded in destroying them all.

Cain turned and left her standing there, walking outside the front door. Judd watched him go and said, "Go after him, Maggie. He needs you."

She wasn't so sure.

Cain was on the stoop, leaning against the pillar that supported the porch. Plunging his fingers into his hair, he shoved it back from his face and looked up at the night sky with a growl of frustration.

"Cain—"

"I almost pulled that trigger," he said when she touched his sleeve. "Another second and I would've killed him."

"But you didn't. It's over now, Cain. Please let it be over."

His eyes filled and he looked away from her. "Yeah. It's over. I'm sorry, Maggie. Hell, I never should've come here."

She turned him toward her. "Don't say that. They'll drop the charges now. We can prove you didn't kill Brent."

He looked down at his hands. "And then what? Wait until the next time? My past won't go away. It's gonna follow me wherever I go."

She didn't like what she saw in his eyes. It sent a shiver of dread through her. "You're not going anywhere. Don't talk like that. You're scaring me."

He took her by the arms, his blue, blue eyes searing into hers. "He could've killed you."

"But he *didn't.*" She searched his eyes, and pulled his mouth down to hers. "He didn't."

She infused the kiss with every ounce of conviction she had. His mouth moved against hers in bittersweet reply and his hands curled around her shoulders—as much to hold her away as to keep her near. And suddenly, she knew.

He would leave her.

The sound of sirens coming up the road rent the still summer night. Red lights flashing, the sheriff's cars that had been at the accident site were only seconds away from Donnelly's.

Maggie watched Cain watch them come. After all he'd been through, there was no surprise in the bleakness she saw in his eyes. He'd spent the better part of the last four years behind bars for a crime he hadn't committed. He'd almost killed a man tonight, and she could still feel the reality of that vibrating through him. It was enough to shake any man. Even Cain who seemed so strong and so good. But he was wrestling with something else as well. Something she had no more control over than she did the stars overhead. She could beg and plead, but in the end, it was his choice. And she was afraid no amount of begging would change his mind.

Morning spilled into Maggie's room through the large windows across from her bed. She rolled over and sighed, unwilling to face the day yet. It took her a moment to remember that last night hadn't been a dream. It was finally behind them. Donnelly had been arrested, and this morning would be arraigned on two counts of felony conspiracy, attempted murder and murder charges. By noon, the state papers would pick it up and bench warrants would be issued for the other men involved in Brent's death and Cain's assault. Charges against Cain would be formally dropped this morning, but informally, he was already a free man.

Only Maggie knew how patently untrue that statement was.

She rolled onto her back to find Cain lying beside her, still asleep. It had been days since he'd had any real rest but when he'd crawled into bed last night, he'd fallen asleep nearly before his head hit the pillow. For her part, sleep had been elusive. She'd spent half the night watching him, and the other half, staring at the moon as it arched a path across the sky and disappeared into morning.

She wished he could make love to her, but it would be weeks before his fractured ribs allowed it. Instead, she contented herself with the fact that he'd slept beside her at all.

She reached out with a finger and traced the strong muscle of his forearm and the soft, dark hair there. Her finger moved down the curve of his wrist and along the bones of his hand to his bruised knuckles. Her exploration ended as his fingers curled around hers.

She looked up. "Hi."

"Hi," he said back, his voice rough with sleep.

"Did I wake you?" she asked, knowing she did. He blinked languidly. She lifted his hand against her mouth and kissed his damaged knuckles. "I meant to."

"Did you sleep?"

"Yes," she lied. "You?"

"I must have. I don't actually remember getting into bed."

"That's because you were practically dead on your feet by the time we got home from the sheriff's office."

On a sigh, he disengaged his fingers from hers and rolled onto his back, propping one hand beneath his head. Maggie curled toward him, resting her head on the smooth muscle of his shoulder and her hand on the flat of his abdomen. The silence between them grew long and awkward. He was staring off at the mountains that circled her valley and probably somewhere beyond.

"Say something," she whispered.

After a minute, he did. "I'm leaving today."

Her heart sank. "Not that."

"It's the best thing, Maggie. We both know it."

"Do we?"

"When you've had a little time to think about it—"

"I've had time. I know what I want."

He rolled away from her and sat up on the edge of the bed. "You think you do. But this will all be headline news by tonight. Everybody in Montana will know about me and my past by tomorrow. I thought I could protect you from it. But I can't."

"So you're going to run away again? Is that your answer?"

He bent his head. "Don't make this harder than it is."

"Hard?" She sat up, tugging the sheets with her. "I'll tell you what's hard, Cain. Loving you and knowing your heart still belongs to a ghost—that's hard. Holding you and knowing you can't imagine a future for yourself or for us. That's hard. I'm in love with you. The past few days haven't changed that. If you run away, I'll survive. It'll be damned hard, but I *will* survive because it's what I do.

"So if you have to go, then go. But don't lie to either of us by saying you're doing it for me. Because you're not. You're leaving because you're afraid that you might actually have to feel alive again if you stay with me and that scares the hell out of you."

"Annie has nothing to do with you and me." He reached for the jeans he'd left on the floor by the bed and pulled them on. Maggie watched the bruised muscles in his back ripple and flex and she wanted him back beside her again, holding her. But leaving was something he'd have to do on his own. She wouldn't help him. She pulled her bathrobe on and got up.

"I didn't know your wife," she said softly, tying the belt around her waist. Cain stalled, reaching for his shirt, then straightened slowly, pulling it on. "I imagine she must have loved you terribly. But you know what I think?"

He didn't answer. He didn't even turn back to her.

"I think she would've hated that what she loved about you died along with her."

Chapter 16

The hot August sun beat down on the back of Cain's neck as he forked the hay out of the pickup truck along the center of his father's pasture. The black Angus cows, torpid in the humid heat of summer, ambled over to the spot, lulled into compliance by the ordinary rhythm of their days. They would do this, Cain thought, until the day they were loaded onto a cattle truck and shipped to the meat factories, never knowing a moment of rebellion or contemplating what might have been if they'd only questioned their lot.

Cain shook his head at the philosophical bent his thoughts had taken. He'd been working with cattle most of his life and had never before contemplated the possibilities of a bovine revolution or, for that matter, the anthropomorphic potential of any animal destined for his dinner plate. But for some reason today, their blind complacency just seemed wrong.

He forked the last of the hay off as Miguel Rios, his father's oldest and most trusted hand, edged the truck forward. When he'd finished, Cain tapped the top of the cab and tossed the pitchfork into the truck bed.

"All done?" Miguel asked, leaning out the driver's window.

"That's it," Cain said, hopping down to jump into the cab of the truck. "They're fat, happy and idiotically grateful."

Miguel nodded with a wizened grin. His skin was brown as old leather and his teeth, yellow from years of chewing tobacco. "They should be. They get food, water, shelter from the storms. Their life is good. Cattle," he said, "their needs are few. People on the other hand, they're harder to please. Take you, for instance…"

Miguel had worked on the ranch since Cain was a kid and knew him better than most. Most days, he kept his own counsel, but today was apparently not going to be one of those days.

"You been home…what? Six weeks?"

Cain stared out the side window. "Five weeks." Four days, seventeen hours.

"*Sí*, and in all that time, you been off the ranch once?"

"Your point?" he asked.

Miguel shrugged as he pulled onto the paved road that led back to the house. "I'm just saying…A young man like you should be out living. Not feeding cows. Señor Mac-Callister, he is worried about you."

He turned in surprise. "My father talks to you about me?"

"You think he doesn't notice how you mope around?"

"I'm not moping. I don't *mope*," Cain said with a scowl. Just because he'd been biting off heads lately at every turn. Or working until the sun went down until he fell into bed exhausted—only to turn around and do it again. That had nothing to do with…anything. "Besides," he said, "I'm doing my job. Earning my keep. Isn't that enough?"

Miguel swivelled a look at him. "Is it enough for you?"

He turned back to stare out at the pasture land as it sped by his window. The fields were burned gold by the late summer heat and herds of Angus dotted the landscape. This was his father's land, land he'd never imagined working again. But it had become a harbor for him for a while.

When he'd left Maggie, he'd flown home with his father. He'd needed a place to heal and Judd had provided it. They'd managed to put the past mostly behind them and Cain had come to know his father not as Judd MacCallister, the dynasty builder who had constructed this little empire, but Judd MacCallister the man. Human. Frail. Just like him.

Sorting through all that had been necessary. Important. Even though every day the restless discontent inside him grew. He'd lost count of how many times he'd relived seeing Maggie in Donnelly's arms with a gun against her ribs. That feeling...that gut wrench was something he'd promised himself he'd never risk feeling again. But there it was, part of him again. Because no matter how much distance he'd put between the two of them, he couldn't shut down the feelings. It was too late for that.

"It's enough," he said at last. A lie, but it would do.

Miguel turned down the road to the house. "You are a lot like him, you know? Stubborn. Certain you are right." A grin tugged at the old man's mouth. "I am old. But life? It is short. Why you don't go and talk to her, *mijo?*"

The question was like a sharp right to the gut. Talk to her? Hell, not a day went by that he didn't think about doing just that—wondering what she was doing, *how* she was doing. But nothing had changed, except now there were a thousand miles and as many reasons between them. "I can't go back there, Miguel," he said, staring out the window.

"I don't mean your wife," Miguel said. "I mean Annie."

The look Cain swivelled on him would have cowed any man who didn't know him so well. *"Annie?"*

"When was the last time you took her flowers?"

The day he'd been released from prison. He'd gone to tell her about the man he'd killed. To tell her he'd keep her with him. Always.

"In my country," Miguel went on, "there is a holiday for it. *El Día de los Muertos.* The Day of the Dead. It celebrates the lives of the ones we lose. People dance and eat sugar candy and leave sweet *pan de los muertos* for the spirits. In my country, we believe our dead should know that in our grief, is also our joy. It is part of the journey. Death, a part of life. And we celebrate our memories."

The old man pulled up in front of the house and stopped the truck. Cain pulled open the door and got out, then leaned back into the window.

"Go and talk to her, *mijo,*" Miguel said. "Tell her your heart."

Cain sighed, grinding his fingers into a fist. "Anybody ever tell you that you were damned nosy for an old cow-puncher?"

"Only your father," he said with a grin. "But he doesn't mind."

A smile curved Cain's mouth. "Neither do I, my friend."

Someone had put fresh flowers on her grave. Roses in a vase full of water. Judd, he thought, surprised again. Cain knelt down beside it, tucking his handful of sunflowers, Annie's favorites, in beside them.

He stared down at the shiny granite headstone. It read Annie Marie MacCallister, Beloved Wife, Lover, Friend. b. June 1,1968 d. July 18,1996.

He brushed a hand against the stone, wiped away a bit of dust and cleared his throat.

"Hey Annie," he said softly. "Sorry I haven't been by

for a while." He squeezed his eyes shut and swallowed past the lump in my throat. "Old Miguel, you remember him? He said I should have a talk with you and I...I guess he was right."

Cain studied the dappled shadow the huge cottonwood nearby threw on Annie's grave. "See, the thing is...I know I promised you that I'd always keep you with me, that there would never be anyone else. But...there is someone, Annie. Her name is Maggie. And you know what? I think you would've liked her. She's brave and sweet and strong. And she needed me. But I walked right out of her life. I thought I could do that and come away in one piece, but it's tearing me up inside, Annie."

His eyes stung and he blinked hard. "Before I left, she said you would've hated what's become of me since you died. And she's right. You would'a kicked my ass."

He stroked the short, clipped grass under his hand. "So I can't keep my promise to you. I gotta start living again, Annie. I've got to let you go. And I hope that's okay with you. Because I need to go back and see if there's anything left to salvage with Maggie. I kind of made a mess of things and I need to try to straighten them out."

He reached into his pocket and pulled a gold band from it, rolling the smooth warmth of it between his fingers. Finally, he placed it on top of the headstone where it glinted in the sun.

He swallowed thickly and stood, brushing a knuckle across his cheek. This moment had been years in coming and now that it was here, he felt suddenly a hundred pounds lighter.

Cain looked up at the rustle of wind past the cottonwood tree. A wind eddy moved across the cemetery, swirling leaves and bits of dust in its wake, meandering toward him like a woman. He waited, transfixed, as it came to the spot where he stood and swirled around him for a handful of moments before it lifted away into the trees and was gone.

He watched it go and smiled. "G'bye, Annie-girl. You take good care."

Maggie moved through the thigh-high hay in the field north of her house, plucking a stem now and then to check the maturity of the golden alfalfa. Behind her, Jigger and Geronimo tagged along like shadows, with the horse stopping every few feet to nibble.

His progress had been remarkable and the scars his accident had left were healing well. He would never be a show horse again, but Maggie had already decided he would never leave her ranch either. He'd grown attached to her and she to him. And Jigger had adopted him. He nipped at his heels, herding him toward her and Geronimo playfully nipped back, prancing around him.

Healing him had filled her days since Cain left and now that he was almost well, she wondered what she would do to keep from going crazy. Not that she didn't have plenty to keep her busy. The training and the work would keep her occupied from morning to night. But it was night that was the hardest. Alone in the house, wishing he was there with his arms around her.

But she'd resigned herself. He was gone. And no amount of wishing would change that. She'd almost gotten on a plane one day. She'd actually made it as far at the boarding gate, but she'd changed her mind. It wasn't enough, she decided, to want him or even to need him. She wouldn't settle again for a man who didn't, couldn't, love her completely. If that meant she had to go it alone, then so be it. Somehow, she'd do what it took.

Jigger pranced up to her with a stick in his mouth, wagging his tail. She reached down and took it from him and threw it. The dog took off like a shot, barking happily.

Geronimo thundered after him in a game they'd invented between them. Maggie grinned. Maybe this was enough, she thought, crumbling the head of an alfalfa stalk between her fingers and turning back to her task.

Jigger's barking grew more insistent. And distant. At first, she didn't pay attention. But the longer it went on, the more curious she got. She turned to find dog and horse nearly to the house. A yellow cab was parked in her yard and a man was walking toward her, past Jigger and Geronimo through the thigh-high golden hay.

Maggie blinked. It couldn't be. He kept walking and she knew it was. No one moved like him.

For a long moment, her heart stopped and she wondered if he'd just come back for the motorcycle he'd left behind. Or perhaps to settle the annulment. But both of those things could have been done long distance. And now, she could see his face, even beneath the brim of his hat. He was smiling.

The yellow cab pulled away and headed down the road.

Maggie moved toward him. Hesitantly at first, then faster. Cain's long strides covered the ground between them in a few more seconds. They both stopped a few feet apart. Maggie's breath was coming fast. He looked good. So damned good. All remnants of his beating were gone. Still there was the smile that stalled her pulse and the look that made her knees go soft. "Cain."

"Maggie. How are you?"

His deep voice vibrated through her. "Fine. You?"

"Better. Now." His gaze traveled over her face until she felt it flush with heat.

"Your...um, ribs?"

"Good as new," he said as Jigger bounced around him like a windup toy, hungry for a pat. He reached down and ruffled the dog's fur. "It's my heart that isn't doing so well."

"Your heart?" she asked worriedly. Had the beating he took done damage they hadn't recognized?

"Yeah," he said. "I've been having this pain—" he fisted his hand just beneath his chest. "Right here. Started the day I left and just kept getting worse."

Maggie frowned, not sure what to think. "Have you seen a doctor?"

He shook his head slowly, the smile disappearing. "Nah. I knew what it was. See, I'd left a piece of it here. And I knew the only thing to do was to come back for it."

Maggie's lips parted and she stared at him. He took a step closer to her as she drank him in.

"Took me awhile, because I'm thickheaded. I had some thinking I had to do. Some things I had to sort through. Know what I found?"

She shook her head.

"That you were right," he said. "I was afraid of letting go of the past, of imagining a future. But see, even the present wasn't workin' for me anymore. Not since I met you, Maggie. Day, night, in the shower, herding cattle—all I could see was your face. The way you always could make me smile. All I could imagine was having you in my arms again, holding you, feeling your mouth on mine."

Oh, Cain...

"So, I got on a plane and came back. Hoping you could forgive me for going. That maybe you still felt something for me." He reached a hand out to her face, but hesitated to touch her. "Do you, Mag? 'Cause this...this pain's getting worse and I'm crazy in love with you."

Maggie steepled her hands over her mouth, her eyes filling with tears. "I thought—"

He pulled her toward him and kissed her, hard and deep. Maggie threw her arms around him pulling him closer still. Oh, how she'd missed him! His taste, the wonderful scent of him and the feel of his arms around her.

Cain broke the kiss before she was ready to give him up and pressed his forehead against hers. "I missed you. So damned much."

She nodded, her throat clogged with tears. "I missed you, too."

He brushed a strand of hair off her cheek. "I know it'll be hard, but I'm asking you to take a chance on me. I'll do everything in my power to make you happy, Maggie. I swear it."

Shaking, she looked up at him. "What about Annie?"

"Annie will always be part of my past. But she's gone. And I'm here. And you're the one I want to spend the rest of my life with."

He pulled a small Tiffany box from his pocket and opened it. Inside was an exquisite diamond ring flanked by small, perfectly cut emeralds. Maggie gasped when she saw it. "Oh, Cain—"

"I never gave you a ring the first time." He took it from the box and put it on her finger. It fit perfectly. She started to cry all over again.

"You don't like it?" he asked, his voice suddenly worried.

"No...it's beautiful. It's just that—" She lifted her gaze to his face. "There's something I have to tell you first. Before you decide."

"Nothing will change my mind, Maggie."

"This might. Some men don't want—" She turned away from him, screwing up her courage.

"Men? What is it, Maggie? You're scaring me."

"I'm...I'm pregnant." There. She said it. It was probably the last thing he expected to hear, considering her assurances that wasn't a possibility. She only known herself for a week.

For a long heartbeat he didn't say anything. Then, "A *baby?*"

He whirled her toward him, on his face a look of wonder she'd never seen before as he stared at her belly. "Are you sure? I mean, how far along are you?"

"Almost two months," she said carefully. "I know I said it couldn't happen, but the doctors must have been wrong because I definitely am, even though honestly, I never meant to get...I mean personally, I'm very happy about it and I want you to know that I intend to keep it and if you're not, well, then I underst—"

He shut her up by covering her mouth with his in a joyous, emphatic kiss. He took her down with him into the deep golden alfalfa, cradling her tenderly in his arms. The smell of crushed hay swirled around them and when she looked up all she could see was the vast indigo sky brushed by gold and Cain's face smiling down at her.

"A *baby*," he repeated against her lips.

"You're happy?" she asked in a small voice.

"Happy? Maggie, three months ago, I didn't really give a damn if I lived or died. I was lost. And here I am, holding you—" his hand traveled down to the curve of her belly "—and our child. You made me remember what it was to be alive again. You gave me a reason to come back. And a baby...well, that's just something I never dreamed could happen for me."

He swallowed thickly, his eyes full of emotion. "Marry me—the right way this time—and I'll spend the rest of my life proving how much I love you."

She pulled him down to her for another kiss. His tongue moved against hers sealing the promise between them. Her fingers moved to the buttons on his shirt, flicking them open one by one.

Above them, Cain heard the Montana wind ruffle the grain with a sibilant sound as Maggie's warm hand slid against his chest. He could hardly believe his luck in finding her, loving her. That she offered herself to him now, without constraint was so…Maggie.

He would make love to her here in the hayfield surrounded by the mountains she loved. In the years to come, he silently vowed, there would be a thousand times like this to remind him that he'd been lucky enough to love twice in one lifetime.

And then he remembered the dream he'd had of Annie and the blond-haired little girl. He smiled against Maggie's mouth.

"What?" she asked.

"I'm thinking we should paint the nursery pink."

She laughed. "What makes you so sure it'll be a girl?"

"Just a feeling," he said, brushing the hair out of her eyes.

Her lips curved. "A feeling, huh? Did I ever tell you about the feeling I had the first time you kissed me?"

He shook his head with a wicked smile.

"C'mere," she whispered. "And I'll show you."

And she did.

* * * * *

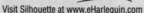

If you enjoyed what you just read,
then we've got an offer you can't resist!

Take 2 bestselling love stories FREE!

Plus get a FREE surprise gift!

Feel like a star with Silhouette.

We will fly you and a guest to New York City for an exciting weekend stay at a glamorous 5-star hotel. Experience a refreshing day at one of New York's trendiest spas and have your photo taken by a professional. Plus, receive $1,000 U.S. spending money!

Flowers...long walks...dinner for two... how does Silhouette Books make romance come alive for you?

Send us a script, with 500 words or less, along with visuals (only drawings, magazine cutouts or photographs or combination thereof). Show us how Silhouette Makes Your Love Come Alive. Be creative and have fun. No purchase necessary. All entries must be clearly marked with your name, address and telephone number. All entries will become property of Silhouette and are not returnable. **Contest closes September 28, 2001.**

Please send your entry to: **Silhouette Makes You a Star!**

In U.S.A.	In Canada
P.O. Box 9069	P.O. Box 637
Buffalo, NY, 14269-9069	Fort Erie, ON, L2A 5X3

Look for contest details on the next page, by visiting www.eHarlequin.com or request a copy by sending a self-addressed envelope to the applicable address above. Contest open to Canadian and U.S. residents who are 18 or over. Void where prohibited.

Our lucky winner's photo will appear in a Silhouette ad. Join the fun!

SRMYAS1

HARLEQUIN "SILHOUETTE MAKES YOU A STAR!" CONTEST 1308
OFFICIAL RULES
NO PURCHASE NECESSARY TO ENTER

1. To enter, follow directions published in the offer to which you are responding. Contest begins June 1, 2001, and ends on September 28, 2001. Entries must be postmarked by September 28, 2001, and received by October 5, 2001. Enter by hand-printing (or typing) on an 8 ½" x 11" piece of paper your name, address (including zip code), contest number/name and attaching a script containing <u>500 words</u> or less, <u>along with drawings, photographs or magazine cutouts, or combinations thereof</u> (i.e., collage) <u>on no larger than 9" x 12"</u> piece of paper, describing how the <u>Silhouette books make romance come alive for you.</u> Mail via first-class mail to: Harlequin "Silhouette Makes You a Star!" Contest 1308, (in the U.S.) P.O. Box 9069, Buffalo, NY 14269-9069, (in Canada) P.O. Box 637, Fort Erie, Ontario, Canada L2A 5X3. Limit one entry per person, household or organization.

2. Contests will be judged by a panel of members of the Harlequin editorial, marketing and public relations staff. Fifty percent of criteria will be judged against script and fifty percent will be judged against drawing, photographs and/or magazine cutouts. Judging criteria will be based on the following:

   - Sincerity—25%
   - Originality and Creativity—50%
   - Emotionally Compelling—25%

   In the event of a tie, duplicate prizes will be awarded. Decisions of the judges are final.

3. All entries become the property of Torstar Corp. and may be used for future promotional purposes. Entries will not be returned. No responsibility is assumed for lost, late, illegible, incomplete, inaccurate, nondelivered or misdirected mail.

4. Contest open only to residents of the U.S. <u>(except Puerto Rico)</u> and Canada who are 18 years of age or older, and is void wherever prohibited by law; all applicable laws and regulations apply. Any litigation within the Province of Quebec respecting the conduct or organization of a publicity contest may be submitted to the Régie des alcools, des courses et des jeux for a ruling. Any litigation respecting the awarding of a prize may be submitted to the Régie des alcools, des courses et des jeux only for the purpose of helping the parties reach a settlement. Employees and immediate family members of Torstar Corp. and D. L. Blair, Inc., their affiliates, subsidiaries and all other agencies, entities and persons connected with the use, marketing or conduct of this contest are not eligible to enter. Taxes on prizes are the sole responsibility of the winner. Acceptance of any prize offered constitutes permission to use winner's name, photograph or other likeness for the purposes of advertising, trade and promotion on behalf of Torstar Corp., its affiliates and subsidiaries without further compensation to the winner, unless prohibited by law.

5. Winner will be determined no later than November 30, 2001, and will be notified by mail. Winner will be required to sign and return an Affidavit of Eligibility/Release of Liability/Publicity Release form within 15 days after winner notification. Noncompliance within that time period may result in disqualification and an alternative winner may be selected. All travelers must execute a Release of Liability prior to ticketing and must possess required travel documents (e.g., passport, photo ID) where applicable. Trip must be booked by December 31, 2001, and completed within one year of notification. No substitution of prize permitted by winner. Torstar Corp. and D. L. Blair, Inc., their parents, affiliates and subsidiaries are not responsible for errors in printing of contest, entries and/or game pieces. In the event of printing or other errors that may result in unintended prize values or duplication of prizes, all affected game pieces or entries shall be null and void. **Purchase or acceptance of a product offer does not improve your chances of winning.**

6. Prizes: (1) Grand Prize—A 2-night/3-day trip for two (2) to New York City, including round-trip coach air transportation nearest winner's home and hotel accommodations (double occupancy) at The Plaza Hotel, a glamorous afternoon makeover at <u>a trendy New York spa</u>, $1,000 in U.S. spending money and an opportunity to <u>have a professional photo taken and appear in a Silhouette advertisement</u> (approximate retail value: $7,000). (10) Ten Runner-Up Prizes of gift packages (retail value $50 ea.). Prizes consist of only those items listed as part of the prize. Limit one prize per person. Prize is valued in U.S. currency.

7. For the name of the winner (available after December 31, 2001) send a self-addressed, stamped envelope to: Harlequin "Silhouette Makes You a Star!" Contest 1197 Winners, P.O. Box 4200 Blair, NE 68009-4200 or you may access the www.eHarlequin.com Web site through February 28, 2002.

Contest sponsored by Torstar Corp., P.O Box 9042, Buffalo, NY 14269-9042.